GOOD
COMPANY

GOOD COMPANY

A Novel

CYNTHIA D'APRIX SWEENEY

ecco

An Imprint of HarperCollins*Publishers*

GOOD COMPANY. Copyright © 2021 by Cynthia D'Aprix Sweeney. All rights reserved. Printed in the United States of America. No part of this book may be used or reproduced in any manner whatsoever without written permission except in the case of brief quotations embodied in critical articles and reviews. For information, address HarperCollins Publishers, 195 Broadway, New York, NY 10007.

HarperCollins books may be purchased for educational, business, or sales promotional use. For information, please email the Special Markets Department at SPsales@harpercollins.com.

Ecco® and HarperCollins® are trademarks of HarperCollins Publishers.

FIRST EDITION

Designed by Michelle Crowe

Library of Congress Cataloging-in-Publication Data
Names: Sweeney, Cynthia D'Aprix, author.
Title: Good company : a novel / Cynthia D'Aprix Sweeney.
Description: First edition. | New York, NY : Ecco, an imprint of
  HarperCollinsPublishers, [2020] | Summary: "A warm, incisive new novel
  about the enduring bonds of marriage and friendship from Cynthia D'Aprix
  Sweeney, author of the instant New York Times bestseller The Nest"—
  Provided by publisher.
Identifiers: LCCN 2020041878 (print) | LCCN 2020041879 (ebook) | ISBN
  9780062876003 (hardcover) | ISBN 9780062876027 (ebook)
Classification: LCC PS3619.W44253 G66 2020 (print) | LCC PS3619.W44253
  (ebook) | DDC 813/.6—dc23
LC record available at https://lccn.loc.gov/2020041878
LC ebook record available at https://lccn.loc.gov/2020041879

21 22 23 24 25 LSC 10 9 8 7 6 5 4 3 2 1

As is everything, for Mike

GOOD
COMPANY

ONE

Flora wasn't looking for the ring when she found it. She was rooting around an old file cabinet in the garage, searching for a photograph from the summer Ruby was five, thirteen years ago. Long years? Short? Both, depending on how she thought about them. Flora had woken up thinking about the photo and she knew it had to be somewhere in the house. The photo had moved from the ugly brown refrigerator door in Greenwich Village to an even uglier brown refrigerator door in Los Angeles ("How do two people on opposite coasts whose houses we are eventually going to live in *both* choose brown refrigerators?" she'd asked Julian) until ugly refrigerator number two shuddered its last breath one August morning and they'd replaced it with a new one that was fancier and stainless steel and wouldn't hold a magnet. She'd moved the photo to a bulletin board in the small enclosed sun porch they called "the office," but the edges started to curl and so she'd put it in a drawer, safe from the ravages of time and the relentless attention of the California sun. She'd cleaned out all those drawers a couple of years ago, right after she got the part voicing Leona the saucy lioness on the animated show *Griffith* and they'd turned "the office" into "the studio," a place she could record her voice-over work at home when she wanted. Where had she put all the stuff from those drawers? She would never throw away a photograph, but especially not that one.

"Don't we already have a pile of presents for Ruby?" Julian asked, rummaging through his bedside table, trying to help but just creating more mess. Their daughter was graduating from high school that night and Flora wanted to slip the photo in a frame and give it to her. A sweet surprise.

"We can probably get rid of a lot of that stuff," Flora said, eyeing the piles of junk Julian was extracting from his drawer and moving to the bed: an assortment of reading glasses, outdated computer cords, empty aspirin bottles, a few battered scripts. He would ignore her suggestion. After twenty years of marriage the lines had been drawn, the places where she was allowed to exert her desire for order and the places she learned to ignore.

"Hey! These will come in handy for Ruby." Julian held up an impressive wad of euros, coiled and fastened with a rubber band. At the end of the month, Ruby was going to Spain with her boyfriend's family, after which she would meet Flora and Julian in upstate New York at the house in Stoneham, the same house in the missing photo from so long ago.

"I wish we could retake the photo this summer," Flora said. "If David and Margot were coming, we could." Julian tossed the euros over to Flora's side of the bed, pleased with himself. Three years ago, standing in front of the currency booth at Charles de Gaulle Airport, they'd argued about whether or not to exchange the euros back to dollars. She remembered exactly.

It was ungodly hot in the terminal because of some kind of air-conditioning malfunction. The three of them were logy and irritable from indulgence—days of cheese and baguettes, foie gras nearly every night, the croissants, the chocolate, the wine. Fifteen-year-old Ruby had been in a mood. "I am *not* being ungrateful. All I said is that the Parisians are pretty *sniffy* for people who can't even get air-conditioning right. What's the big deal?"

Ruby had never done well in the heat from the time she was a baby. Her early years in Greenwich Village during the summer were a nightmare. Ruby begging to leave the playground, refusing to wear a hat, her fair cheeks flushed red, the stinging heat rash between her meaty toddler thighs.

"Next year can we *please* go to the beach in July? Somewhere with *air-conditioning*, somewhere I'm not sweating through my clothes by noon?" She lifted one arm and gestured angrily toward the sweat stain at her armpit. "This blouse is ruined, Mom. It's brand-new and I won't find this silhouette in Los Angeles and it's *ruined*."

"Okay, okay." Julian had placed a placating hand on Ruby's shoulder. "Let's find something cold to drink." He had winked at Flora then, a signal, reassuring her that they were on the same side. They both heard in that moment how much Ruby sounded like Margot. *Silhouette, sniffy*—not Ruby's vernacular.

That Ruby loved—worshipped—Flora's best friend was a good thing. And it was no surprise that Margot, who had no children, and Ruby, who was an only child, were thick as thieves. The *ruined* blouse had been a gift from Margot, bought at a small boutique in the Sixth, not a place Flora would ever deign to shop. Too expensive. Too intimidating. She and Margot had had a testy exchange about it at dinner in a tiny bistro the previous night, where they'd probably been a little too drunk, a little too loud. Margot and her husband, David, had taken Ruby for the afternoon and then reappeared laden with shopping bags. Ruby was bright-eyed and high-spirited and not complaining about the heat for once.

"This is too much," Flora said as Ruby opened bag after bag displaying her haul—the very sheer pink blouse, a pair of white gladiator sandals that Flora thought horrendous, a black scarf from some high-end designer covered with tiny skulls, a suede fringed handbag. "Is this in style now?" Flora said, running her fingers through the brown suede. "Mom," Ruby said. "Obviously."

Everything was impressive. Everything was expensive. Flora was annoyed at Ruby for accepting so much while also realizing how stubborn Margot could be, wielding her generosity like a bludgeon: *Here! take this, take it, take!* Sometimes it was impossible to resist the force of her.

"It's nothing." Margot waved Flora off, tucking the shopping bags beneath their crowded table. "Everything was on sale." David shrugged, his affable, agreeable self: *what Margot wants—*

But Flora was already feeling sheepish about the apartment they were renting. As always when traveling with Margot and David, it was obvious those two were covering most of the costs; there was no way Flora and Julian's "half"—the very reasonable figure Margot quoted as their share—was 50 percent of the spectacular, sprawling flat blocks from the Jardin du Luxembourg. "Maybe she got it with 'miles,'" Julian joked, when they were unpacking, referencing Margot's insistence that she would take care of everyone's plane tickets because she had airline miles she needed to use.

That day in the airport in France, Flora didn't have the energy to argue with Julian over exchanging the currency they could have used for the cab fare from LAX to home or for takeout that night. She'd just wanted to keep the peace. Get home. Regain her daughter's attention, because if everyone was being honest the real reason Flora was testy over the clothing purchases was ten days of Ruby hanging on everything Margot said, mimicking her gestures, her intonation, even one night—jokingly but also kind of accurately?—calling her *mon autre mère*.

Flora went downstairs and poured herself a cup of coffee, adding some almond creamer that Ruby had convinced her to use instead of half-and-half. ("Sorry, Mom, but at your age dairy is basically poison.")

She looked out the living room window. It was early, the sun barely rising, turning the sky a watery Monet blue and backlighting the downtown skyline. Early June in Los Angeles. June gloom. A thick, low marine layer shrouded the houses down the hill, making the neighborhood look like the hidden village of a fairy tale.

Julian grabbed his backpack and car keys and kissed Flora good-bye. His last day of shooting before the summer hiatus. She still wasn't used to the slightly longer hair, the massive sideburns he'd grown for his new job playing a cop in 1970s New York City. A good cop, of course; the cop who was furtively building a case against corruption and cover-ups. Julian was almost always cast as *good*, he had one of those faces. His show had just been renewed and for the first time in all their married lives, they both had desirable parts, season renewals, almost two months off without worrying what the rest of the year might bring in the way of work. Julian pulled Flora close and spoke into her ear, "Tony, Tony come around. Something's lost that must be found." The old prayer to St. Anthony that her mother used to recite at top volume whenever anything was lost, as if St. Anthony lived in the apartment upstairs and she could summon him to rush down and look for her reading glasses or a misplaced glove.

Julian was teasing her, and though she no longer prayed to St. Anthony or anyone anymore she did have her little superstitious rituals around lost things. One was to rub her thumb along the thin line of her mother's wedding ring, the modest band of white gold that she'd worn on her right hand since her mother died. She did it now. A tiny comforting gesture.

Where could the photograph be hiding? Then a flash, an idea. When they'd built the recording space in her office, she had moved a bunch of folders and papers from the house to the garage, mostly into the large file cabinet they'd owned since she was pregnant with Ruby, one they'd found on Twenty-Third Street in Manhattan back when the area was littered with office supply stores and they were supposed to be shopping for furniture for the baby's room.

"It's perfect," Julian had said, standing in front of the bright white metal file cabinet.

"For a nursery?"

"At least it's white."

Flora balked. They had a hand-me-down crib and changing table, and she wanted to buy something new for the tiny space that would be Ruby's nursery. She wanted a rocking chair or a bookshelf or a toy box; it didn't seem right to stick a filing cabinet in a corner of the baby's room, and this was back in the earliest of the aughts, before decorating a nursery became a reflection of the good taste and intellectual rigor of the entire family, before Danish ceiling pendants and murals of enchanted forests and curated bookshelves and those little square lamps that reflected the sun, the moon, and the stars on the wall all night.

But the file cabinet was needed and practical and, she had to admit, had been a smart purchase. A prominent piece of Ruby's "nursery," it was in constant use. Flora and Julian had moved the cabinet from the snug apartment in the West Village to their first rental house in Los Angeles, where it seemed to shrink once it was settled into a larger space. When they bought the house in Los Feliz, the stalwart cabinet was relegated to the garage nobody ever needed for a car because there was no snow and it had barely even rained the last few years.

The file cabinet had been a compromise of early marriage between Julian's near hoarder-like tendencies and Flora's love of purging. The "archives," Julian only half-jokingly called the contents of the cabinet. Half-joking because he'd confessed to her once that he began keeping and cataloging everything of his when he was a young boy because he thought he'd be famous one day. She hadn't been surprised by his confession; she'd indulged the same fantasy when she was young: that she'd grow up to be an actress and that meant, to her kid self, some degree of fame, but it had never occurred to her to actually plan for the eventual telling of her story.

Once, she'd mustered the confidence to say her dream out loud to her mother when they were at the sink doing dishes. Josephine had laughed. "Every little girl thinks she's going to be a star." Flora didn't believe her. It wasn't possible that *every* little girl thought she would—or even wanted to—be famous. Minnie Doolin with her perpetually runny nose and saggy knee socks? Rosemary Castello, who in fourth grade was scolded in front of the whole class by Sister Demetrius for stuffing her bra because she'd used colored Kleenex that showed right through the white school-uniform blouse? Flora didn't buy it.

That Josephine believed *Josephine* was going to be famous was not only understandable but accepted family folklore, the story Josephine told about her younger self most often. The auditions, the casting agent who loved her and wanted her to fly to Los Angeles. "They wanted me to be the next Elizabeth Taylor." Glossed over were the years where she continued—unsuccessfully—to audition for Broadway, for radio and television commercials. Marrying Flora's father and the quick dissolution of that relationship. The apartment Flora grew up in was like a shrine to her mother's brief theater career. Crossing the threshold of the small two-bedroom above a bakery in Bay Ridge, you'd never know that Josephine had worked as an actress for only four years and a hotel telephone operator for thirty-five.

"Okay, Miss Rich and Famous, try again with this." Flora's mother handed her the copper-bottomed spaghetti pot. "You need the special cleanser. Make it nice and shiny, so you can see your face."

Remembering now, Flora wondered if that was a common story: little boys who wanted to be famous started carefully and precisely cataloging their lives—*the archives*—and little girls were encouraged to use a variety of cleaning solutions on one sauce pot.

⌒

FLORA HATED THE GARAGE, which had often been claimed by rats over the years; it was a place she tried to pretend didn't even exist. She administered a little pep talk to herself about rodents and their nocturnal habits, mustered her courage, and headed out to the freestanding structure at the end of their driveway. She lifted the heavy door with both hands and paused, listening for any signs of life. When they'd first moved into the house, the entire yard was infested with rats. An older woman had lived in the house for decades and at the end had been too weak and ill to maintain the property. Before they bought it, Flora used to pass the house all the time on her morning walks. It looked like something from a Grimms' fairy tale: vaguely Tudorish, lots of half-timbering, a big cobblestone chimney, and leaded windows. The modest house felt exactly right for the three of them, but it was the extravagant yard that Flora had fallen for. Two looming eucalyptus trees planted long before the house had been built flanked a small patio. At the edge of the lawn, the most beautiful copse of fruit trees she'd ever seen: fig, lemon, tangerine, grapefruit. It was like a Bible color plate of the Garden of Eden. The first time she saw it, it left her breathless. It still did. She never stopped feeling like she'd stepped into someone else's life when she walked outside and smelled the bitter morning air perfumed with eucalyptus, saw the hummingbirds darting in and out of the flowing bougainvillea and the tiny yellow finches eating seeds from the wild rosemary.

And then there were the rats. The fruit was an abundant year-round supply of free food for all the neighborhood rodents. She and Julian had put up a fence, cleared ground cover, baited traps, plugged holes in the garage and house, and she hadn't seen the heart-quickening blur of brown in years. Still, she worried. But all was quiet today.

She made her way back to the file cabinet and opened the top drawer. It was jam-packed with manila folders, all from Good Company's early years back in New York. This was a wormhole she couldn't afford today, but she couldn't resist the program right in front: *Jason and Medea*—the production that Julian and his partner Ben had staged around a defunct city pool in Williamsburg, a retelling of Euripides's *Medea* set in modern-day Brooklyn. The cover of the program was a drawing—the silhouette of a woman carrying a small child in a blood-soaked T-shirt, the blood the only color on the cover. She'd always hated the image, so cold and ruthless. The critics had loved the production—well, the indie critics, the ones from the *Voice* and *Time Out*. But nobody had bought tickets.

"The play is so sad," Flora'd said to a disappointed Julian one night.

"Life is sad," he'd snapped at her.

In the second drawer, theater and drama books: Stanislavski, Hagen, Adler, Meisner, Strasberg. Julian didn't pledge fidelity to any particular method; he was a drama atheist with all the certainty and scorn of atheists. He loathed idolatry. He believed actors should use whatever worked.

She moved on to the third drawer. All of Ruby's old school records and progress reports. The art projects Flora had saved. She used to have to clean out Ruby's backpack and toy box when she was asleep, making sure to bring the garbage outside to the curb that same night. If she didn't, Ruby was bound to open the trash bin and spot something of hers—a broken doll, a drawing, a graded spelling test—and be pierced with longing and indignation. "You're throwing out my *Valentines*?" she said one June morning when Flora had finally dug deep into her school bag, trying to return it to some kind of order. "And my valentine *candy*?" Nearing the final days of the school year, the candy hearts were mostly dust, but Ruby acted like Flora was discarding rare books, fine chocolates.

Flora would apologize. "Oh, honey. I didn't mean to. Good thing you looked." But Ruby would be chilly to her for the rest of the day and protective of every single one of her possessions for weeks, not forgetting. "Where's the paper umbrella they gave me at the restaurant?" "What happened to that yellow ball?" "What did you do with my party hat?" she'd ask Flora, sharp and accusing.

Finally, Flora pulled open the bottom drawer. She dragged an old stool over, a red metal one from Ikea that they'd bought for Ruby to stand on to reach the kitchen counter when she was three. It was paint spattered and scratched but still sturdy. She sat and started rifling through the papers. A jumble of envelopes, not a single one labeled. One held a bunch of faded receipts, one a stack of postcards from various art museums and churches, all meant to serve as inspiration for what exactly she couldn't remember—sets, or costumes maybe.

Under the folders, a large manila envelope that Flora recognized. She pulled it out and saw her own handwriting on the outside: KEEP. Ah, she remembered! She had gathered a bunch of photos and placed them here for safekeeping. She opened the envelope and the one she wanted was right on top.

The photograph had been taken at Ben's sprawling family property upstate during rehearsal for a summer production that was an off-shoot of Good Company's work in Manhattan. Ben and Julian founded and ran Good Company together, but from its earliest days Ben was fixated on mounting an outdoor show up at Stoneham. He pitched the idea late one April night over many beers in Flora and Julian's living room. A piece of classic theater, site-specific, staged for one night—and only one night.

No tickets, no critics. A chance for all their friends who were unemployed and not auditioning in August to get out of the city, get their hands dirty, have complete control over something. *True* community theater.

"I don't know," Julian said. "Seems like a lot."

"If it doesn't work, it doesn't work. Worth a try, right?"

What began the first summer at Stoneham as a lark, an experiment, quickly cemented into annual tradition.

The year of the photograph, one of the actors had documented the entire week of madness. Charlie was a big bear of a guy, bashful, the camera around his neck an obvious shield for his offstage unease. One night while Flora and Margot were sitting on the porch steps, shucking corn for the nightly "family meal," he'd grabbed Julian and David from the lawn, corralled Ruby, who was running around with a dish towel on her head pretending to be a princess, and tried to arrange them all on the steps of the house's front porch.

Flora and Julian sat on the top step, Margot and David just below. Flora barely got Ruby situated next to her when she squirmed away and settled herself onto Margot's lap. Ruby's Margot fixation had started that summer. She followed Margot around the property like a duckling following her adopted mother. Margot looked back at Flora apologetically. "It's fine," Flora said, though it wasn't. Julian moved closer to Flora, kissed her bare shoulder, looped his arm through hers. "Hey"—Flora reached over Margot's shoulder and tapped Ruby's arm, trying one more time—"you don't want to sit on Mommy's lap?"

Ruby shook her head no, but grudgingly reached up to take Flora's hand. Charlie was fiddling with the lens and Ruby was restless, so Flora counted off on Ruby's fingers, saying, "This little piggy went to market, this little piggy went home."

"No, Mama!" Ruby said, but she was laughing. "You need my toes."

"Okay," Charlie finally said, "everyone look up."

And miraculously, everyone had.

Flora and Julian's heads were bent together, smiling straight into the camera. On the bottom step, David was slightly hunched forward, the conscious furling of a very tall man, his elegant surgeon's hands clasped in front of him, his face half-turned to Margot, who was tan and blond and gleaming, her fingers laced together in front of Ruby's buddha belly, her chin on Ruby's head, her smile dazzling the camera. Ruby's legs with their slightly dirty knees entangled with Margot's longer ones. Ruby's hair a mess of curls. Ruby shyly grinning, a finger pulling down the corner of her mouth, her other arm raised and that hand firmly implanted in Flora's, a conduit between her mother and Margot.

They all looked so enmeshed and content and endearing and young. A family.

Flora put the photo in the pocket of her sweater and took a minute to savor her triumph—because this was what Flora did. In the division of labor, emotional and otherwise, that was their marriage, Flora was the finder of lost things. The household St. Anthony. It was a point of pride for her (and a source of irritation for Julian) that when he declared something truly lost, she could usually find it within minutes by following the circuitous routes of his disheveled brain and figuring out his paces in real life. Was that how every couple functioned after time? Seeing the contours of someone else's intelligence so much more easily than your own?

She started putting all the folders and envelopes and notebooks and pens back in the cabinet drawer and decided to do a quick cull while Julian wasn't standing there to object, telling her to save it until he had a chance to look at everything himself, which would be approximately never. This was another area of her expertise, winnowing their lives down to essential parts, appointing herself judge and jury of the detritus of their past, deciding what would survive and what could go. They were so sentimental, her husband and daughter.

Flora did a quick check of the mostly empty notebooks. The cryptic scribblings couldn't have any meaning anymore. Trash. She tested all the markers, half of them spent of ink. She took one that worked and wrote general descriptions on the envelopes (POSTCARDS, FAMILY PHOTOS, PLAYBILLS). From the very back of the drawer, she pulled out a brown envelope stiff with age and something shiny and bright slipped out, a glint of gold on the cracked concrete floor. A ring.

A ring?

Flora immediately recognized it as Julian's wedding ring—*one* of Julian's wedding rings. To her chagrin, he was constantly losing them. How many so far? Three at least. The ring almost always went missing on set or in a theater because he had to take it off if it wasn't right for the part he was playing and also because he was so absentminded. She slipped the ring onto her thumb. Having an extra wouldn't hurt as he was sure to eventually lose the one he was wearing now.

Back in the kitchen, she removed the ring to take a closer look, and that's when she noticed something: the ring was engraved. The only ring they'd had engraved was the first one, because after that who had time? She was holding Julian's original wedding ring.

The chill started low and slow, deep in her gut. It took some seconds for her brain to catch up to the creeping realization

moving through her body. Julian had lost the ring she was holding the summer of the photograph. He'd come to her one afternoon, sheepish. He'd gone for a swim in the pond and somehow
the ring had fallen off in the brackish water.

"Oh, well," Flora had said. "We'll have to get a new one."
She didn't want to make him feel any worse than he did, so she
didn't let on how sorry she was that he'd lost the ring. She was a
little heartbroken. She'd loved that ring, which was too expensive but so pretty. The band was wide and flat with tiny little
beading—milgrain—along the top and bottom. When she'd
slid the ring on his finger the day they married and looked up
at him, at his beautiful face, she'd thought, *Mine*.

And yet. The ring was right here in Flora's palm. It had been
in an envelope at the bottom of the file cabinet in the garage.

Flora was perspiring in a different way now, a cold sweat despite her exertion and the rising sun. She had a sudden, sharp
desire to call her mother, who had been gone for over a decade.
She could almost feel her mother at her side, peering down at
the ring with her familiar scowl, her booming voice full of dis-
may: *Flora. What in the name of g-o-d?*

TWO

⁓

The entire time Margot was being interviewed by the girl (What was her name? Maura? Molly?), a complete stranger sitting on the opposite side of the café had been taking pictures of her with his phone. Some people tried to be surreptitious but they rarely succeeded because in addition to being painfully obvious—the slump, the awkward angle of the device, the studied casualness of a teenager up to no good—Margot, like almost everyone she knew who had a recognizable face, had a sixth sense for being spotted, even when the person was standing behind her in line or on the sidewalk outside of the restaurant or on the other side of the street. Some actors said they felt it as a tingling on the back of the neck or in the tips of their toes. Some, Margot knew, felt joy (*I've been seen! I exist!*) in spite of their complaints. Margot's brand of intuition presented as inexplicable sadness. There she would be: grocery shopping, eating in a restaurant, hiking with a friend and she'd feel a wave of gloom and think, *What's wrong now?*

It was always a camera. Always. And now that there was a

camera in virtually everyone's palm, the surveillance felt constant, the existential sadness a daily battle.

What a world. When someone wanted to take a picture of her and her glass of lemon water on an ordinary Wednesday morning in a little café on Larchmont. The spaces where she felt safe, invisible, were becoming scarcer and scarcer, and this café had been one for nearly all the years she'd lived in Los Angeles. One of the reasons she and David had eschewed the Westside—Beverly Hills, the Palisades, Santa Monica—was because her neighborhood didn't feel as *Hollywood* as those other places. And although it was true that she wasn't bothered by trolling TMZ buses full of tourists (*yet*), this recent, constant intrusion was confounding.

"That must be so annoying," the girl had said when she noticed Margot angling her chair away from the person snapping away with his phone. As with every interview, Margot ran what she wanted to say (*No more annoying than having to talk to you!*) through her survival filter and came up with the blandest reply: "Sure, sometimes it's frustrating, but it comes with the territory and, you know, I'm lucky anyone cares." *Light laugh, shy duck of the face.* The guy with the phone had re-angled himself right along with her. What would he do with all those photos? Text them to someone? Post them somewhere? Make a shrine? Something more perverted?

What a world.

Margot was doing press because she was one of the original cast members of *Cedar*, a network hospital drama about to conclude its ninth season. She played Dr. Cathryn Newhall—Dr. Cat—who, as the audition sheet proclaimed all those years ago, was "a pediatric oncologist waging a war against cancer *and* longing for love." Margot's contract was up for renewal, and this time—this time, *dammit*—she was insisting that her salary be brought to parity with her costar's: Charles Percy, aka Dr. Langford Walker, who had joined the show two years *after* Margot and still made more money than she did. Charles was the chief of surgery at the fictional Cedar General in the fictional northwest town of Cedar. Charles started back when Bess, the show's creator, still lathered all her attention and affection on the show, back when she called it her "baby," before she had an actual baby. He started before Bess began building her empire of *Cedar* spin-offs: *Willow*, a drama about the medical examiner's office helping to solve crimes, and *Cypress*, which focused on a trauma center of a major city hospital. "*Cedar* is still my first baby," Bess loved to say the first day of each season when she showed up to give her inspirational talk to the entire cast and crew. "I might not *physically* be here all the time, but I am always here in spirit, and—I have a lot of spies." The line always got a laugh from the newcomers and an inward groan from the veterans because she did indeed have spies.

"Charles is a real *get*," Bess had told Margot excitedly when he signed on. "Fresh from Broadway. Tony nominated."

Margot resisted reminding Bess that two years prior she'd been fresh from a Drama Desk nomination *and* a successful run on the West End. Bess had the memory of a sparrow, only able to contain what she needed in that moment. And Margot was genuinely excited to work with Charles. They'd crossed paths a lot in New York and had worked together once during an out-of-town run at the Guthrie. She liked him, and he did bring a certain prestige to the show. She was glad to have him as her television love interest. She just wanted to make the same amount of money that he did.

"Now's the time to push," Margot had told her manager,

Donna, the previous week. After a few years of mediocre story lines, the past season had been a strong one for Margot. Dr. Cat and Dr. Walker had realized their many-season dream of having a child—twins via surrogate—and Bess had given Dr. Cat non-birth postpartum depression. "Is this really a thing?" Margot had asked.

"It is, because I had it," Bess told her solemnly. Of course. For reasons that were never quite clear to Margot, Dr. Cat's story arcs usually mirrored Bess's real-life story arcs. When Bess fell in love, so did Dr. Cat. When Bess couldn't get pregnant, neither could Dr. Cat. So, if Bess had non-birth postpartum? Well, Margot would play the hell out of it despite never having been pregnant and never having had a child and never regretting either for a single second.

"We need to get you out there, Margot. Prove to Bess that Dr. Cat still means a lot to viewers and then set our terms. An Emmy nomination would be fucking fantastic," Donna'd said, wistful, because those days were over for the cast of *Cedar*. Long gone were the summer months where Margot would drive down Sunset Boulevard and see her towering face on the For Your Consideration billboards. The show had been around too many years and felt too old-fashioned. Standard network fare.

So here she sat, at interview number five, offering up Margot's Favorite Moments—scenes, costars, story lines, wardrobe— from nine seasons at Cedar General. No detail seemed too mundane, and in an effort to try to not ask the same questions everyone else was asking, the queries had become absurd. This morning she'd had to send a description of one of her "favorite things" to her publicist, Sylvia, for an article that would appear God only knew where.

She'd chosen a candle from an old pharmacy in Florence,

one she gave away as gifts all the time because the candle itself was so pretty and the scent of the one she favored wasn't overpowering. *It smells like Sunday mornings in Italy*, she'd written, *redolent of roasting coffee, lemon blossoms, and pine groves.* She'd written about coming across the shop as a teen during her family's annual summer trip and how the candle reminded her of those magical months in the Italian countryside. She'd enjoyed the exercise, for once. But then Sylvia had emailed back that the publication was featuring the *entire cast's* favorite things, and the woman who played her little sister, Kelsey Kennen, a fairly new addition to the show and someone Margot was trying very hard not to loathe, had also chosen a candle and *Sorry!* but Kelsey's candle was not only more affordable—*Do you really pay seventy dollars for a candle?*—but was also made by Syrian refugees, so could Margot pick something else? *It would be great*, Sylvia had written, *if whatever you choose could come from a war-torn nation. A handbag maybe? Sandals? I don't want to put words in your mouth, of course.*

Or shoes in my closet? Margot had written back.

Lol. But—seriously. Maybe something from Bosnia? This from a woman who spent hundreds of dollars a week to have someone blow-dry her hair and couldn't find Bosnia on a map if you offered her a case of seventy-dollar candles.

Usually all it took for Margot to steer the conversation during an interview was to retell her shopworn tales about what it was like to play a doctor on television while being married to a doctor in real life. A not-very-amusing coincidence that was endlessly entertaining for the media. She knew all the questions by now: Did she run her scripts by her husband? Did he help her rehearse? Did he watch/like/respect the show? And she had all of her answers down pat (longer versions of no, no, yes).

But this girl (Mia!) had done her homework, and she was a good interviewer, keeping Margot off balance by threading her puff-piece questions with genuinely interesting ones. She'd dug up some of Margot's old work, including her first television show that had filmed in New York, the one where she played a smart, eccentric single woman—also named Margot—in her early thirties *not* longing for love, never mind a cure for cancer. The creator and director were young and exciting, but the single-camera show was scheduled to premiere two days after 9/11, which of course didn't happen. By the time it did air, some weeks later, nobody was paying attention, and the light-hearted take on Manhattan felt wrong given the context of the world. She told herself that was the reason *Margot* was received poorly, even by the critics clamoring for something better and smarter than the standard sitcom pabulum. They'd had a twelve-episode order, but the ratings were so dismal the show had been cancelled after six. Nobody other than the people involved in making *Margot* had seen the last episodes. Apparently they were in the Paley Center for the Media.

"I'm wondering how it felt to go from your theater days in New York to working on *Margot* to a hospital drama like *Cedar*. As good as it is," Mia said (young but smooth), "it's very different from your work in New York."

Like night and day was what Margot wanted to say to her. *Like fucking night and day.* Her work before becoming Dr. Cathryn Newhall was interesting and literate and challenging, and *Cedar* was a nighttime soap opera—fun and ridiculous and the pay was great. She could see the audition description as if it had manifested on the table in front of her: "Cathryn Newhall (Dr. Cat) is pretty (*feline pretty a plus*) and approachable, kids love her on sight, brilliant but a little flaky; did she remember to wash her hair today?"

Mostly, *Cedar* was the thing that got her and David out of New York when they needed to leave. But she wasn't chatting with a girlfriend. This was an interview, and it was her job to be interesting for sixty to ninety minutes but not say anything of real interest.

Before she'd even had a chance to flex the old muscles of that particular narrative (*had enough, wanted a different life, Los Angeles beckoned*), Mia mentioned the Jensen case and stopped Margot in her tracks. "I know you moved out here in part so your husband could open his stroke clinic, but I also came across something about a patient of his who died during surgery. Abbie Jensen? And I was wondering if that played into your decision to leave New York." (Not just smooth, *devious*.) "I'm sure this is a sensitive topic," Mia continued, "but I was wondering, with some distance, if you'd care to talk about the Jensens. Are you ever in touch?"

Now Margot wondered whether the girl was actually fucking with her, because why in the world would they have stayed in touch with the Jensens? "I'm sorry," she said, using her gentle voice, the one she'd cultivated for the scenes where she had to tell a family the test results were *not what they'd hoped*, "but I thought this was a profile about me and *Cedar*."

Mia had the courtesy to blush. "I was doing research on your New York days, and it seemed like the dates might be significant."

Margot sat there with a perfectly benign expression on her face, trying to imagine what vein of "research" would have brought this girl to the Jensen case. The hospital had done a good job keeping it out of the news; they'd settled quickly and the Jensen family hadn't wanted that kind of attention. The agreement was sealed. She held Mia's gaze; she'd learned how to hold a silence to the point of discomfort, a journalist's favorite trick and one that never, ever worked on her. She could outlast anyone. It wasn't a fair fight, really. She stared at Mia. She was pretty in a blond and possibly Midwestern way, her nose a little flat, her cheeks a little broad. Twenty-five? Twenty-six? No makeup, but her skin was blinding. She took care of her skin, just like all the young people who were the most talented and the most beautiful—often both—in their hometowns who flocked to Los Angeles only to discover a city brimming with identical specimens. Mia's studied casualness didn't fool Margot—the lowered pitch, the widened eyes. She was dressed in her version of what an entertainment journalist should wear. A flowery, flowing dress that could have come from a revival of *Little House on the Prairie*, lace-up leather boots, a long loose braid, a bomber jacket. A costume. Margot looked at Mia and thought, *I know you.*

The waiter came over, and Margot asked a bunch of inane questions about the menu to buy some time even though she never ate during interviews. She'd made that mistake once, years before, and the reporter had peppered his article with descriptions of her breaking off pieces of her scone as "raccoon like." Margot looked at her watch, almost noon. "I don't suppose," she said, lowering her voice conspiratorially and flashing her widest smile, "that I could persuade you to have a glass of wine with me. They have the most delicious Gavi di Gavi here."

"Gavi?" Mia said, hand fluttering to a slender chain around her neck, eyes widening. "What is that?"

"Oh, you're in for a treat. Two glasses," she said to the waiter, and, breaking her rule, "Why don't you put together a nice antipasti platter for us?" She turned back to Mia. "Did you know I spent summers in Italy as a kid?"

"THIS IS SO DELICIOUS," Mia said, raising glass number two to her lips. The wine had loosened her up, and now Margot was asking *her* questions, about her job, her boyfriend the aspiring actor, her hopes and dreams. "I would *love* to go to Italy," she told Margot, polishing off her wine.

"You have to," Margot said, "and when you do, I'll give you my personal list of restaurants." And then, "Hey, are you busy tonight? Because there's a premiere at the Hollywood ArcLight for that new Clooney movie, and the whole thing takes place in Italy. I've heard good things. I was supposed to go, but I'm hosting a party for my best friend's daughter. I can definitely get you and your boyfriend on the list if you're interested."

"Are you kidding me?" Mia put her glass down a little too hard. "I don't know how to thank you. That would be amazing. You are *so unbelievably nice.*"

Mission accomplished. Margot had diverted the conversation without giving Mia any ammunition to write about her unwillingness to discuss David or the Jensens because that reluctance would take on a life of its own. Another reporter would read about her not talking about the Jensens and then another, and pretty soon there would be a full-fledged piece somewhere dredging up the painful past—an event juicy enough, even a decade later, to feed the bottomless pit that was entertainment journalism.

"Wow," Margot said, looking at her watch. "It's late. I'm afraid I have to run."

"Oh, shoot," Mia said, picking up her notebook. "I had a few more questions."

"I have time for one more."

"Okay," Mia said, relieved, looking down at her notes. She turned the pages of her Moleskine, stopped, looked back up at Margot, and smiled. "Okay. One last question. Any regrets?"

She used the word lightly, as only someone so young could. Margot choked back a laugh. Where to begin with regret! She wouldn't know where to start. Or rather, she would: she would go back to the morning of David's stroke, when they were still in their place on East Eighty-fifth street. Him coming into the kitchen fresh from a shower, her picking the moldy raspberries from the container and putting the perfect ones into a bowl. His hands around her waist. "No," she said to the girl. So young. So unsullied. So poreless. "I have a wonderful husband, a job I love, a great life. I'm so *lucky*."

On the sidewalk after the interview, she stood wondering where to go. She was hungry and she had the beginnings of a wine headache. She could go home, but she was hosting Ruby's graduation party tonight and her house was full of catering staff. Plus a florist. She should go home and supervise, make sure everything wasn't too over the top, or else Flora would—well, she wouldn't say anything, but she'd get that look on her face, the disapproving pinched mouth, the tense set to her shoulders. She wouldn't even try to hide the slight eye roll. Lately, this seemed galling to Margot, to have to continue to pretend she didn't spend money in an entirely different way than Flora and Julian did, because the monetary gulf had narrowed in the last few years, now that both Flora and Julian were steadily employed.

Flora, after years of commercial voice-overs, had a part as

a main character on *Griffith*, an animated musical series that was about Los Angeles, only all the characters—Hollywood players and not—were animals living in either Griffith Park or the neighboring zoo. After season one, the show had the all-important word-of-mouth and a season-two renewal. Margot had caught up on the episodes yesterday. Flora was phenomenal as Leona, a lioness preoccupied with getting older, losing her looks, and worrying that her singing voice was deteriorating. The show was funny and dark and although it was geared to adults—the cages in the zoo the perfect symbol for how actors were pigeonholed, *kept* the story lines also managed to be sweet and hopeful.

Julian had moved up to series regular on his cop show. He had to be making decent money, and she didn't think he helped finance Good Company anymore. Why would he? He was never there.

She understood Flora and Julian's habits were engrained, their priorities different, but why did that mean she had to feel sheepish about wanting mini lobster rolls for Ruby's gradua-tion? What she'd *really* wanted was to host a good old-fashioned clambake, fly in a crew from her favorite restaurant on Cape Cod to orchestrate the entire thing. But she'd seen the look on Flora's face when she described the enterprise. Picnic tables covered with layers of butcher paper, the food strewn down the length of the table: clams, lobsters, crabs, corn, potatoes, pots of melted butter, everyone digging in with their hands. But it was Ruby's party after all. The guests were her friends and Flora and Julian's friends, so she'd downgraded. Burgers (Kobe beef), dogs (Wagyu), and Flora was going to have to deal with the mini lobster rolls.

She was walking slowly, pretending to window-shop. She

had to assume Mia could be sitting in her car, observing Margot's post-interview self. The Jensens. For years, Margot had thought about the Jensens every day, wondering what they ate for breakfast, if they'd return to their jobs, and if they would ever try to have another child. She would think about them on holidays and weekends. She wondered if they'd moved to another place, left the city. She always expected to run into one of them, because it seemed like the rule of New York City was that you would mostly run into people you were dying to avoid, but she never had. She'd been tempted to look them up on the internet, see what their lives were like now, but she was afraid she'd be opening some porthole of darkness that would swallow them, invite back the shadow that seemed to retreat a little when they moved to Los Angeles.

She meandered down the street and stopped into the bookshop she loved, entered the side annex where all the art and photography books were. She'd bought Ruby a fancy digital camera for graduation because Ruby loved photography; she had an artist's eye. Maybe she'd buy her a book, too. As she browsed the tables, she saw a man on the sidewalk outside, watching her, angling the camera, checking the phone to see if the photos he'd taken were acceptable. Cameras. She couldn't escape them. She turned away from the window and opened her handbag and rooted around for her phone to text Flora. In her peripheral vision, she could see the bearded guy showing a woman the photos on his phone, then pointing to real-life Margot inside.

What a world.

THREE

The ring sat on the kitchen table like a piece of kryptonite, and Flora stared. How had she not sensed it under her roof for all those years? How had she not felt its heat, smelled its stench of broken vow, because why else would Julian have hidden it away? The treacherous telltale heart.

When Flora was a young girl she used to try to "fix" moments in her memory. The notion that years of her life would pass and she would only remember snippets, seconds of the whole, distressed her. She came up with a plan and at various times— walking home from school or out with friends or just sitting at her desk she would think: *This. Remember this. It's 1978, 1981, 1993*, and *this* happened: walking down Bay Ridge's Third Avenue glistening with Christmas lights; sitting under a tree in Fort Hamilton Park in the shadow of the Verrazzano bridge; Sunday dinner, the table groaning with platters of spaghetti and eggplant parmigiana and stuffed artichokes. It worked, in a fashion, except she lost the specifics of the moment—the smells,

the sounds, the people, her mood. She was left with a fistful of
memories, containing her fierce desire to will a memory.

But this moment? This moment was one she knew was going to stick. How to make sense of the object in her hand? She
wanted coffee. How odd, she never drank coffee after her one
allotted morning cup anymore; it made her too shaky. As she got
the grounds from the refrigerator and started scooping them
into a filter, she realized what she was doing. She was conjuring
her mother and her aunts, her protectors, all dead now. The
surest way to get the attention of the Mancini sisters—even in
the afterlife—was coffee in any of its stages: percolating, freshly
brewed, stale and burnt, reheated in a microwave. The life cycle
of a pot of coffee was the smell of her mother's apartment. She
didn't know how they did it, those women. They lived on coffee and cigarettes and cooked food all day they barely touched.
They ate two forkfuls of pasta, they munched on a crispy corner of breaded veal while standing at the stove poking at the
cutlets simmering in a cast-iron pan of oil. They ate half a
cannoli, the heel of a loaf of bread dunked in a pot of tomato
sauce. They *picked*. But their appetite for coffee and cigarettes
was bottomless. She wanted to feel them around her now, now
that—

Well. Now that *what*?

If someone had put the photo from Stoneham in front of
Flora and said, "Quick! What do you remember about that
summer?" Julian's lost wedding ring might not have made the
list. She picked up the photograph and looked at Julian's hand.
Julian's ringless hand. When he confessed he'd lost the ring in
the pond, he was so upset that *she'd* ended up consoling *him*. It
was only a thing, she'd said, just a band of gold. They'd get a
new one. Even though they both knew it would be a while be-

fore they could squeeze a replacement into their budget. Every time that year she saw the tiny strip of pale skin where the ring had been, it made her sad.

When she remembered that summer, she thought how it was only months before David's stroke, and though they couldn't know it at the time, it would be the last summer Margot would perform at Stoneham. She remembered it was the summer Ben insisted they stage *The Crucible*—in spite of everyone's moaning and groaning that they weren't high school sophomores anymore—because, he insisted, it was the perfect allegory for Guantánamo Bay. It was the year Ben had generously offered them the Little House for the entire summer and he and Julian had planted a few hemlock trees to give the front porch a little shade and privacy. Julian had strung lights on the one right in front that was the size of a small Christmas tree. Ben insisted Ruby flip the switch to light the tree every night at sunset and because it was also the summer Ruby became obsessed with the stack of Frank Sinatra albums in the Little House, she'd make the gathered crowd sing along to *That's Life*. "Her Mancini blood," Flora told Julian as they watched Ruby belt out her version of the lyrics: *I've been a puppet, a parrot, a poem, a popcorn, a pong, and a KINGGGGG.*

Flora remembered that it was the summer of the seventeen-year cicadas clinging to the tree trunks with their vulgar transparent wings and creepy red eyes—they terrified Ruby. It was also the year a million tree frogs took up residence around the pond ("What's next? Boils?" Margot asked) and everyone who could would catch a frog and bring it with cupped hands to Ruby, who kept them all—unsuccessfully—in a big red pail. She remembered how Ruby lost her fear of swimming that year, and when Flora tucked her into bed at night, she'd bury her nose in the fatty folds of Ruby's neck and smell the pond, clean and grassy with a slight undertone of rot.

That summer was also the summer of Margot and Ruby. One afternoon as Flora and Margot were watching Ruby play with two dolls on the front porch, Margot perked up and shushed Flora and said, "What is she saying?" They crept closer and listened and looked at each other in disbelief over what would become the summer's best party trick, five-year-old Ruby reciting Margot's lines from *The Crucible*: "'John, I counted myself so plain,'" she had one Barbie doll say to the other, "'It were a cold house I kept.'"

But Julian's missing ring? It hadn't seemed like a part of the story she needed to notice.

Flora wouldn't know exactly what she was dealing with until much later today because Julian was going to the graduation straight from work and then they were all going to Margot's. She wouldn't call him on set; even if he could answer and was alone and able to speak freely, this was not a discussion to be had during one of his breaks.

Flora stepped outside because the walls of her kitchen felt like they were vibrating, contaminated by the presence of the ring. The room she usually took so much comfort in because of its wall of casement windows and tiny breakfast nook. She would sit there in the morning and read the news, and depending on her day, do her vocal warm-ups and exercises. Drink her hot water and honey. Watch the ridiculous pageantry of wildlife right beyond the glass. The delicate yellow butterflies that always flew around as a couple, darting in and out of one another's path. The mellow honeybees hovering in the lavender along the side of the house. The fence lizards doing their show-off push-ups on the concrete retaining wall. The vivid pink-and-orange bougainvillea, the neighborhood libertine, intruding into every available space. It was like living on the back lot of a movie studio, only everything was real, all hers.

Her phone buzzed, and she ran back to the kitchen to grab it. She wouldn't intentionally disturb Julian, but if he called her—

It was a text from Margot.

> Where are you? You wouldn't believe the day I'm having.

Well, that makes two of us, Flora thought. She ignored the text. She didn't need to hear about Margot's horrible interview or her complaints about the questions and, invariably, a rant about people-in-public-with-phones. Margot would never admit it, not to herself or anyone else, but the only thing she hated more than cell phones was being completely ignored in public. Flora had seen Margot drop an iced coffee, fake a stumble, increase her volume so people had to look to see who was being so damn loud—just for that moment of recognition, the double take, the surprised smile, the approach.

Flora wasn't in the mood. She needed to walk.

When they first moved to Los Angeles, it was the walking that allowed Flora to find her way into her West Coast life. She more than anyone was aware of the irony. "Los Angeles!" everyone said, alarmed, when they'd announced their move. "But the traffic! The smog! The dearth of intelligence!" It was almost funny, the way her world of New Yorkers reacted. "Better you than me" was a thing she heard nearly once a day, even though so many of their friends would leap at the chance to be cast on a series, to make some real money for a change. At first it was amusing, but quickly became annoying. "Don't people understand they're talking about my life? Would they say that if we were moving to London?" she asked Julian. "To Chicago? It's downright rude."

"I agree. It's rude."

"If I said we were moving to *Tulsa*, would people say, 'Better you than me'?"

"If we were moving to Tulsa? Maybe."

Flora was exasperated. "You know what I mean."

"I do. But also, let's not be hypocrites. How many times have we sat right here in our eat-in kitchen"—he gestured grandly, taking in the tiny space, barely big enough for two adults never mind their daughter, who seemed to be growing visibly lately, her limbs a little longer every morning when she came out of her bedroom, which back in some previous iteration of the apartment building had been someone's foyer. "How many times have we sat here and felt superior to Margot and David because we stayed in New York? Because we had the fiber to last."

Flora knew he was right and also that her sudden swing to staunch defender of the West Coast rose from an inability to admit to herself how hard it was going to be to leave New York City, the West Village, her home, her heart, her people. Relocating had started as a lark, one she'd been happy to indulge because it seemed so improbable. Flora in Los Angeles? Julian in Los Angeles? They were the quintessential Manhattan couple, knowing how to work the city with their rent-controlled apartment in a neighborhood with a good public school and exactly one child, whose tiny bedroom would suffice.

For years, they would visit Margot and David and watch their lives take on a different hue, feel their souls expand to fill the sun-drenched vistas of Los Angeles. They'd watch Ruby run around on the lawn, swim in the pool, pick lemons from the tree in the yard. David would grill steaks in February, and after dinner they'd sit around the fire pit with blankets on their laps, sipping some decadent California red wine. Mornings were for hiking or a trip to the farmers' market to buy fresh strawberries and fava beans and sweet peas. (In March!)

On the way back to New York, they'd all be quiet, partly tired, partly contemplative. But as soon as the plane approached the city, Julian would take Ruby on his lap, make her watch the descent over the skyline and say to her—in what became a practiced routine, Abbott and Costello—"What do you see, my girl?" And she would press her nose against the freezing window of the plane and say what he'd taught her: "I see the best city in the world, my daddy!"

And they believed it. Even the year Ruby sobbed all the way to the airport in Los Angeles because she would miss the lizards in Margot's yard. Even the year they opened the apartment door after a week at Margot's to the unmistakable smell of not one but many dead mice. Even the year they got home in the middle of a late spring snowstorm and the dryers in their building were broken and Flora had to drag their wet laundry through the slush to a local laundromat. She'd stood in the laundromat folding clothes that wouldn't see the light of day again for months, and pictured Margot at that very moment, moving through the rooms brilliant with sun. She thought of how David could walk out to the front yard and pick an avocado. As she matched Ruby's Hello Kitty socks and eyed the snow outside that was starting to turn to sleet—the freshly dried clothes would get wet again on the walk home—she envied Margot the most basic convenience: being able to open a door and walk outside. Outside wasn't an excursion that required coats and boots and locking up an apartment and a destination. What would it be like to have a washer and dryer *in* the house, not down the street or in the very creepy basement of their building that was always freezing and reeked of mildew and was certainly the source of all the rodents that found their way into her kitchen? What would it be like, she wondered, to wake up almost every day and know the sun would shine, the lemons would ripen, the hummingbirds would flit, to walk into a room in your own house and load the washer and then step outside to pick a tangerine for breakfast?

But if she and Julian allowed themselves their moments of envy, they were quick to pivot. The leaf blowers! God, they were awful. The racket, how could you stand it? The cars, the traffic. And wouldn't sunshine pouring through the windows every day be wearying, wouldn't it bleach your soul and your mind? All the furniture in Margot's house was faded on the side that faced the windows and basked in the sun all day. All the deep blues and greens on one side of her beautifully upholstered chairs reduced to shades of white and gray. "See?" Julian said, turning the chairs to metaphor, "that sun—it strips away all the texture."

And who moved out of a rent-stabilized apartment? It was like giving away the last seat on the last plane out of Saigon. It was a thing you would regret for the rest of your days. The only constant of New York was that if you let go, the city would speed along without you. If you stepped off, you would never be able to afford to slip back in. Were they willing to do that? They thrived on the energy and frustration of New York; it was what made them interesting, kept them sharp. Los Angeles wasn't a real city.

No edge, Julian would say.

No energy, Flora would say.

And yet.

And yet—

No matter how often Flora tried to pinpoint the moment their feelings changed she couldn't, because like most things it wasn't a moment but a series of moments that felt like a trail of breadcrumbs leading them somewhere new. Flora wasn't sure how or why or even exactly when, but Julian's hunger for everything that was Good Company and his brooding discontent for anything that wasn't had mellowed. It seemed that as things got easier, the ties loosened. Finally, Good Company was ambling along—not making any great amount of money but not hemorrhaging money, either. Like so many small downtown theaters, they rented a modest space for rehearsals and readings. Over the years, Julian and Ben had done enough work on the building and bartered enough repairs that it was in decent shape, no longer requiring mass infusions of cash they never had. The meager credit line they'd talked a sympathetic banker into extending them was paid off. As their reputation grew, they got regular residencies at bigger theaters and had figured out how to mount shows that mostly broke even. For two consecutive years they'd even made a little money. Julian had stepped back from the day-to-day responsibilities. He didn't sweep the floors anymore or run off programs at Kinko's at two a.m. or plunge the funky toilet. Julian was the de facto artistic director, choosing scripts, casting shows, courting directors, trying to steer Ben's sometimes contradictory impulses into choices that might interest the right people, bring an audience.

Eventually, younger members of the company were eager to pitch in, take over the more burdensome responsibilities. Anything he still wanted to do he could do from Los Angeles with occasional visits back east. Ben's attention had almost completely shifted to the summer production at Stoneham (after the first year, he'd tried naming it Stoneham Soup, but nobody bit; it was always just Stoneham).

At first Flora didn't know how to feel about this twitch of the rudder, the taking away of her nemesis. As long as she had resented Good Company (and *loved*—she had loved Good Company like an unruly favored child who doesn't love you back), without it her ire was free-floating. And who were they without Good Company—the irritant and the binder? Who would they be?

Less time running Good Company meant more time for auditions, which meant Julian booked more work, and when the callback came for a new show that would be filming in Los Angeles it didn't seem like a conundrum. Most of the time the callback was the achievement, the odds of getting the part so slender. But then it was a second callback and another and then the call from his agent that the producers wanted to fly him to Los Angeles for a chemistry test with a potential costar.

"This would probably be the time to tell them we don't want to relocate," he'd said to Flora, after Ruby was asleep. They were sitting in what they called the Great Room. A twelve-by-fourteen living room that was also kitchen and dining room and library and workout room and whatever else they needed that wasn't their bedroom. It paid to be in the theater when living in a tiny apartment. Lara, the company's set designer, knew a handful of carpenters who were always looking to pick up extra work. Everything in the apartment had dual functions. The pneumatic coffee table converted to a dining table or a desk. Ruby's Murphy bed flipped up to give her space to play. The kitchen counter was hinged and could lift up against the wall to create more dining space. It was ingenious, but it also felt like she was on a stage all the time, waiting for a few stage-hands dressed in black and wearing headsets to run out and snatch the flowers off the dining table while they broke it down to a park bench.

It was a warm spring night and the two windows in the living room were open and she could hear the sounds of the street. The rush of traffic, the impatient bleat of a horn, laughter from people leaving the restaurant down the block. She could smell someone grilling meat, getting a jump on summer. She thought about how they'd brought Ruby home to this place in a Moses basket. How before Ruby was born she had believed the apartment was keeping her from carrying a successful pregnancy.

"Maybe if we moved," she said to Julian late one night, unable to sleep, unable to stop crying. "Sometimes I think my body knows there's nowhere to put a baby. Maybe if we had more room . . ." She knew she was being irrational, and Julian was so solicitous, so eager for her to regain her equilibrium, that he made an appointment with a realtor to look at a bunch of two-bedroom apartments that weekend. It was laughable, what the prices for the extra space were in their neighborhood.

"Should we be looking in Brooklyn?" Flora asked the realtor.

"If you want," the woman had said, disinterested. She'd sized them up the minute she saw their reaction to the prices on the spec sheets. "You and everyone else in Manhattan. It's madness out there."

"I shouldn't let them fly me to California if I'm not willing to consider it," Julian said, pulling her back to the present, to their living room, their apartment, their life. "Flora?"

"Are you considering it?" she asked, picking up on the different tone of his voice.

He shrugged. "I could be persuaded to consider it."

Surprising herself, she said, "We could at least sleep on it."

⌒

FLORA TRUDGED UP HER FAVORITE path to the Griffith Observatory, which usually had a calming effect. She was out nice and early, so she ran into all the regulars on the trail. The tall, freckled man with reddish-blond hair walking two Irish setters that looked so much like their owner they all seemed to have stepped from the pages of a children's book. The dapper gentleman in his eighties, a dead ringer for Gregory Peck, who wore khakis and a sweater tied around his neck and appeared to have suffered a stroke on his left side. He walked every day, as far as Flora could tell, slow and determined, dragging one foot along with enormous effort. The elderly Yoon sisters up the block, dressed to protect themselves from the sun, including a kind of veil that descended from the brims of their hats, making them look like petite beekeepers. Her friend Lopez, who was up at the Observatory every morning and would hang around at the head of the trail, talking up the pretty young ladies, flirting bombastically with the older ones, high-fiving the runners, spreading his abundant joy all over the hillside. Julian had come with her a few Saturday mornings, and he was always perplexed by the cheeriness. "How do you *know* these people?"

"I don't. We're park friends." Some mornings she'd be out early enough to see the scraggly, unkempt coyotes ending their evening of hunting, like the morning she'd left the house as the sun was rising and a coyote had jogged past her with a large black cat in its mouth. She'd screamed, and the animal had sped up. Her instinct was to give chase, but for what? To try and wrestle the undoubtedly feral kitty from between the animal's teeth?

She could feel the ring against her leg in her pocket. She pulled her baseball cap down low over her face. Put in her headphones even though she wasn't listening to the music playing. What was she going to do? Ruby's graduation was that very night, then they were all going to Margot's house, which would be full of people celebrating Ruby's graduation, including Ruby's boyfriend and his parents. The odd assortment of friends in Los Angeles who stood in for the family they didn't have in the city. Flora had never been good at masking her emotions. She knew she would walk through Margot's door and Margot would take one look at her and say *What's wrong?* And she would crumble.

Whatever you do, little miss, keep your eyes open. People aren't always what they seem. Some mothers might have offered words of encouragement or advice or—even when Flora got married, especially in her Catholic neighborhood—unneeded reassurances about the *wedding night*. Not Flora's mother. Josephine's advice from the minute she and Julian were serious up to and including her wedding day could have all been gathered under the heading: *Be Suspicious.*

It wasn't hard to understand how the ring had also summoned Josephine; she might as well have been standing right next to Flora at the top of the trail, drawing down a Benson & Hedges Menthol Light 100. She could hear her perfectly: "He's too handsome. I told you day one that was going to be a problem. And actors! My God, you didn't learn your lesson with your father? They don't know how to be with one person. It's not"—and here the ghost of Josephine jabbed herself on the side of the head—"it's not in the equipment. The only equipment that works on those fools is down below."

Flora had been raised to be suspicious and distrustful, and when she started dating Julian that was her default method of assessing his intentions: to be a relentless sneak. Reading mail, listening to phone messages, scouring daily planners and whatever receipts she happened upon. Even though she was caught twice, she kept it up until she realized what any other person would have discovered a lot sooner: that her snooping always, *always* made her feel worse. Not because she ever found anything she was looking for but because the act of looking into someone's life with suspicion gave everything the whiff of dissolution.

Once they were married and Ruby was born and (this is how she thought of it) their adulthood and marriage began in earnest, she stopped believing there was truth in Josephine's words. She began believing, finally, that Josephine's fate was not her own.

She stood at the railing of the Griffith Observatory and fingered the ring in her pocket. She could take the ring in her palm, rear back with her arm, and let it fly into the scrubby dirt hillside, peppered with chaparral and wild fennel and black mustard. If she arced the ring just right, it would fall into a shrub or in the small runoff ditch on the side of the road. Maybe picked up by a hawk or the same coyote who favored cats. Maybe a park ranger would find it and there would be a notice on the information station: *Lost ring, gold, engraved:* J AND F.

If she threw it away, she wouldn't have to face whatever truth came with the ring. She thought about the day they bought the ring, how Margot and David had come with them, how

Margot had liked a fancier ring, something platinum and hammered, but instead Julian had chosen the gold band.

Margot. If this were anything else, she would have already called Margot to discuss. But she couldn't until she knew what it meant. And maybe there was a perfectly logical and innocent reason that the ring had been sitting in their file cabinet for thirteen years instead of where it was supposed to be: on the bottom of the pond at Stoneham, resting among the twigs and slugs and whatever other objects had been lost during the many summer productions that had been staged on Ben's property. Somehow she doubted it.

.

FOUR

⌁

O n the sidewalk outside the school auditorium, the endless graduation ceremony finally over, Ruby threaded
her way through the crowd looking for her parents. She
was trying to walk elegantly, but her feet were killing her. She'd
been thrilled when Margot had offered to lend her the expensive
pair of heels, but she couldn't wait to get them off and put on a
pair of flats. Looking around, she saw how nearly all the graduates had made the same mistake and the girls were delicately
navigating the grass and the cracks in the sidewalk, clutching
onto one another for balance, looking like agile fawns, their
faces a blend of exhilaration and fear.

It was a cinematically beautiful June night, the setting sun
infusing the world with a vivid orangey pink, making everyone and everything luminous and bright, if only briefly. She
could smell the heady flowering of night jasmine, and even the
distant thrum of a helicopter sounded romantic to her. Ruby
hadn't expected to be so emotional during the ceremony. Although her school had long since shed its religious affiliation,

it had been founded by a Scotsman, and the bagpipes were still dusted off and trotted out for any formal occasion, a tradition Ruby and her friends had always mocked. But tonight, after all the families were seated and the keening pipes filled the coffers of the room, as the girls slowly processed down the navy carpeted aisles, Ruby was unexpectedly moved, caught off guard by a wave of nostalgia. Darrow Academy had been a constant in her Los Angeles life. As she walked past where she knew her parents and Ivan were seated, she couldn't even look at them, afraid she'd start crying, and she couldn't imagine anything more mortifying. Ruby liked being the comforter, the friend who could lend a shoulder and crack the right joke. She was not going to perform her sadness like all the girls around her ostentatiously crying, fanning their faces with their hands, aware of themselves and the pretty sight they made, flushed pink with tears.

Moving through the clusters of families on the sidewalk, Ruby was dreading seeing her mother a little; she was worried Flora would be crying. Because if, when she found her parents, her mother turned to her and was weepy, there was no way Ruby was going to be able to keep it together. The entire summer was going to be one long good-bye—this she knew was inevitable—but she wanted tonight to be celebratory, not melancholy. Ruby had a hard time differentiating her moods from the miasma of her mother's emotions, which infiltrated her like the morning fog, the storied marine layer that crept over Los Angeles at this time of the year.

"It's not your job to worry," Julian would tell her all the time, taking her head in his hands and using his two thumbs to soothe the anxious wrinkles on her forehead. But wasn't it? The three of them were a tight unit, and if one of them was unhappy, how could the other two ignore it? Flora would tell Ruby all the time how one of Nana Jo's favorite admonitions to her daughter was, "You are only as happy as your unhappiest child." The point of the story being that Flora was an *only* child and, therefore, was not allowed to express unhappiness. And even though her mother said it in a joking way, a way that made clear she'd *hated* the burden of the sentiment, why did she repeat it if she didn't think it was at least a little bit true? So it *was* her job to worry, how could she not if her happiness was the defining feature of her parents' happiness?

And wasn't the reverse also true? Many times Ruby had felt she could only be as happy as her unhappiest parent. She felt it more keenly when they lived in New York because life had become easier in California, but she'd never lost what Julian called her tuning fork—the thing inside her that was always calibrating the mood in the house. "Ruby's an old soul." How many times had she heard Flora describe her that way to another person?

Ruby was pretty sure she was just an only child, a kid who spent a lot of time around adults and was comfortable with adult emotions, a thing she would never say to Flora because she didn't want to pick that scab with the words *only child*. Not that Ruby cared (she felt herself insisting to herself); she never wished for siblings. Well, maybe sometimes. Maybe it would be nice to have a sister where they could borrow each other's clothes and makeup. Maybe on Christmas Day when she wanted to play with a board game or a dollhouse, it would have been nice to be with someone other than her parents, who just wanted to sit in their pajamas all day, reading the books they'd invariably given to one another. Maybe it would be nice to feel that another person was responsible for their family happiness.

As she walked, Ruby spotted David, waving his hands over his head to get her attention like a football referee calling a play. He'd been at last night's award banquet with Flora because Julian had to work. When Ruby's name was announced as the winner of the Senior Biology Prize, David had hooted and hollered. He'd grinned for the rest of the night and started calling her "Doc."

On the sidewalk next to David, Margot stood surrounded by a small circle of admirers. She was shaking hands, and she had her pleasant-but-not-too-friendly face on. Tonight was probably the last time Ruby'd be able to show Margot off. Would anyone in college care that she was practically related to one of the stars of *Cedar*? Probably not. She hoped not. She was going to college back east in the hopes that nobody would care about television or film or pilot season or auditions or any of the things that her friends at school talked about as if they were the ones looking for work. Although sometimes they *were* looking for work, and that was a whole other disordered world, the high school girls who were already in show business.

"Wait. You know Margot Letta?" Although Ruby pretended to be annoyed every time someone saw her with Margot and remarked, she was quietly thrilled. Her school started at seventh grade, and Ruby had moved to Los Angeles at the beginning of eighth grade. As soon as she toured Darrow, she knew it was where she wanted to go, and she started her campaign to apply. In New York, private school was never even an option, not anything they could afford to consider. Julian and Flora didn't even want Ruby to look at Darrow, but Margot had encouraged her to at least take the tour. Margot had asked around—"If you had an incredibly smart daughter, where would she go to school in Los Angeles?"—and she said Darrow came up again and again. That the school was in Margot's neighborhood was another mark in the plus column. Her father's job would make finances easier, but Ruby didn't need to be told for the millionth time that television (her dad) and voice-over (her mom) work weren't reliable. Her parents could be flush one year and struggling the next. The ups and downs of money had defined her childhood. If she wanted to go to Darrow, she would need some kind of financial aid or scholarship. She didn't work as hard on her *college* applications as she had on her application to Darrow. Her teachers in Manhattan loved her and helped her, and when she got accepted with a generous financial aid package, Flora and Julian softened their stance. Even they had to admit the school was impressive, the girls so composed and confident.

Ruby was terrified her first weeks of school. Everyone was perfectly nice, perfectly polite, momentarily curious about the girl from New York City, but several weeks in, she still didn't know where to sit once she filled her tray at lunch with a salad and an apple and maybe a cookie. She still waited for the bus every afternoon, mostly off to the side, headphones on, watching the other girls in groups talking. She buried herself in her studies and observed, waiting to see how she might penetrate. She joined a few after-school clubs, but it was slow going. Until the Thursday afternoon, about six weeks into school, when Margot pulled into the parking lot in her white Jaguar convertible and honked and waved. She got out of the car and gave Ruby a big hug. As they drove away, Ruby knew they were being watched. In the world of high school in Los Angeles, celebrity was common. Some of her classmates were the daughters of people far more well-known than Margot. And successful? She guessed so. She didn't want to be disloyal to Margot even in her thoughts, comparing her to other actors—like the group of girls who had spent their lunch break one week ranking every single school parent who was in show business based on how famous they were.

But so many girls at school watched and loved *Cedar*. Margot made a habit of picking Ruby up when she could and soon she was taking Ruby and her friends out for ice cream and cheerfully answering their questions about the show and her costars, and even though social currency wasn't Ruby's *thing*, she couldn't help it—she lit up with pride and affection every time she saw Margot's car cruising up the school driveway.

Ruby's *thing* was being a good student and figuring out how to get into the college she wanted and not letting her parents know how eager she was to go, to take flight. So many times she imagined herself as a soaring bird, like one of the hawks from Griffith Park that lazily circled above their house, only she was a hawk on a mission. Tucking her head and squaring her shoulders and flying three thousand miles east, just north of New York City. She couldn't wait. She wanted her life to start so badly she couldn't bear to sit still long enough to read or even watch television.

"What are you *doing*?" Flora would ask her as she paced around their house. "Are you okay?"

She was okay. Ruby was almost always okay. She was also bored, thrumming with anticipation. She knew Flora and Julian were proud but also slightly confused by her declared intention to be a doctor, and she wasn't even sure she believed it herself, but she'd quickly deduced that her best chance of distinguishing herself in her school was by becoming a STEM girl, so she threw herself into math and science. It seemed like every other girl in her school wanted to be an actress. The drama club was so overflowing with students they had to add an extra play to the year's productions because of the wealthy parents who freaked out when their daughters didn't get cast once.

She'd lived around theater people her entire life, and the girls from drama—*the thespians*, she and her non-theater friends called them—were a little too much for her with the tears, the singing in the hallways, the exquisite trembling and cheering and overly exuberant hugging. It was all a little distasteful to Ruby. And if she wasn't an old soul, she was certainly a girl who had spent all her years listening to the ups and downs of her parents and their friends. The auditions, the rejection, the melodrama of drama. It was fascinating to watch, but Ruby had been very young when she knew it wasn't anything she wanted in her life. She couldn't imagine choosing a life that promised— guaranteed—so much rejection and where success and failure were so ephemeral.

Back in their apartment in New York City, where there was no privacy, where she could hear every word her parents said beyond the flimsy drywall of her makeshift bedroom, she couldn't help but know what a source of angst their work was for both of them. They worked hard to protect Ruby, but it was impossible for her not to deduce that in the constellation of her parents' marriage, Flora was the one who made sacrifices and Julian was the one who didn't compromise. Until California. She remembered the look of surprise and wonder on her mother's face the day Julian had come home and announced he'd been offered the part and maybe they should consider a stint in Los Angeles. A stint. She'd liked that word.

"Really?" Flora had said, looking unsure of whether she was supposed to be happy or sad.

It hadn't been simple, of course, because her parents were nothing if not thorough, and so there had been many conversations, some with Ruby included, some overheard, about the *pros and cons*. Should they sublet the apartment? Where would Ruby go to school? What neighborhood? Should they ask Margot for advice or wait because once Margot got her teeth into this idea there would be no talking her out of it? Would Julian regret it? "Are you sure," Flora said one night, "are you sure you're ready to leave the company?"

The company! Those two words were probably among the first Ruby learned. She came home one day in kindergarten and told Flora that her friend Liza's parents must know Daddy.

"I don't think so, honey," Flora said.

"But they do."

"Why do you think so?"

"Because Liza can't have a playdate tomorrow because they have The Company."

The company—Good Company—was the defining law of their existence. Whether Julian was in a show or directing a show or just working to support the show or thinking about the next show, the next season. Hiring interns, dramaturgs, actors. Teaching.

"Why aren't you in the company?" Ruby had asked Flora once when she was finally old enough to realize that her mother was also an actor, just one who worked off camera.

"I didn't love it the way your father does," Flora said. "Besides, I wanted to spend more time with you. The Company of Ruby."

Ruby knew Flora's work kept them afloat. So many voice-overs—a lot of local work, industrial films, occasionally a big national commercial—but rarely enough so Flora didn't start worrying right after Labor Day about hitting the year-end SAG minimum for health insurance. She would double down on auditions for union gigs then and not be able to pick Ruby up from school. Mrs. Packer, an older woman in their building, would be the one standing with the other moms and nannies on the sidewalk at three thirty p.m., and although she was nice, Ruby hated those afternoons because Mrs. Packer's house smelled like mothballs and Campbell's soup and cat litter.

"Did you get a job?" she'd ask her mother on those days, not wanting to spend any more time with Mrs. Packer and Grace the cat.

"Maybe. I read for one burger joint, a hardware store, and two banks." Her mother would sometimes read the lines for Ruby in a silly voice to make her laugh. "Fingers crossed for one of the banks, Rubes."

The years Flora did hit the minimum before December, they'd have a big celebration and let Ruby pick the restaurant. The two years they didn't, Ruby remembered overhearing the worried conversations about whether they should buy insurance for all three of them, or just for Ruby, who was prone to strep throat. Those years she tried to be extra careful, always wearing her hat and a scarf so she wouldn't get sick.

The nights the anxious timbre of her father's voice roused her from sleep and she put her ear to the wall, they were almost always talking about Good Company. If the discussion was general, situated around finances, audience attendance, casting choices, Ruby would go back to sleep. But if it was a more specific conversation about Julian, his career, his future, his frustrations—she would listen. And worry. And make two promises to herself: 1. If she ever had a child, she would live in a house big enough so that the child couldn't see and hear everything, including sex. Julian and Flora were careful; she didn't hear much, but as soon as she was old enough to understand, she knew what was happening when the door to the bedroom was shut. 2. She would never be a *thespian*.

When she thought about it, it was hard for Ruby to determine who had the better deal, the more enviable life: Julian's work seemed gratifying if maddening and also, until Los Angeles, not very lucrative, not very *known*. She had told her parents about the girls at the lunch table ranking the other parents but hadn't told them how she'd heard one of them say, "Isn't Ruby Fletcher's father an actor?" and another say, "Yeah, but he's not famous." She'd been livid all day. Those girls didn't even mention Flora, who had been the one supporting them—with acting!—for Ruby's entire life. Ruby got a little lift, a little thrill, whenever she thought about Flora's job on *Griffith*. After one season, people were writing about the animated show and even her friends were watching. Ruby hoped more than anything that Flora would get some real recognition. Maybe do some panels, even an interview like Margot. An Emmy! As she was getting ready to leave for college, she wanted her mother to be busy. She wanted her mother to be happy.

Ruby headed toward David and Margot, waving to the occasional friend or stopping to hug the parents of the girls she knew best, the places she'd had sleepovers and pool parties and pre-prom gatherings. Ruby wasn't sentimental, but she would miss this bright enclave of girls, mostly smart, mostly well-meaning, mostly set for promising things.

She tried to approach so she could see her parents before they saw her. Get a beat on the mood, so to speak. Her father was talking to a man she didn't recognize, probably someone he knew from work. All the parents at her school were connected by the filament of show business. It was a tiny, incestuous group. Exotic when a girl's parent was a doctor or a plain old executive somewhere. She spotted her mother, who, uncharacteristically, didn't seem to be looking for Ruby but was watching Julian. Something in her mother's posture made Ruby slow her pace. Julian turned to Flora and winked. Flora, so subtly that only Ruby would notice, stiffened and slowly pivoted away from Julian, and in the few seconds it took for her to spot Ruby, Ruby got a good look at Flora's face, which instead of being weepy or sad or melancholy—all the things Ruby expected to see in Flora's features—looked undeniably, *vividly* furious. Her mother was pissed.

FIVE

~

Flora almost didn't go to the party the night she met Julian. *She almost didn't go.*

In all the years that followed, she would occasionally say to him—half in wonder, half in fear—"What if I hadn't gone to your party?"

"It was just our first way to meet," he'd say, certain in the belief that they would have met somehow, some other day, that life would have broken in his favor concerning her.

She almost hadn't gone because the only person she would know at the party was her roommate (and *friend*—she and Margot were becoming genuine friends, to Flora's astonishment and joy), who was coming from another gathering and would be late. Flora would have to go alone, and she dreaded walking into a place full of strangers clustered in conversation. She'd feel awkward and unwelcome whether or not it was true. Maybe some women in their twenties had a lot of experience walking into parties alone, but not Flora, who had broken her engagement to her first, her only, boyfriend only nine months earlier. She'd known Patrick since they both knelt at the same altar at Holy Sacrament when they were seven and received first communion side by side (Flora Mancini and Patrick McGuire; the alphabet was their matchmaker). Going to a party alone was novel and scary, and Margot's friends—like Margot—all boasted some kind of pedigree that Flora most certainly did not. Juilliard (Margot) or Yale Drama or Tisch or trust fund. Flora had spent two years at Hunter College before running out of money and interest and throwing herself into musical-theater auditions, and as far as she could tell, Margot and her friends—well, they were not a musical-theater crowd. They were Chekhov and Ibsen and O'Neill and Albee and maybe the Davids (who she'd finally figured out were Hare and Mamet and Rabe). They *tolerated* musicals. She could occasionally find a Sondheim kindred spirit, but Flora often felt adrift in their company, a little in over her head. The last time she'd gone out with Margot and her friends, she'd been stuck at one end of the table between two men who spent most of the evening arguing about Brecht's theory of alienation versus Aristotelian logic. "You should really read *Poetics* if you haven't. As a starting point," one of them had said to her as they were putting on their coats.

"Oh, they're both asses." Margot had laughed it off on the way home. "They'd kill to have your job right now, trust me."

This was true! Her miraculous new job as a fairy in *A Midsummer Night's Dream*. Flora was still pinching herself, still dumbfounded. She was a good singer and a passable dancer, but she was not a classically trained actor. Nobody would think to put Flora and Shakespeare in the same sentence, not even Flora. She wouldn't even have known about the audition if Margot hadn't called her at work, demanding she leave the office on her lunch break. "I can't. I just took lunch," Flora said. "Besides, Shakespeare? That's not for me."

"It *is* for you; it's Shakespeare in the Park—looser, more fun. You've been to the Delacorte, right?"

Well, no. Flora had never been to the Delacorte. She'd heard of Shakespeare in the Park, of course. She sometimes read the reviews in the *New York Times*, but she'd never gone. For all the times her mother complained about the cost of Broadway, all the penny-pinching to take them to shows, not even the free admission was enough to lure Josephine to stand in line for hours to sit outdoors. *The mosquitoes! The humidity!* Alfresco was not Josephine's style. Her style was a nice dress, good shoes, a matching handbag, and a center orchestra seat.

"Maybe once," Flora lied to Margot. "When I was younger, I think. I don't remember. But they're going to want a mono-logue. I don't have a classical monologue."

"Not a big deal," said Margot. "They're seeing non-equity actors for a few hours tomorrow. I'm putting your name on the sheet. We'll work on a monologue tonight. Flora, the fairy chorus is an *actual chorus.*"

"I thought the fairies were usually children."

"Not always. Not this time. And every fairy needs to sing. The setting is going to be a Vegas nightclub or something. Very Rat Pack. Very Ella." Well, okay. Almost all the songs in her audition binder were Porter, Berlin, Gershwin, Arlen—the American standards, her favorites.

When they were both home later, Margot opened her book of Shakespearean monologues and mumbled to herself as she turned the pages. Flora had seen Margot work in a couple of small productions, a one-act downtown, a small part in a revival of *Agnes of God* in Connecticut, but that night—in their living room over a takeout pizza and Diet Cokes—was the night she saw what she imagined Juilliard had seen in Margot. Every few pages, Margot would stop and toss off a name of a character or play.

"There's Beatrice from *Much Ado*, but I hate that play. Adriana? Katherine from *Shrew*?" Then she would answer her own question. No. No. No. Too predictable, too romantic, too whatever. Sometimes she would read a few lines, stop, and read them again with a slight adjustment or a completely different attitude. Her voice got stronger, filled the room, and her face and body would become angry or disbelieving or sorrowful. It was a remarkable thing to watch, how she could look regal or defeated with a gesture, a posture, hitting a word in just the right way. Margot in real life was a restless soul, fidgety and impatient. But onstage, even when the stage was the small alcove off the small living room that became her bedroom every night, she was focused and magnetic. A star. Flora could have watched her for hours.

"I think this is the one," she said. "Hermione from *A Winter's Tale*. 'Sir, spare your threats. The bug which you would fright me with I seek.'" Her voice switched back to conversational Margot. "It's short and sweet. What do you think?"

"I think you're going to be very famous." Margot looked up, surprised and pleased. "You're so good. I don't know how to do *that*," Flora said, gesturing at Margot. "I don't have it in me."

"Sure you do," Margot said, sitting down on their sofa and patting the cushion next to her. "Sit and we'll break it down. It's not that hard."

But it *was* hard; they worked for hours with Margot directing her. Flora was too angry, then she was too weak. "Hermione is defending herself, but she's not ashamed or sorry. She's strong.

Try again." They worked until almost two in the morning, and the next day Flora was so tired she didn't have the energy to be nervous. She went into the audition room—it all seemed so improbable!—and did it as they'd practiced the night before. Well enough not to be cut off after ten seconds with the dreaded *Thank you, that's all.*

Then it was time to sing. She had an old-fashioned alto voice, bright and clear, and when she started snapping her fingers and tapping her foot and swaying her hips a little while singing "Fly Me to the Moon," she saw the musical director look over at the show's director and smile. Days later, after rounds of cuts and more songs and more cuts and more singing, she and Margot and five others were left standing on the stage when the director said to all of them, "Congratulations, fairies. We start next week."

Flora was deliriously grateful to have been plucked from the downtown law firm where she worked in the word-processing pool from three to eleven p.m. five nights a week and dropped into a group of young, eager strangers bound together by gossamer fairy wings. Rehearsal at the Shetler Studios started the following week, they would move to the Delacorte in May. She would be that much closer to having her equity card when she was done. Her world was about to bloom. For the first time in months she wasn't brooding or burdened by her unhappy, claustrophobic relationship. But going to a party alone? She'd rather sit home and read.

"Come on, Flora," Margot persisted. "Both guys giving the party are my friends. Both are single."

"Not interested. Not one iota. I am giving myself at least a year to date, *at least.*"

"What's wrong with a distraction? A transition? A little love affair." This was the kind of old-fashioned expression that didn't sound strange coming from Margot—a *love affair*—it sounded romantic. "A few people from *Midsummer* will be there. It would be good for you to meet them. I heard *Oberon* will be there."

Flora laughed. "I'm sure Oberon and I will have so much in common, so much to discuss." The actor playing Oberon was the second-most-famous person in the production. The first being the woman playing Titania, who had recently won an Oscar for a movie about sharecroppers in the South in the 1930s. The billboards of her sweaty and dirt-stained face had plastered the sides of city buses for weeks. "I'll be there around ten p.m., and I want to see you the minute I walk through that door. Don't disappoint me, Flora. Don't disappoint *yourself*."

FLORA SMELLED THE STRAWBERRIES BEFORE she saw them. She was walking down Broadway, on her way to get something to eat. (She was *not* going to the party.) But then she smelled the strawberries and they had no business being as beautiful or fragrant as they were, not in March, not given that they had to have made the journey from California, across an entire country, over a bridge or through a tunnel, before they were unloaded and displayed outside of the Fairway. Pedestrians gathered around the display, stupidly grinning as if they were watching a litter of puppies, fingers floating above green boxes stained red at the bottom.

"Six dollars?"

"I just saw them at Pioneer for only two dollars."

"But not like this."

"Like what?" said a middle-aged woman, lifting her half-moon readers, which were dangling from a piece of butcher string around her neck, to take a better look. "Are they made of gold?" She took one of the berries and popped it into her mouth. Everyone watched her brow soften, her eyes brighten a little. She nodded, granting permission. "They taste like summer," she told them, while putting quart after quart in her plastic basket.

Summer. When it was summer, Flora would be on stage in Central Park. She saw herself walking into a party where she knew no one and casually saying, *This summer? I'll be at the Delacorte. Strawberry?* Even though she hadn't left the house to go to the party (she hadn't!), she was wearing her good jeans, the black ones that made her legs look longer, and a new bright pink blouse she'd found on sale at Bolton's. The color brightened her olive skin and dark hair, and okay, she'd put on a little makeup and taken some care with her head of unruly curls, and maybe it would be a waste to eat all those berries by herself. Maybe she should stroll by the party and check it out. It wouldn't hurt to take a look, would it?

⌒

STANDING ON THE SIDEWALK OUTSIDE the small apartment building where the party was taking place, Flora held two quarts of the berries in her hands. She'd spent half the money she had in her wallet, money that was supposed to last for at least the next five days. She hoped this was the kind of party where they had food that could pass for dinner. Not just snacks. She was hungry.

She could hear music and the din of voices snaking out of the upper-floor window. While she was looking up, hesitating (she still had time to bring the strawberries home and eat them alone while reading a book), a guy in a plaid flannel shirt leaned out the window and tossed a slice of pizza toward the sky. From behind him, she could hear a woman's laugh. "Julian! You're insane."

He looked down as Flora looked up. "Hey!" he yelled. Something inside of her, hungry heart or hungry gut, she couldn't tell, soared to meet the arcing slice. She stood watching it. "Friend!" the guy in the window sounded urgent now, "Watch out!" She heard a careening through the tree branches above her, scurried back, and the slice of pizza landed at her feet. Pepperoni. Well. At least they had dinner.

Flora climbed the two flights up to the party. The stairs were creaky beneath the worn carpet that had been beige once; the wooden banister was faded and dull from all the hands running its length. On the second floor, one of the apartment doors was wide open, the party inside high-spirited. Standing on the threshold, she could see through the crowded living room into the small galley kitchen. The thought of making her way past all those people kept her rooted in place. She could feel her brow start to sweat, her chest and neck flush. From her vantage point, everyone inside seemed to know everyone else. She couldn't imagine walking up to any of the people in that room and interrupting, introducing herself.

Oh, this had been a mistake. She stepped away from the door and took a few steps down the hall, considering. As easily as she'd traipsed up to apartment 2B (*to be or not to be!*), she could run back down. Nobody would know; nobody would miss her. She could plead a headache or an upset stomach to Margot later (who wouldn't be fooled). She could hear Margot's voice as if she were standing next to her. *Why are you so afraid? They're just people. Show folk. Our folk.*

But Margot moved through the world in an entirely different way than Flora did, especially the world of *show folk*. She was an insider, with all the ease of an insider. A blithe spirit incarnate. How many times had Flora been out with Margot at an audition or a show and seen her establish some kind of connection, sometimes with complete strangers, within minutes? Maybe they'd crossed paths at Juilliard or they'd been in a workshop together or the person knew her theater-world-famous mother or they were all regulars at the same annual Thanksgiving parade brunch on the Upper West Side that everyone *loved so much*. Margot had been acting since she was a preteen; she'd accompanied her mother every year to this or that summer stock production. She knew costumers and stage managers and directors and musicians. It was intimidating. And Flora sometimes thought of herself as Margot's mascot, the person who gave her a deeper kind of legitimacy because Flora had no pedigree, or rather Flora's pedigree was—as she'd heard Margot say once when she didn't know Flora was listening—*hard-core outer borough*.

When Flora met Margot she was pleased they had their Italian heritage in common, until it became clear that Flora's brand of Italian-American (Sunday sauce, weekly Mass, the Immaculate Heart of Mary statue front and center on the dining room buffet) differed wildly from Margot's (Friday night at Elio's on Second Avenue where Flora's father casually ordered in impeccable Italian, summers in Tuscany, back-to-school shopping in Rome).

"Hey!" Flora looked up and the guy from the window, the

pizza thrower, was standing at the open door to the apartment. "It's you."

She smiled and shrugged. "Here I am."

"Here you are." He had a kind smile. He walked down the hall until he was standing in front of Flora. He was taller than she was, but not by too much. His shoulders were broad, and he had a long face and a strong jaw. He looked perplexed. "Why are you down there?"

"Deciding," Flora said.

"Ah. Okay." His eyes narrowed in concentration. "I know you. How do I know you?"

"From a few minutes ago on the sidewalk?"

"Well, that, yes. Beware of flying pizza. We had a bet on how far it would go, and I lost. Turns out pizza is heavier than it looks. But no, I know you from somewhere else. Have I seen you in something?"

Flora very much wanted to be able to say yes at that moment, that maybe he *had* seen her in something, but the odds were slim to none, and besides, she knew what this was; it happened all the time. Still.

"It's possible," she found herself saying. He brightened. "Maybe you saw me last year in the Bronx Children's Theater production of *Peter Pan*. I wowed them as a Lost Boy with striped stockings." He smiled, shook his head no. "Afraid I missed that one."

"Then maybe my starring role as a wandering Christmas caroler at Bloomingdale's last December? Green velvet bonnet with matching muff." She sang a few lines of "Joy to the World." My God. She was flirting. She knew how!

"Haven't stepped foot in Bloomingdale's since my mother dragged me there for an eighth-grade graduation suit."

"You're not missing anything. I'm Flora Mancini." She took a tentative step forward. "I'm a friend of Margot's."

"Is Margot here?"

"Not yet. She's coming later."

"That must be how I know you."

"No, we've never met." She would have remembered. She would have remembered that laugh, the head of curls so dark and glossy she wanted to reach out and touch. The smooth skin and ruddy cheeks and hazel eyes. "I have one of those faces," she said.

"What kind of face is that?"

"The kind of face where everyone thinks we've met before. It happens all the time." The entire time she was talking, he was looking at her face.

"It's a good face," he said, "the kind of face that puts people at ease." Flora hoped he couldn't tell she was blushing. "Okay, Flora from the sidewalk." He extended his hand. "I'm Julian Fletcher and this is my apartment and I think you should come inside. It's much nicer than the hallway." She couldn't stop the stupid grin that took over her face, the dumb, eager smile. His hand was a good fit. "What's the verdict, friend? You in?"

She was in. She couldn't remember ever feeling so *in*. She nodded and he released her hand. The hallway went dark. "These lights," he said, looking up. He jumped up a little and gently tapped the long fluorescent fixture. The hallway brightened again. "That's better. Shall we?"

Hours later, when Margot finally arrived, the party had taken the turn the best parties take, where the partygoers were a similar degree of drunk, the same degree of flirtatious, fanning mutual desires. The boxes of pizza were picked over and the few remaining slices congealed. The party was on a second wave of food; someone had ordered Chinese and a delivery-man was picking his way through the living room, where half the guests had formed an impromptu chorus and were enthusiastically singing something. Was it something from *A Chorus Line?* Margot never knew the songs everyone else knew. *Show folk,* she thought wearily. She gave a quick look to see if Flora was part of the singing group, but she knew that was unlikely. One of Flora's best qualities was her reluctance to be *on* all the time. If not for Flora, Margot wouldn't even be at the party. She was tired and irritated and wanted to be home, but if Flora *had* shown up and Margot didn't, she'd never hear the end of it. The dinner party Margot had come from was a complete bust. She'd only accepted the invite because a certain director she would love to work with was supposed to be there, but he hadn't shown and she'd spent the entire night fending off the advances of a no-name producer who claimed she was *exactly the look he needed* for a ridiculous-sounding new show he was trying to workshop. Margot was also annoyed because Anton, who worked in casting for Shakespeare in the Park, had been at the party, and he'd been rude about Flora. "Remind me who she is?" he said when Margot told him they'd cast her friend and said what a great find she was.

"Flora Mancini. Great voice, reddish curly hair"—she leveled her hand at her chin—"so-high."

"Ah, right. Flora. The zaftig one."

Margot frowned. "Flora is a perfectly normal-sized human being."

"Oh, relax. We were thrilled to see someone with a little skin on her bones after a parade of willowy blondes. No offense. She has a funny face. We needed a little comedy in the fairy troupe."

"Funny? Flora looks like she stepped straight out of a Botticelli."

"Hmmm," Anton said, spearing a cube of cheese with a toothpick and examining it before frowning and placing it back on the cheese plate. "Maybe from the *school of* Botticelli."

Margot walked through the living room, waving to a few friends. She could see the actor who played Oberon commanding the kitchen—he had come!—and, incredibly, the Oscar-winning actress was standing next to him, laughing appreciatively at whatever story he was telling that had the room in its thrall—he was Irish and a joy to listen to and knew how to weave a spell.

Margot wondered where the booze was. To her right, a few people were dancing on the worn wooden floor. She saw Julian first. His back was to her, but she recognized his elegant shuffle—he was a good dancer. She maneuvered herself a little and tried to see who his head was bent toward, who he was listening to and laughing with. The song ended, and he and his partner executed a dramatic dip. They came up and the woman turned, and Margot couldn't believe her eyes. Flora.

"Who is *that*?" Margot turned toward the voice—Sydney Bloom. Margot wasn't in the mood for Sydney tonight.

"Julian?" Margot said, knowing that's not who Sydney meant.

"No, I know who Julian is. We"—Sydney waved a finger back and forth, pointing to her and Julian—"We had a *thing*." *You and probably ten other people in this room*, Margot wanted to say, but didn't. Sydney was trouble. Constantly bothering Julian and Ben for work. Weirdly possessive. She always seemed to be stirring a pot. "I mean who is the woman attached to him?"

Margot looked over to see Julian take Flora's hand and kiss it. She couldn't help but laugh. "*That* is my roommate. Flora."

"Huh." Sydney made a beeline toward Flora and Julian. Julian didn't look happy to see her; he looked resigned. He crossed his arms and stepped back a little, half listening to what Sydney was saying, half keeping his eye on Flora, who had seen Margot and was heading toward her, smile wide.

"You're here." Flora hugged Margot, swaying a little. She was drunk.

"Yes," Margot said. Flora had been sad and guilty for a long time. She liked seeing Flora like this. This lit up. "You look like you're having fun. You seem to have made a friend."

Flora held on a little too tight. She was damp around the hairline. "You were right," she whispered in Margot's ear. "I *do* like one of them."

⌒

THE MORNING AFTER THE PARTY, Flora overslept. She'd stayed out so much later than her standard embarrassingly early bedtime. Cinderella, Margot called her for her habit of leaving a bar or a party without a word of good-bye. Not last night. Last night she'd stayed until the end and had slept fitfully, the way you sleep when you have too much liquor in your system and a healthy premonition. She'd slept until ten o'clock! She couldn't remember the last time she'd slept in; she was an early riser, up with the sun.

Her head hurt. She needed water and aspirin. She listened at the door to her bedroom, which opened onto one half of the living room. The other half of the decently sized L-shaped prewar living space was Margot's makeshift bedroom. When Flora moved in, she'd offered to give Margot the bedroom and take the alcove, but Margot loved the space she'd fashioned directly in front of one of the two second-story windows that faced West Seventy-Sixth Street. She had three black lacquer oriental screens that expanded to give her some privacy and had furnished the space with cast-offs from her parents—a brass daybed, a round antique table with inlaid wood that she used as a vanity and was always covered with lotions and cosmetics. Above the table, a large silver-framed antique mirror. A moth-bitten oriental rug in faded shades of pink and green covered the floor. The effect of all the old furniture and the bits and pieces of Margot's wardrobe and piles of scripts with Post-its somehow combined to make the ordinary space look glamorous, the same way Margot's beauty seemed effortless. When Margot was sleeping—even though she slept like the dead; Flora could probably lead a marching band through the room and Margot wouldn't wake up—Flora was still considerate, keeping to her own tiny bedroom. As casually elegant as Margot's space was, Flora's was pristine and clean. White walls, a carefully made bed with white sheets and a white duvet. A few belongings on a tiny desk. The only color in the room came from all the books on the floor-to-ceiling shelf the previous tenant had built.

Flora opened the door to an empty room. Margot hadn't come home last night. Before she had time to consider what she could do with a Sunday morning alone in her apartment, she heard the key slide into the lock, the latch release, and the door swing open. Margot entered, looking a little green around the gills. "Don't ask," she said, making a beeline for her bed.

"Can I get you anything?"

"A time machine? A pill that makes you forget the last twelve hours?" Margot threw her purse in a corner, grabbed a brush, and yanked it through her tangled hair, wincing.

"What happened?" Flora asked. Margot's usual morning-after demeanor was smug and satisfied. Flora wasn't used to seeing her distracted and irritated.

"Question," Margot said, pulling her dress over her head, undoing her bra, throwing both in a heap. Her comfort with her body astonished Flora, who had grown up surrounded by women and had never seen a bare breast other than her own. She tried hard not to stare at Margot's breasts, which were small, tidy, perfectly shaped orbs (of course they were) but with incongruously large, brown areolas. Somehow Flora thought everything on Margot's body would be pearly pink. "When I got there last night—" Margot's voice was muffled, as she dug through a pile of dirty clothes looking for something. She pulled out a sweatshirt, sniffed under the sleeves, and put it on. "Didn't I say to you, 'Whatever happens, don't let me go home with Quinn'?"

"Quinn was there?" *Quinn*, the man who had been the subject of so many conversations, all along the lines of how bad he was for Margot: conceited, arrogant, selfish, but handsome, *dangerously* handsome, and talented, *incredibly* talented. "I wish I'd known he was there. What was he wearing?"

"Sheep's clothing." Margot threw herself down on the bed for effect and groaned. "That hurt," she said, putting a hand on her forehead. "I would have introduced you, but you were otherwise occupied, Flora."

"Do you want water or aspirin?" Flora said, moving into the kitchen. A minute ago she'd been wishing Margot were here to talk to, but now she realized she didn't want to discuss last night with Margot. Not yet.

"Both," Margot said. "Four aspirin, please."

Flora brought her a large glass of ice water and the aspirin.

"Sit," Margot said. "I can tell I'm not going to be able to sleep. I have some questions, Florentina."

"I can't," Flora said, surprising both of them. "I have church."

"Florentinaaaaa," Margot drew out her name, disappointed. "It's Sunday. Let's hang out and order grilled cheese or something."

Flora would have loved a grilled cheese or something. She didn't want to pull on her shoes and coat and go to church, but she also didn't want to confide in Margot. By the time she was ready to leave, Margot was sound asleep, lightly snoring. Flora watched her for a minute. She loved her friend, but she was going to follow her instinct and keep last night and Julian to herself.

What got Flora out of the house that morning was the same thing that got her out of bed most Sundays, a basic truth of her life: weeks that began with Sunday Mass were qualitatively better than weeks that did not. If church buoyed Flora when she was down or burdened, it wasn't because of what was said at Mass—she barely listened, and after years of Catholic school she'd heard it all before—no, what she loved were the smells and sounds of a church, any church. The comforting scent of burning candles and incense, the feel of the solid wooden pew beneath her, the squeak and thump of the kneeler, the soaring notes of an organ. And she liked the performance—a group of strangers who came together once a week and played their parts. As she left the apartment, she thought for the hundredth time how *this* was the most secretive, the edgiest thing about her—that she sang in a church choir on the Upper West Side every Sunday.

Flora had broken some hearts in the past year. She had cut herself off from the only life she'd known, from familiarity and comfort. She avoided her old neighborhood because with every subway stop back to Bay Ridge she felt herself becoming less Flora and more Florentina Rose. But she could still participate in this shared language. The songs, the rhythms, the call and response, *We ask this from you, oh Lord*—they could connect her with what she'd left behind, with what she didn't want to lose, but loosen.

She grabbed a coffee and a banana at the bodega on the corner of her street and headed uptown. The church wasn't far, and it was still warm, springlike. She got to the church early and sat on the steps, nodding to the other parishioners whom she was on a nodding basis with, watching the parade of mostly well-to-do Catholics, so different in bearing and appearance from her church in Bay Ridge where her mother was probably sitting by herself right now.

She wanted to think about Julian (*Julian!* Just thinking of his name gave her a quiet, intense thrill, especially for a girl who'd grown up surrounded by Patricks and Johns and Marks and Christophers) and every clever exchange and how she'd made him laugh and how when other people (girls!) came up to talk to them he would deftly send them away or steer her back into a private conversation. She thought of how she could feel his eyes on her as she moved around the room with her bowl of enchanted strawberries; she was the bearer of berries, the stainer of lips. At the end of the night, when she was drunk and enflamed and willing, Julian had followed her into his bedroom, the room where all the guests' coats were piled on his bed. Flora looked for her coat and wondered what to do, how to handle a good-bye. She wanted to see him again, but how to make that clear and not embarrass herself? Could she just ask? Write down her phone number? Suggest dinner? She didn't know how these things worked.

"I had a great time," she finally said, pulling on her jean jacket, unable to say anything more specific. "I'm glad," Julian said. They stood, smiling at each other, and she thought for a minute that he was about to kiss her. She stayed still, held his gaze, trying to telegraph permission, want. But then a voice at the door. "Sorry! Am I interrupting something?" A woman, Flora didn't know her name, who had been vying for Julian's attention all night. She thought he looked annoyed, but maybe she just wished he did.

"Of course not," Julian said, stepping away, breaking the spell. He extended his hand for the second time that night and shook Flora's. "It was a pleasure, Ms. Mancini. A true pleasure."

Sitting on the church steps, sipping her stale coffee, Flora wondered what that meant exactly—*a pleasure*. Was it hopeful or dismissive? Would she hear from him? She'd wanted him to kiss her so badly she could feel the desire deep in her body. She could hear the organ warming up inside, the opening chords of "Be Not Afraid"—which was her solo for today. She closed her eyes for a minute and thought about dancing with Julian last night, how assured he was, how confidently he moved. It was nothing like dancing with Patrick, who was too tall and too self-conscious and constantly stepped on her toes. She and Julian were a perfect fit. He'd hummed in her ear and spun her and dipped her and wheeled her back in. Flora understood the meaning of the word *quicken* for the first time because her heart was doing something she'd never felt before. She'd like to kiss Julian, but she also wanted him to undress her, to run a hand down her body, slip a finger inside her— She flushed as Mr. and

Mrs. Vincenzo made their way up the church steps and waved to her. She was sure everyone could see the desire on her face, the sin of lust. For the first time in her life, she could imagine herself being sensual in front of someone, feisty even. She could see herself coolly undoing her bra like Margot and standing in front of Julian, letting his appreciative eyes roam, watching him get hard. What had gotten into her?

She stood and walked down the steps and threw her coffee cup and her banana peel in a nearby trash can. Someone else could sing "Be Not Afraid." Like Edith Connelly, who was always jockeying to sing but was a little tone-deaf. She'd be thrilled to take Flora's place.

Flora was five blocks away from Julian's apartment, and she somehow knew that if she walked down his street, she would see him. She knew it the same way she knew it was Sunday morning. And sure enough, as she turned the corner onto his block, there he was, sitting on the stoop, looking in the opposite direction. She stopped and almost chickened out. How to explain why she was on his block. But why did she have to explain? It was New York City, her neighborhood, too, and she could be wherever she wanted. He didn't own the street. She was out for a walk. Nothing wrong with that. She squared her shoulders and kept going, and her nervousness vanished when he turned in her direction and spotted her and she saw the look on his face—absolute joy.

"Flora Mancini," he said, standing. He was wearing the same clothes from the night before. He looked tired but happy. "It's you."

"Here I am," she said and shrugged a little, tried not to throw her arms around him and plant a kiss on his lovely face. "I'm here."

SIX

Flora needed to keep it together for a few more hours, but she felt fragile. The graduation ceremony had been unexpectedly beautiful. She knew it would be moving—how could any transition as ripe and fraught as a school graduation not be? But she hadn't expected to be caught up in the pageantry of the whole thing. Sitting in the new auditorium in Ruby's school, the one that had been built after a capital campaign to expand the campus that had mercifully taken place before Ruby was admitted (Ruby missed the construction; her parents missed the aggressive fundraising), Flora didn't know how to feel about how different Ruby's life was from hers. This confusion wasn't new, but somehow it felt particularly acute that night. She remembered touring the school when they were planning their move. She couldn't get over the girls. A constellation of bright and pretty things buoyed by the certainty that the world was going to continue to bloom in front of them like exotic lily pads just because they were bright and pretty. Their optimism and ballerina-like bearing were unnerving—they *flitted* from place to place, not stopping so much as *presenting* themselves.

"Where are they keeping all the awkward girls," Flora said, only half-kidding, "the ones with unruly hair and bad skin? In a hut behind the ballet studio?"

But Ruby hadn't been intimidated; she'd been enthralled, and that simultaneously thrilled and worried Flora. She wanted her daughter to be comfortable everywhere. Wasn't that what she and Julian had told themselves? The reason they'd stayed in Manhattan for so long? They were so proud of her intelligence and curiosity and delightfully delicate manners. They'd tell each other Ruby stories over and over, even though they'd both been witness: Seven-year-old Ruby riveted, on the edge of her seat, at an evening performance of *Guys and Dolls*. "I'm the only kid here," she said, looking around, wide-eyed. When Julian asked her how she liked the show on the subway ride home, she said, "It was good, but those girls weren't dolls. Why do the boys call them dolls?"

They marveled over how they could bring her to any restaurant and she'd try almost any food; she'd scarf down olives, caper berries, and stinky cheese and lovingly suck on a piece of lemon. "This is delicious!" she'd say, or "No more, thank you." They thrilled at her love of books, how emotionally connected she was to what she read. When she was ten, Flora found a copy of Hans Christian Andersen fairy tales hidden at the bottom of a stack of pots and pans in the kitchen. When she opened the book, she saw that Ruby had crossed out "The Little Mermaid" in the table of contents with a pen. "What happened here?" she asked when Ruby got home from school. Flora had found the beautiful secondhand hardcover at the Strand; she was angry Ruby had marked it up.

"That story makes my heart too sad, Mom," Ruby said. "The mermaid gave up everything and got nothing back. So I crossed out the title, but then the cross-out made me think of the story. I hid the book in my dresser, but every time I saw the dresser, I thought of the little mermaid. So then I put it somewhere I never look."

"Did it work?" Flora asked, trying to think of a way to spin a happy end to the girl who gave up her freedom and literal voice for a man who didn't love her back; it *was* a terrible story.

"No," Ruby said. "I could still feel her in that drawer."

Watching Ruby's transition to Los Angeles was a parenting triumph of sorts. Now she was finished with high school and leaving home, not for good but surely they were approaching *for good*. Sitting in Margot's backyard, sipping a glass of wine, Flora felt the grief of Ruby leaving seize and catch her by the throat. She couldn't hold back a hiccup of a sob. Flora would have felt somewhat heartbroken even if she hadn't found the ring, but now—the graduation with all its talk of new beginnings, the path ahead, the choices in front of you, the brightest of futures, the world yours for the taking, she couldn't help think about what *her* future was now. What would it be?

"Shit," Flora heard her friend Samantha say at the exact moment she spotted Samantha's ex-husband enter Margot's kitchen. She quickly stood. This was not good. She hadn't invited Edward to the graduation party at Samantha's request. They were in the middle of an acrimonious divorce, and Flora had been assured by Samantha that her son Logan was fine with meeting up with his father a little later, after Ruby's party.

"I'm sorry," Flora said to Samantha, keeping her voice low, Logan just a few feet away. "I didn't invite him. I don't know why he's here."

"Because he's a total shit, that's why."

Flora could see the panic on Logan's face as his mother headed into the kitchen. Only a few people were aware of the heated conversation that ensued. Flora could hear snatches: *my son*, *not your call*, *sick to death of this*—it made her queasy.

Julian came over and put a hand on Flora's back. "Do you want me to go over, try to handle this?"

"What are you going to say?"

"I don't know. I'll think of something."

"I'll go, too." Even though the party was at Margot's, she and Julian were the hosts. As they approached the kitchen, Julian stopped and leaned into Flora and said, "What's his name again? The husband?"

"Seriously?" Flora threw Julian a look. "We've been to their house maybe seven times?"

Julian was taken aback by her tone. "I'm sorry. I don't remember."

"Because you don't try to remember. It's *Edward*."

"Hey, what's wrong?" Julian said, as they both heard Margot's voice cut through the tense murmurings in the kitchen. "Edward! What a surprise. How nice to see you."

Of course Margot knew Ed. He was a network executive in charge of *Cedar* and all of Bess's enterprises. Margot had described him to Flora once as an obtuse egomaniac with the discernment of a horny teenager. "Not that it distinguishes him."

Flora watched as Margot deftly guided Ed to the outdoor bar she'd insisted on having even though none of the kids were old enough to have alcohol. She'd devised a nonalcoholic beverage that was served on dry ice so all over the yard the graduates looked like they were sending up tiny smoke signals of distress from their cupped palms.

Logan, mortified by his parents, was sitting with his head in his hands. Ruby and Ivan were kneeling in front of him. Ruby looked serious. She had a hand on Logan's arm. Her lovely, ministering, empathetic child. She was no doubt saying something soothing.

In the kitchen, Samantha was sitting on a stool alone, deflated.

"How are you?" Flora said, handing Samantha a full-to-the-brim glass of wine.

Sam took a greedy gulp. "Thank you for that," she said, putting down the glass. "I'm fine, I guess. I don't know." She looked out the window. "Logan is going to be furious. Not at Ed, of course—at me."

"I'm sorry."

"Christ, Flora. I don't know how many times I've heard other people say this, but looking at someone you married, someone you *loved*, and feeling unadulterated *hatred*—it's an unimaginable thing."

The dissociative dizziness Flora had been fighting all day came roaring in. She fought to keep her face placid. "I can't imagine."

"Of course you can't. You and Julian. You two figured it out, didn't you?"

"Did we?" Flora said. She knew her smile was shaky. "I'm not so sure about that."

"The thing that kills me," Samantha said, "is that I took him back the first time. I believed him."

"It happened before?"

"Right after Logan was born. So predictable. I had a hard time with an infant. He had an understanding friend from college, blah, blah, boooring. The woman called me at home one night to tell me she loved Edward and I should let him go." Her laugh was joyless, tight. "*Let him go.* Like I was chaining him to the dishwasher every night. We talked. We went to therapy. We had Logan's little brother. I thought, you know, tough times, but we did it. We made it through. Do you want to know what's really messed up?" Flora didn't, but also didn't know how to stop the unwelcome invective without seeming awful. "The *new* person? It's the *old* person. The woman from college. They stayed friends, and now they're—*more than friends,* as the kids would say."

"I'm so sorry, Sammy."

Sam shrugged. Refilled her wineglass. "You have to watch out for those old girlfriends—the Camilla Parker-Bowleses of life." Samantha and Flora laughed. Flora couldn't help but picture Ed with a towering British woman on his arm wearing an outrageous hat. "They're dangerous. They already know the way in."

"I'll keep that in mind." Flora's gut was churning.

"Oh, please." Samantha waved her off. "Remember last year's school auction? With the awful Beach Boys cover band? Our entire table noticed you and Julian dancing. You looked like you were in high school. I remember Sophie Levin saying, 'Those two are the real deal.' Even in our happiest days I'm pretty sure nobody ever observed Ed and me and used the words 'real deal.' I never thought we were perfect. I don't believe in *meant to be.* But I always thought we'd fight for each other." Samantha picked up the wineglass and polished it off. "Now I don't even like him. I guess I'll call a car to go home." She kissed Flora on the cheek. "You're lucky."

HALFWAY THROUGH RUBY'S GRADUATION PARTY, Samantha safely tucked into an Uber, Flora took shelter in Margot's bedroom. She went upstairs to look for Band-Aids for her blistered toes and finally found them in the walk-in linen closet that was the size of a small bedroom and which, in addition to its impressive first-aid section, also shelved stacks of precisely folded white sheets, each set tied with a different-colored satin ribbon. A laminated index card attached to one of the shelves served as a color key: the blue ribbon denoted California king, green was king, pink was queen. "You did this?" Flora had asked Margot the first time she'd visited the newly renovated house. She realized by the look on Margot's face—had it been pity or embarrassment? Maybe both—that of course she didn't tie satin ribbons around her sheets, she paid someone to do it.

Flora grabbed the box of Band-Aids she needed, the ones designed specifically for blisters on the toes, wondering when Band-Aids had gotten so specialized, and wandered into Margot's bedroom because the room was quiet and dark and far away from the party. Both she and Julian agreed that as Margot's houses got bigger they somehow also got increasingly subdued. "Fifty shades of café au lait" was how she'd described the current decor to Julian after her first visit. The house resembled every other renovated mansion Flora had been in, as if a memo went out to all the decorators in town to choose the same brass midcentury light fixtures and French bistro chairs and sisal rugs and those carefully placed pillows lending a splash of turquoise or green or pink to each room. The house was beautiful and polished but somehow devoid of personality, blank. Flora liked the bedroom, though; she could have spent the rest of the evening on Margot's silvery velvet sleeping sofa. Flora was tired. She didn't think anyone would notice if she closed her eyes and rested for twenty minutes, but after two minutes, she realized that being alone with her thoughts was the last place she wanted to be.

She got up and moseyed (*noseyed*, Ruby would accuse) into Margot's closet, which was nearly the size of her and Julian's entire bedroom. It probably *had* been a bedroom back when the house had been built in the 1920s, before people could dream of wardrobes expansive enough to fit entire rooms. Flora found herself appraising the inventory, still slightly awestruck even though she knew Margot's wardrobe almost as well as her own. It was different seeing everything together, the shelves of cashmere sweaters, rows of hanging silk blouses, the drawers that she knew were full of lacy, silky things. The dresses, the blouses, the jeans, the handbags, the shoes, God, the shoes. She saw an empty spot where the shoes Ruby had borrowed must live, next to a dozen nearly identical nude high heels. She looked around the room and realized she could identify which items were Margot's—things she'd chosen for herself—and which were more suited to Dr. Cathryn Newhall. Not for the first time she thought how strange it must be for Margot to have played the same character in the same television show for so long that it was almost an alter ego.

Flora moved to the bedroom window and looked out on the backyard where the graduation dinner was in full swing. Margot's people (oh, that was a horrible word, but what was the right one? Her staff? Her caterers? Her helpers?) had done a beautiful job, and Flora was relieved that Margot hadn't gone too overboard. Her original idea, to fly in (*fly in*—the carbon footprint alone!) some crew from Cape Cod to stage a classic New England clambake, had been ludicrous. She'd showed Flora photos, the picnic tables covered with butcher paper, all the food piled in the middle: lobsters, salted potatoes, clams, corn. It looked like something out of a Renaissance painting: *Before the Fall of the Roman Empire*. Although if she was honest with herself, she'd been tempted. Sometimes it was hard to know where to draw the line with Margot. When Flora was being unnecessarily obstinate, making a point, or when a point really needed to be made for Ruby's sake. They'd tried very hard to keep Ruby grounded in the face of the extreme wealth of so many of the families at her school, and Margot spoiled her enough as it was.

Being upstairs looking down felt like the perfect way to observe the world right now. She felt she'd been observing herself all day, floating somewhere high above. Flora remembered so clearly the night of the school fundraiser. How she and Julian had walked around the silent auction tables laughing at the items for sale: one week at a private house in San Miguel de Allende for "only" three thousand dollars (airfare not included!); dinner for six in someone's private wine cave for five thousand dollars (six courses!); lunch with Margot Letta on the set of *Cedar* (priceless!). How when the band started playing "God Only Knows" Julian took her hand and they danced and although she wasn't aware then of Samantha and her compatriots watching them, she *was* aware of being observed and she liked it. So sure of herself and her marriage. She and Julian had gone home that night a little drunk and had stayed up talking about what life would be like when Ruby was in college, all the things they would do, all the places they could go. Then Julian had slowly unbuttoned her shirt and pulled her onto his lap and they'd had sex in the living room, right on the sofa, lights on. "I should close the curtains," Julian had said. "Don't," she'd said. "Stay right here."

The next morning, feeling sated and smug, she'd thought exactly what Samantha had urged her to believe: that she was lucky.

She didn't know what emotion to land on, fear or hope. She didn't know if everything was going to change or nothing, if this day would be remembered as a near-miss, a silly misunderstanding or the first day of the end of her marriage. Ruby had confronted her in the parking lot after the graduation. "Mommy?" When Ruby called her *Mommy*, she was either in a very good mood or a very bad one. "Mommy, what were you mad about earlier?"

Ah, this was the loosening-up *Mommy*, for when she wanted information. Flora frantically thought over the past hours: she had been diligent, avoiding being alone with Julian, avoiding thinking about the conversation they were going to have later. "When earlier?"

"On the sidewalk outside of the school when Dad was talking to someone. You looked so mad!"

"I did?" Flora laughed, shook her head. "I've no idea."

Ruby eyed her. "Okay," she finally said. "I just wanted to be sure."

Looking down now, she felt an undeserved pride at Ruby's group of friends, not a truly objectionable human being in the lot. She even liked Ruby's boyfriend Ivan (*the terrible*, Julian would add when Ruby wasn't around, which never failed to make Flora laugh, because their major complaint about Ivan was that he barely spoke above a murmur; he seemed, in fact, slightly terrified of Flora and Julian). She saw that Ruby had ditched the ridiculous shoes for flip-flops. She and her friends were gathered around the fire pit. A few had guitars, and they were all singing a song Flora didn't recognize, harmonizing beautifully. It was corny and heartwarming and young.

She still couldn't believe she'd agreed to let Ruby go to Spain with Ivan for a month. She and Julian had disagreed when Ruby came home bursting with the news that she was invited to Madrid! Barcelona! Mallorca! The summer was going to feel short enough before they took her to college at the end of August. Flora had been looking forward to the three of them being at Stoneham for the first time in years, back in the Little House. But Ruby and Julian had worn her down. Julian thought they shouldn't deny Ruby the opportunity—they liked Ivan and Ivan's parents, who were responsible, thoughtful people. Ivan's mother had called Flora to say that Ruby could share a hotel room with her own daughter, Rachel, if Flora wanted, but Flora hadn't insisted on an arrangement that would have had Ruby sneaking around hotel rooms in Spain every night. Ruby wasn't one of those kids who confided every little detail of her life to her mother (thank the Lord) but nobody thought she and Ivan weren't having sex, and that wasn't Flora's objection to the trip.

"She outgrew Stoneham years ago," Julian rightly pointed out—it was one of the reasons they hadn't been in years. "She'll be back in time for the show, the fun stuff. The timing is kind of perfect." So Flora had said yes.

On the other side of the yard, Margot and Julian were sitting side by side on one of the outdoor sofas. Margot had her feet tucked under and was listening to Julian, who was pitched forward gesticulating. No doubt they were talking about work. His job or hers. Maybe Julian was filling her in on the upcoming summer at Stoneham, how they were doing *The Cherry Orchard* and how he'd be playing Lopakhin. Flora didn't remember when Margot became his main confidante about work. After Ruby? When Flora stopped being involved in Good Company or, eventually, anything else that their group would consider legitimate theater? Although she'd mostly been relieved to step away from Good Company, she was also annoyed—no, she was *affronted*—at how easily her departure had been absorbed. She waited for Julian to come home despairing, missing her efforts—the notes she took during rehearsal, the schedules she carefully wrote up and emailed out, the elaborate system she'd developed for cataloging incoming submissions to be sure everything got read at least once (until they realized most incoming submissions were awful and didn't need to be read even once). But no, the minute she left, fools rushed in.

A group of young company members—all women, of course—fell into formation like a chorus line executing a series of perfect kicks. One became his de facto assistant, another a self-appointed company secretary, a third kept petty annoyances at bay. "Did you organize all this?" Flora asked, knowing how unlikely that was. "No, it just kind of happened," he'd said, equal parts admiring and amused. "But it didn't just happen," Flora snapped at him—he could be so infuriating! Was it a thing, Flora wondered, that *just happened* to charismatic men—or maybe all men—how the world around them seemed to bend to their wants and needs? He laughed at her good-naturedly, unaware of his luck. "But it *did*."

Flora watched Margot stand and place a hand on Julian's shoulder. He held on to it for a minute. Not too long, not inappropriately. Still. She could hear Sam's voice: *You have to watch out for the old girlfriends.* But Margot wasn't an old girlfriend. She'd never been interested in Julian. Had she? Flora sent up a little prayer to Josephine, a thing she still did occasionally: *Whatever this thing with the ring is, please don't let it involve Margot.*

Flora sat on Margot's bed and gingerly bandaged two toes that were blistered from the unsuitable sandals she'd worn. One of these days she'd get over her vanity around wanting to be taller. Maybe when she turned fifty? Wouldn't that be nice, if the fifties offered her freedom from all the habits she'd developed to compensate for her self-ordained physical shortcomings: the too-high heels; the preponderance of slimming black; the Spanx. How was it that at the same time women were being told it was no longer fashionable or necessary to wear nylon stockings, an entire new bondage industry rose in its wake? A stunning array of body-crushing tubes to encase them from breasts to knees.

"How am I supposed to go to the bathroom in this?" Flora asked, the first time she was presented with a new age girdle, one that promised to take an inch off her waist. "Easy," the saleslady said, turning the piece over and expanding the narrow slit in the crotch of the multilayered nightmare with her fingers. "Squat and pee. Isn't it ingenious?"

Flora looked at the opening, stunned. It took a minute for her to remember what it reminded her of. When they'd gone to Italy with Margot and David some years ago, they'd toured an old prison in Venice and come upon a gruesome display of iron chastity belts. Those medieval torture devices had the same menacing slit in the bottom, only lined with iron teeth. This garment in her hand seemed sprung from the same impulse. Still. She'd bought it. And one day before an awards dinner, Julian had walked into the bathroom and found her bent at the waist, trying to unroll the thing up over her midriff.

"Have you lost your mind?" he'd asked. "Take that thing off." She should pile them up and burn them. Julian would applaud.

"There you are!" Margot said, coming into the room and flipping the light switch. "I've been looking all over for you. What are you doing sitting here in the dark? Are you okay?"

"Fine." She pointed to her toes, forced a laugh. "Cruel shoes."

Margot walked over to the window and looked down on the scene. "It looks like a movie from up here, doesn't it? Those kids around the fire pit. Are they for real? I didn't think kids sat around singing and playing the guitar anymore. I thought they stared at their phones all day."

"They do that, too."

Margot sat on the bed next to Flora. "I had *such* an upsetting day. I texted you."

"I know. I'm sorry. I was running around." Flora tried not to bristle at Margot's assumption that she should always be available.

"I had the most annoying interview."

"How so?"

"This girl. The interviewer. She was like fourteen and had dug up all my New York stuff."

"That doesn't sound so terrible."

"Yeah, well, including somehow knowing about the Jensens."

Flora turned to Margot. She shouldn't assume Margot was always complaining for nothing. The Jensens. "I'm sorry. That is terrible."

Margot groaned and lay back on her bed, fanning her hair out behind her, her pelvic bones jutting out from her jeans. Like Flora, Margot was also on the cusp of fifty, and her stomach was still flat as a board. "I'm so tired. I hate all of this, all of the positioning and the pretending and the interviews. It's such bullshit. I should have walked into Bess's office and said, 'Bess, I deserve this amount of money and it's what I need to stay on the show. End of story.'"

"Why didn't you?"

"Because"—she made her voice raspy and low, imitating Donna—"*that's not how it works, kiddo!*" She stood up and went back to the window. "Not how it works because she needs her 10 percent."

"You'll get the raise. Or, you'll get *some* raise."

"I guess," Margot said. She turned to Flora, who had closed her eyes and was pressing her thumb and forefinger onto her eyelids. "You okay?"

"Just a headache. You know, a long day—"

"Oh, but look at her, our girl. Come here and look." Flora stood and went to Margot's side, and Margot put an arm around Flora's waist. "I mean, *look at her*. She is fine. We'll miss her, but we'll be fine." She opened the window, not without a little effort, and the screech of the old wood made some of the kids look up and pause and wave. Flora didn't think she imagined that their voices all got a little brighter, a little louder, including Ruby's, when they saw Margot was listening.

"Are they singing 'Landslide'?" Margot asked.

The melody drifted up, and Flora could hear the words ("Can I sail through the changing ocean tides? Can I handle the seasons of my life? Oh-ohhhh—"). She laughed. "Yes, enjoying those lyrics as only eighteen-year-olds could."

"They don't get how sad it is."

"Or," said Flora, "they think they know what it means to be sad."

"Ruby has a beautiful voice. She sounds like you!"

"By all means do not tell her that. I asked if she wanted to sing with me this summer at Stoneham and she recoiled like I'd thrown a slug at her."

"I miss Stoneham," Margot said. "I wish I could go back this summer, too." They stood there for a few minutes listening to the closing notes of the song. All the girls singing harmony. "Thank you," Flora said to Margot. "Thank you for this party. It's beautiful. Thank you for everything you've done for Ruby, for us." She was overcome with gratitude and shame for thinking so unkindly of her friend earlier. Margot had done more for them than she had the courage to tally.

Back downstairs, everyone gathered around the outdoor farm table for cake and presents. Ruby was almost done opening gifts when David handed her a tiny box. She lifted the lid and took out a gold chain with a small anatomical heart dangling at its end.

"This is incredible," Ruby said, turning it in her palm. "Look at this detail."

"It's a locket, too," David said, a little shyly, pointing. "It opens right next to the pulmonary vein." Margot watched him fumble with the locket. His desire for Ruby to follow in his early footsteps—well, she guessed it was sweet, but it was also a little baffling given how it all ended. He handed the unlatched heart back to Ruby, and she opened it wide.

"David!" She turned the locket so everyone could see. "There's a tiny ruby inside. Look."

"Where did you find that?" Margot asked, amazed. He hadn't shown her the delicate heart, hadn't even told her he'd bought a gift. Such a David thing to do, go off by himself to find the perfect one-of-a-kind present.

"A shop near the hospital. I couldn't believe it when I saw it."

"It's amazing. I love it." Flora helped Ruby with the clasp. "This has been the best day," Ruby said, looking around at her family and friends, the tiny heart resting right below her throat.

"There's more?" Ruby asked when Flora handed her a small package, wrapped in bright blue tissue paper with an emerald-green satin bow—Ruby's favorite colors.

"A little something extra for your dorm room."

Ruby unwrapped the gift carefully. Gently removing the bow and placing it on the table. Slowly opening the corners of the gift until she could see the back of a picture frame. "Mom. Is this going to make me cry?" Ruby's eyes were already glistening with tears, her lip trembling, just like when she was a toddler and would cry after every denial for one more round-the-block on the bike, one more cookie, one more bedtime story, one more piggyback ride into her bedroom.

"I don't think so," Flora said.

Ruby turned the photo over, almost fearfully, until she saw a picture she immediately recognized and her face lit up with delight. "I haven't seen this in *forever*." She clasped it to her chest. She turned the photo around, extending her arms so everyone around the table could look.

"You found it," Julian said. "You didn't tell me."

"Surprise!" Flora said. It came out harsher than she intended, and Julian looked at her, confused.

"Oh, Flora." Margot took the photo from Ruby, and she was the one who unexpectedly burst into tears. She tried to compose herself, but oh! How much the four people in that photo didn't know. "God, I was so thin," she finally said, trying to lighten the moment. As if she'd gained weight since then. As if she still couldn't wear a pair of capri pants from Old Navy and a halter top from the Gap if someone put a gun to her head.

David was looking over Julian's shoulder. "I think we look better now," he said. If David had learned one thing in his years of marriage to an actor, his life full of actors, it was leaping to the rescue of any egos. "I mean it," he said. "We all look like we could use a little fattening up. Someone give this man a chicken." He pointed to Julian in the photo.

"I love it, Mommy," Ruby said, taking it back from Margot and standing it up on the center of the table and smiling. *Mommy.* The happy one.

SEVEN

⌒

fter Ruby's party was over and all the guests had left, Margot swiped half of a bottle of wine from behind the bar as they were breaking it down to bring up to her bedroom. She never knew what to do when the caterers were cleaning up, what was expected of her. She was tired, and she didn't want to make small talk to a bunch of twenty-something aspiring whatevers. She hung around long enough to be nice, to appear interested, to pick up a few plates and listlessly bring them to the sink until someone rushed over and said, "We'll get that." She made a few jokes and thanked the crew profusely and gave everyone envelopes full of too much cash and ordered them to take any leftovers they wanted, so that when they talked about her in the catering van on the way to wherever they were going with all that leftover lobster, they would inevitably say how terrific she was. She would go on the list of "good" celebrities—generous and easy.

Margot only allowed one photo of herself to be hung on

the wall of her home because she thought that stuff was tacky. Some of her *Cedar* co-actors had their walls lined with photos of themselves wearing their doctor garb, as if they actually practiced medicine. Charles, in particular, was enamored of his publicity stills, especially the one where he was covered with blood and struggling to subdue a gunman in the ER. He'd had it blown up to the size of a movie poster and hung it on a wall in his double-height entryway, beneath a crystal chandelier.

The only photo Margot allowed in the house was from the third season of the show, the year she was nominated for an Emmy and *Variety* had put her on the cover with the caption: "Is Margot Letta the Nicest Woman in Hollywood?" She framed the cover and hung it in her front hallway partly as a goof, because anyone who knew Margot knew, sure, she was nice, but she was also adept at *performing* nice because it was important to her to be seen that way. The cover also served as a suggestion to those who crossed the threshold and didn't know her: Was she was the nicest woman in Hollywood? *Yes.*

The catering crew gone, she opened the fridge to find some cake. It had been neatly cut into sections and put into Tupperware containers. She cut a slice smaller than she wanted, but bigger than she should eat. She was mortified that she'd cried in front of Ruby's friends, which she knew was ridiculous. Seventeen and on the brink of leaving home, eager and terrified, they'd never be so at ease with tears, their own or others, again. They'd all rushed to comfort her.

The photo had pierced her. It had. She didn't have any pre-stroke pictures of David around, because she couldn't look at his old smile, the one that was wide and strong and minus the tiny droop at one side that was a constant reminder of what in their world had changed. And all she could think, staring at her younger self, was how everything good was already behind that woman in the photo, and how she didn't know it yet.

"I'm going upstairs," she said to David, who was in his office sitting at his desk.

"Okay," he said, not looking up from his computer. She stood for a minute and watched him. His brow furrowed with concentration. "Hey, that necklace was perfect."

He looked up, pleased. "It's an ingenious little construction. I don't know if you saw, but the chain is threaded through the superior vena cava and left pulmonary vein, so the heart hangs at a slight angle, exactly the way it does in the body." He cradled an imaginary heart in his hands and positioned it in front of his chest.

"No," she said, laughing, "I didn't notice that, but I noticed Ruby loved it. Good job."

"I'll be up soon." He turned back to his computer and started clicking away. She didn't have to look to know he was playing Scrabble. After the stroke, he took up a number of games to strengthen his brain's neural pathways and help with memory retrieval and word retention. He still played them religiously.

Upstairs, she changed into sweats and pulled up her hair and dutifully scrubbed her face with a ridiculously expensive exfoliator before applying the ridiculously expensive moisturizer that Bess had talked her into buying. Bess had gasped when Margot told her she used Noxzema cold cream to remove her makeup, but Margot loved the smell—it smelled like her youth. Like backstage and musty dressing rooms and summer stock and show openings and bone-tired nights when she couldn't wait to leave the theater but couldn't sleep because she was so wound up from the show. The slight sting of the cold cream made her feel at home. She took the wineglass into her bedroom and sat on the bed. Early summer, she could hear the kids from the house next door in their pool. Marco? Polo! *Marco? POLO!*

She used to think about the morning of the stroke all the time, trying to will herself back for a do-over. David had returned from a conference in London the previous night. Jet-lagged, he'd been up with the sun and had gone out for a run along the East River. She'd gotten up early with him and had gone to the little French bakery down the street to buy croissants and brioche and coffee beans that she assumed were a lot nicer than what they usually picked up at Gristedes. She had put some raspberries in a pretty china bowl they'd received as a wedding gift and never used. She'd bought flowers, enormous magenta peonies, and put them in a water pitcher on the table.

"What's the occasion?" David said, coming into the kitchen, freshly showered, smelling like lavender soap and toothpaste and filling the room with his good humor and vibrant energy, even though he'd only slept a few hours.

"A little welcome home to show how much I missed you."

He was wearing a new shirt he'd bought on Jermyn Street. No matter how busy his schedule, he always found time to shop. David loved clothes, and she loved that about him, his streak of vanity, the bright colors he favored. His new shirt was ivory with broad violet stripes that did something warm and good to his coloring. He kissed her, not a good morning kiss, a kiss with intention. Looked at his watch. "I have about an hour, you know."

She would always regret not taking him up on that invitation instead of looking at the spread of treats she'd assembled and deciding they should sit and eat, have a nice breakfast, because wasn't there all the time in the world for sex? An entire lifetime? She hated the banality of her thoughts, the constant worn groove of the moment that changes everything, but how else to remember that exact thing? She watched him pouring two cups of coffee. He added sugar and cream to his and handed her the cup of straight black coffee, except it never made it to her hand—the cup shattered on the floor, hot coffee splattered everywhere. "Yikes," she said and grabbed a roll of paper towels and started mopping up the shards of porcelain and coffee and looked up to see him standing stock still, holding one arm with his hand, looking bewildered.

"David?" His face was blurred with confusion, an expression she'd never seen on him before. "David?" She stood up. "Are you okay?" And the foreign string of consonants and vowels that came out of his mouth next were so confusing Margot couldn't even approximate them for the doctors later. "It was nonsense," she told them. "Like baby talk." She'd made him sit down. She knelt in front of him. "David, talk to me." When he didn't, she picked up the phone to call 911, but then he spoke.

"Hold on. Give me a minute." His voice was a little stronger, much clearer. He sat at the table, clenching and unclenching his fist. "I'm okay," he said, but then he winced. He stood and went to the bathroom. She wanted to follow, but she was also frightened. "Do you need something?" He closed the door behind him, and she could hear the water running, the medicine cabinet opening. She stood there wondering if she should call an ambulance. She heard the toilet flush. He came out, smiling, reassuring. "I'm fine. I think I have a jet-lag migraine coming on."

"Are you sure that's it?"

"Yes, I felt it while running, too. The wading-through-water feeling. Everything feels like an effort, like handing you a cup of coffee." He laughed, and she watched his face carefully. He looked okay. "I'm also probably dehydrated. Should have had more water before and after that run."

He *did* suffer from terrible jet-lag migraines. The entire time they'd lived in London and he'd had to travel all over Europe and Asia he'd struggled with those headaches. Sometimes they'd last for days and he'd have to take breaks in a darkened room. Her racing heart started to slow. "Maybe we should call Doug," she said. Doug was one of the partners in his practice, older and a mentor to David.

"I'm fine. I'm completely fine."

But he wasn't fine, because he was still clenching and un-clenching his fist. That was the moment she lingered on in spite of knowing she shouldn't. Why hadn't she insisted? Why hadn't she listened to her intuition that something serious was wrong rather than let David talk her out of it? But he was so reassuring. He laughed. He'd had a tiny brain blip. Man, did he need some sleep. It made a kind of sense. Also? Margot wanted to believe he was right. A messenger had just delivered a script for a new play, and she was itching to sit in a quiet room and read it from start to finish. She was eager to get back to work after coming home from London and spending the summer in Stoneham. She was looking for something different, not her usual part— the pretty but caustic wife, the knowing big sister, the wise-for-her-years friend. She didn't want to get pigeonholed, and her agent said this new play was it: a slightly ribald comedy by a new female playwright, something daring and different, and they were interested in her for the lead. She was impatient for David to leave so she could take it in, start to think about how she might approach the audition. And now he was loading the dishwasher and whistling and he was David, vital and strong.

If she had insisted on an ambulance. If she had made him stay home that day and let someone else cover his surgeries. If she had pressed him on his symptoms. If she had called Doug and said, *Hey, a little heads-up. Can you check on him?*

If. If. If.

If only she could have known that he was having what would be described to her later that day as a *tiny* stroke—a warning for the graver event to come only hours later while he was standing in the operating room, his gloved hands making an incision in ten-month-old Abbie Jensen's heart, which was the size of a walnut.

Even though everyone involved in his care told her she probably could not have prevented the larger stroke (*probably*, such a tenacious snag), if she had, maybe she could have stopped it all: the surgery, the malpractice suit, the complete cessation of his career as a pediatric heart surgeon, the subsequent depression and the lasting personality changes from the stroke.

"Why didn't *he* know what was happening?" she'd asked Doug in the early days. It was a question she would never muster the strength—or cruelty—to ask David. "Doctors," Doug had said to her. "They spend medical school imagining they have every disease in the books and the rest of their lives thinking they're invincible. Especially surgeons. Especially David. He talked himself out of it."

His doctors would eventually discover David's birth defect: a patent foramen ovale. When he was born and took his first breath, the tiny hole that every newborn has between the upper chambers of the heart didn't close the way it does in most babies. Some people went through their entire lives with a PFO and never knew; some had strokes. The moment David had taken his first breath, that day in the operating room had been foretold, his heart betraying him as he held the heart of Abbie

Jensen in his hands. She would have appreciated the symmetry of the story if it hadn't been her life.

The hospital had settled, there was no question that they'd go to court, and for all the ways they'd been unlucky, the way in which they were very lucky was that the Jensens were not out for David's blood. No trial, no terrible days sitting in a courtroom looking at Abbie Jensen's parents, who had lost their baby. The number the hospital offered could never be enough—what was the price of a child?—but it was a lot and the Jensens wanted to move on.

David had never loved New York City the way Margot wished he would. He loved *her*, and he loved his job. Working on his recovery after the stroke, life in the city became even harder. He was constantly confused. The noise and traffic and sheer number of pedestrians were difficult to navigate. So while all her friends traipsed up to Stoneham the August after the stroke to do Ibsen's *A Doll's House*, she and David flew to Los Angeles to spend time with his family. David's brothers were as focused and competitive as David had been (*would be*, she insisted on telling herself), and they made his recovery their project. When they weren't working—they were also doctors, both top of their fields—they kept David busy for hours, made a schedule of his day for the physical therapist and worked with him themselves on memory, language, fine motor skills.

She had been welcomed into his childhood home like a long-lost daughter, and she reveled in the attention. The *time*. But it was also hard. One afternoon, hearing uproarious laughter from the backyard, she went out to see what game they were playing. David was hooting and high-fiving his brothers. "Only took him a few tries to clean up, and he just learned this morning."

"Amazing," Margot said, walking over to give David a kiss

on the cheek. Looking at the game, her heart fell in on itself a little when she recognized it as Concentration, one David had taught to Ruby the previous summer. She'd had to leave the house and walk around the baking streets of Pasadena for an hour before she was composed enough to go back.

His recovery, by anyone's standards, was impressive. He still got frustrated and would lose his temper or—far, far worse for Margot—cry easily, but he'd regained a self-awareness of what he was saying and no longer blurted out rude comments about what someone was wearing or how they ate. He stopped saying inappropriate things about Margot in front of others. "Did Margot tell you how horny I am?" he'd asked their home health aide one morning in front of Flora and Ruby during the early days of his recovery, preening like a frat boy. They'd laughed it off—what else could you do? But she cringed when she heard Flora out in the hallway trying to explain away "horny" to Ruby while they waited for the elevator.

He worked so hard and gained so much, but he wasn't the same headstrong, deliberate, *arrogant* man she'd married. He came back, but he came back different. He was, she admitted to herself in her lowest moments, David-*like*. Like the man she'd married, but not.

In addition to what the stroke robbed from David, it also made Margot less fearless. All her life she thought she'd been protected; a circle of ease and luck seemed to surround her, and when she met David she recognized the same thing in him. It was stupid, she now understood, to think that privilege translated to protection. To mistake privilege for grace.

But that summer, as she watched the California sun heal him, she realized he'd never let on how much of a sacrifice it was to remain in New York City for her. So when she was invited to audition for *Cedar*, she did. When they offered her the part, she took it.

"I don't know how to thank you," David said. She'd never seen him so grateful, so dependent, so soft. She hated it.

When *Cedar* got a twenty-two-episode order, David's brother brought him into his private practice and they started up the stroke center. David became a consultant, a lecturer, an advocate for stroke patients and the doctors who treated them. It was important work, and she was almost always involved in the fundraising bit. At galas or dinners or conventions, when she was available she would introduce him by telling the story of the morning of the stroke. How scared she was. How easily they both brushed off the warning signs. Then David would tell his story and talk about the research the stroke center was supporting, highlight any notable and recent advances in recovery, make his pitch for money. She stood by his side, smiled for the cameras, and went off to work every day to play at being a doctor. So (she thought when she couldn't stop herself) did David.

⁓

ANY REGRETS?

Margot wished Flora hadn't brought the photo tonight; she would shake it off tomorrow. She could hear David now, downstairs, setting the security alarm. Running the faucet for a glass of water. Locking the front door. She quickly downed the rest of the wine and turned off the lights. She settled herself in bed, facing away from the door and feigned sleep.

EIGHT

⌒

Flora wanted the party to be over as much as she didn't want it to be over. Safe in the liminal space between knowing that she'd found Julian's wedding ring but not knowing what it meant, she was intentionally dragging out her good-byes at Margot's.

As she had been doing intermittently all day, Josephine reappeared as the last of the guests were leaving. *The party's over,* she could hear her mother singing, swanning around the room, picking up plates with leftover cake and abandoned wineglasses, *let's call it a day!* One of the many qualities she and her mother shared was a mutual love for an event concluded. It was an inclination she fought all her life. She loved a party best when it was over and the house had been restored to order and she could sit in the quiet and replay the evening. Too often, she looked forward to the end of something—to beginning the remembering—more than the thing itself. Her best self emerged as she was saying thank you and good-bye, all cheerfulness and light because she was so close to the exit. One of the things she most appreciated about Julian was that he was all present tense all the time. She knew her eagerness to get through a thing instead of linger within it sometimes irritated him. Tonight, she would have been happy for the party to go on forever.

On the way home with Ruby in the back seat, they talked of the day, the ceremony, the "killer" lobster rolls. Back at home, Ruby changed out of her dress and she and Ivan headed out to more parties, a long night of celebration. Julian walked them out to Ivan's car. She could hear him humming on the sidewalk, the clang of the front wooden gate as he said good-bye to Ruby. She went into her office and found the ring, which she'd tucked in its envelope into a bookcase. She went back out into the kitchen and moved the pile of Ruby's presents from the center island to the dining room table.

Flora's love for her marble-topped kitchen island was almost indecent. She never got tired of its gray and white striations and how the porous marble ended up being a canvas for what went on in their kitchen, the various spills and stains that never completely disappeared, fading a little as they seeped into the stone but leaving traces of this dinner or that party. Some of them she recognized. The night she left half a lemon cut-side down and accidentally bleached a spot near the faucet; Julian had made margaritas while she was cooking and they never even got around to dinner before going upstairs for a little tequila-fueled sex and passing out. The red wine stain from the dinner party where David had knocked over a glass of Cabernet and nobody noticed for hours. Tiny blotches on the spot where she and Ruby would roll out cookie dough.

Flora had been so thrilled by the kitchen when they'd bought the house. An island! Was there any surer sign that their fortunes had changed? The island—not even that large for Los

Angeles—would have barely fit into their living room in the West Village, never mind the galley kitchen. She recognized her musings for what they were: stalling. How would all of this look in the morning?

"Hey." Julian stood in the doorway, a satisfied smile on his face. "Ready for bed?"

In that moment, she wanted to forget about the ring. She wanted to say, *Yes! Ready for bed*, and go upstairs and do what they did most nights. Chat a little about the day. Talk about all the plans they had started making, starting with parents' weekend at Ruby's college in October. Maybe they could go somewhere else after. London? Paris? These things were finally possible thanks to both of them having good jobs at the same time, a thing that had not happened before in all their years, and the thought of ruining it before it even started was gut-wrenching. But what kind of life would that be?

She opened the envelope and took out the ring. "I found this today." She put it on the marble slab. "When I was looking for the photo in the file cabinet. It fell out of the envelope." Julian was standing stock still. He picked up the ring and looked at Flora and although she searched, prayed, there was nothing quizzical in his expression. She felt something inside plummet to a cold, dark place.

He sighed and put the ring down. He walked over to one of the kitchen cabinets and opened it and for a moment she thought he was going to present her with some kind of counter object, a thing that would explain the presence of the ring, make her suspicions silly. But he grabbed a glass, filled it with water, and drank it in one smooth gulp. Refilled the glass and drank again.

"Julian?"

He ran his fingers through his hair—his beautiful black hair, glossy and fine, all those curls barely touched by age, hardly any gray—and closed his eyes and grimaced and she saw then what all those casting directors saw when they cast him as a social worker, a therapist, a priest, and twice as the Messiah himself. He looked exquisitely beautiful when pained. Pierced but beatific. "Flora," he said. "I love you. You know how much I love you."

"That bad?" She could feel the tears but tried to stop them. She couldn't start crying before she even knew what was wrong.

He opened another cupboard and grabbed a bottle of good whiskey; one he'd brought back from Ireland years ago that they saved for celebrations. He sat at the table and gestured for her to sit. "It's not good," he said.

NINE

~

On the first day off David had in forever, he got up early and gave his tiny New York City apartment a meager clean—a Windex clean, his mother would call it, because at his childhood home there was always a housekeeper to do the real cleaning—but in between her twice-weekly visits, if necessary, his mother would take out the bottle of Windex and give everything a quick shine. After the cursory housekeeping, David thought he'd go to the Metropolitan Museum of Art, one of the few (only?) places he'd frequented in New York because looking at paintings calmed him, took him out of his head and out of the hospital. It was ridiculous—but not unusual—that nearing the end of his surgical residency he'd seen so little of New York City outside the confines of New York Hospital and its surrounding blocks.

"New York!" his family from California would say, excited to hear where he was living. "What's it like to live there?"

"Beats me" was his usual response. He always had grand plans for his days off that usually ended up with him sleeping as much as possible and maybe seeing the occasional movie with a group of friends and then going to the same old bar on East Seventy-Ninth, the one with foosball and tabletop bowling and bartenders newly arrived from Ireland. All of them—the newly arrived, the passing through—trying to figure out how to occupy a place as vast and varied as New York from the comfort and safety of the bar stools at Flanagan's. But as he headed toward the Metropolitan, he got distracted by the park. David never minded the summer stickiness in the air. He'd grown up in bone-dry Southern California. Ambling up Fifth Avenue, he could see the banners from the front of the Metropolitan stirring in the slight breeze. He slowed and made a sharp left onto one of the paths into Central Park. Screw it. He'd like a long walk; maybe he'd risk his digestive tract with a street hot dog, maybe even stop for a beer at the Boathouse if he could figure out where it was.

As he got farther away from the noise of Fifth Avenue, farther into the meandering paths and magically appearing bridges and streams, he appreciated the value of walking and thinking in pseudo-nature. Nearing the end of his surgical residency, he was preoccupied with what came next. His mentor was pushing for a fellowship in pediatric heart surgery, which he was considering, but it was hard to think straight in the midst of his current life: the hours, the pressure, the lack of sleep. He couldn't help fantasizing about an easier surgical specialty. But when had he ever taken the easy path? Also, he knew he would make a good cardiac surgeon. He had the exact combination of traits the work demanded. His fingers were long and slender, and he had naturally good spatial and eye-hand coordination. He had legs of steel—he could stand in the operating theater for hours. He loved the mechanics of cardiac surgery, the logic of it, the way the heart was a machine that could be fixed. He liked working at the center of things, on the engine.

On the other hand, his girlfriend wanted them to leave New York, move back to the West Coast, where she'd also grown up, and start their lives. He couldn't quite understand how he'd gotten to this point with Patricia except that the hospital was its own contained world, and it felt logical, natural, that they met and started sleeping together and then they were a couple and now four years had gone by and there was an assumption that their lives were moving forward in tandem. How had that happened?

"It's not that complicated," she'd said to him the previous night as he was waffling about their "next steps," as she put it, as if she were ordering a series of diagnostic tests. She'd just come home from a run in the park and was sitting on the floor in the middle of their living room, sweaty and flushed. Her legs spaced wide apart like a gymnast, she'd bent forward at the waist, fingers extended. Then she raised her arms up high and leaned first to the left, then to the right; she was frighteningly limber, an athlete, and as such was going into orthopedics. She rightly wanted to be out west, where people were active year-round, more active in general. She hopped to her feet with disarming ease and grabbed her right foot in her right hand, pulling back in a deep quad stretch, wincing a little. "What do you *want*?" she asked.

He'd equivocated, but what he should have said to Patricia (and this couldn't be a good sign, a mark in the "pro" column, that he hadn't wanted to say it out loud) was that *want* was nothing but complicated. It seemed so linear to her, desire and outcome, but nothing about it felt that way to him. He wanted many things. He wanted many contradictory things: to leave New York, to

stay in New York; to begin life as a surgeon, to study longer to
be a cardiac surgeon; to look at paintings in the Met, to walk in
the park; to commit to Patricia Casey, to move on.

Desire was nothing more than impulse and potential, with
paths leading off into separate but possibly equally satisfying
destinations. Like right now, somewhere in the middle of Central Park, should he go left or right? Who knew where either
would lead, but picking one meant denying yourself the other.
How to know which to prefer? The path to the left was crowded
with a bunch of children on a field trip, wearing neat blue-and-
white school uniforms, making a fuss over something to the
side of the walk. A bird or a squirrel.

To the right, an elderly couple walked arm in arm. They
were dressed almost alike, both wearing jeans that hung a little
too loose and were cinched with leather belts, both wearing
faded polo shirts—his once a bright green, hers once a vivid
turquoise. They were nearly the same height and were ambling
along pleasantly until the man said something that made his
companion stop and turn and look at him and slap him gently
on the arm, laughing, as if he'd been fresh. *How nice*, he thought,
*to be together until old age and still make each other laugh, surprise
each other.*

He veered right.

David sat on a bench with not one but two hot dogs in hand,
recklessly courting heartburn, but they were good. They were
delicious. As he was finishing up, washing his mustardy hands
in a water fountain that barely trickled, he heard someone calling his name. "Pearlman! Pearlman!"

How was it possible that he'd come to New York City not
knowing a single person and yet it seemed he could never leave
his apartment without running into someone from the hospi-

tal? Or worse, a patient, someone who remembered him and expected a courtesy recognition, which David could rarely provide. He went from case to case and patient to patient and was not proud to admit that he didn't concentrate on faces or names. He did in the moment, but then the information was dumped from his brain to make way for what he needed.

He turned and saw Sandra, a resident on urology rotation. She started lightly jogging toward him and arrived a little breathless. "Hey, Pearlman. Do you have plans tonight? Because after standing in line for three hours, I just got a ticket for *A Midsummer Night's Dream*"—she waved it in the air—"and Rosen paged me and I have to scrub in tonight." Any other theatergoer might have been disappointed, but she, like all the surgical residents, was chuffed. *Called to scrub in* was a thing they wanted more than a day off. She held the ticket out. "Yours if you want it."

The decisions never ended, even the simplest ones. Did he want it? "Where is it? On Broadway?" he asked, with only a vague idea of where "Broadway" was in relation to Central Park.

"No, the theater is in the park. Right over there." She gestured vaguely over a rise and toward a copse of trees that didn't look like a theater.

"There's a theater over there?"

"The Delacorte," she said patiently. He seemed to recall she'd grown up in New York, like many of the other residents who had a shorthand about the city he never understood. He looked at her blankly. "You have heard of Shakespeare, right? I'm telling you this is a hot ticket. Lots of people in line behind me didn't get one."

Here was an opportunity to do something quintessentially New York. "Sure. How much do I owe you?"

"It's free, dummy." She handed him the ticket, shaking her head. "Public theater. In the park. Jesus, Pearlman, how long have you lived here?"

"I don't get out much, obviously."

"'Lord, what fools these mortals be,'" she quoted with relish. He recognized that at least. "I'm bummed to miss this even though I don't really love the comedies. More of a tragedy girl myself. Give me *Othello*, give me *Hamlet*, give me *Lear*. Okay, I'm boring you. Have a great time. The director is terrific. Pay attention! I'm going to want a full report."

He pocketed the ticket and thanked her and made his way toward where she indicated the theater was so he'd know where to go later. He could see the seats from a little opening over the box office, the banks of theater lights. He felt unaccountably excited. He wasn't a theater guy per se, but this would be fun, something to report on to the family back home. He had some hours to kill. Maybe that beer at the Boathouse after all.

BECAUSE THE STORY WOULD BE TOLD so many times after that night, it was sometimes hard for Margot to remember how it happened, and she and David always disagreed on the exact unfolding, but she knew her version was—if not the most accurate—the best.

Act II, Scene I. Margot was onstage ready for her big fairy moment, her *over hill, over dale* speech to Puck, played by her longtime family friend Theodore Best. He was a slightly older-than-usual Puck, but so elfin and mischievous and lively onstage—so beloved at the Public—that he stole the show. By late July, the cast was accustomed to working with the noises of the city in the distance, the rush of traffic, a helicopter over-head, the boom of a radio or wail of a siren. The more insistent intrusions of revelers in the park: children arguing over a ball, teenagers shrieking, the occasional smash of a bottle of beer morphing into a million glittering emeralds on the pavement.

But on that night, as Margot finished her speech, Theo-as-Puck was looking at her in clear distress. Or was he? She didn't know what to do except what her training told her to do, center herself and focus and carry on, but as she waited for Theo to say his next line—*The King doth keep his revels here tonight*—he fell to his knees.

"He was so pale backstage. He said he was tired," one of the Rude Mechanicals—the actors who staged the play within the play—said later, trying to wring portent from the moment. Actors were the worst unreliable narrators, assigning meaning in retrospect, embellishing facts with imagined significance. At least five people would tell Margot the story of Theo fall-ing that night, and they were all different: he'd clutched his chest or he'd clutched an arm; he'd said *Help* or he'd said *Fuck* or he'd said nothing; he'd put out one hand beseechingly; his eyes had rolled back in his head or they'd darted around look-ing for a specific someone. None of them true. She had been right there!

"I can't believe I wasn't there for him," the woman playing Titania had said later that night, in tears. "I was standing off-stage and the way he looked at me like *What is happening?*" A story she stuck to for the rest of the run and probably the rest of her life even though it was impossible for her to have been back-stage at that moment and, also, everyone knew Theo loathed her and what he called her Tinsel-Land ways.

What was indisputable was that the actor playing Oberon, awaiting his entrance in the wings, was the first person to fully comprehend that Theo needed help, and he'd come out onto the stage and turned to the audience and yelled—theatrically, if that was even possible given the setting—"Do we have a doctor in the house? Is anyone a doctor?"

The reason Margot could narrate the rest with a fair degree of certainty, beginning with David standing and saying loud enough for Margot to hear, "I'm a doctor," was not—as she would later claim (she wasn't above revision)—because she stayed downstage to guide whomever might be able to help, but because she was rooted to her spot in terror. She'd never been the kind of person to rush toward trouble. She was the kind of person to go running in the other direction and look for someone far more capable and far less squeamish to help. In that moment, she was terrified to even look at Theo, whom she loved, whom she'd loved ever since she'd seen him in the first Delacorte production her parents took her to. Her mother had performed with him several times. When she arrived at the first day of *Midsummer* rehearsal, he'd puffed up with pride, like she was his own daughter. His affection bestowed a legitimacy on Margot that elevated her above the other newcomers. She should kneel and take his hand, comfort him, see if he was breathing. But she couldn't move. Some of the audience members were standing, some were already leaving, most were sitting in their seats, riveted by the very real drama unfolding on the stage. And making his way down the stairs was a tall, lanky blond, taking the steep steps two at a time. He reached the perimeter of the stage and looked up at Margot and said, "I'm a doctor." She stepped forward and offered her hand and he took it, gracefully leaping up, Julian right behind him. Julian, who was in new-boyfriend mode and seeing the play—and Flora—for the fifth or sixth time.

"Why did *you* come up onstage?" Margot asked Julian later.

"I love Theo. I thought I could help." He shrugged. "I know CPR."

David always insisted he *wasn't* the first on the stage, that he'd followed the path of a young woman who was in front of him, a nurse, and *she* was the first person to attend to Theo. But Margot didn't remember the nurse getting to Theo first. She remembered that someone on the lighting crew had picked up David's path, moving the beam along with him, lighting his way. She remembered how David took off his sweatshirt in one smooth movement and tossed it aside, like Clark Kent tearing open his reporter's white button-down shirt. How as he knelt and put an ear to Theo's chest, the backstage crew came out and started arranging themselves. Margot understood immediately what they were doing and she waved to Flora and the rest of the fairies to join her and they all linked arms with the crew and formed a barrier to give Theo privacy. By then, the stage manager had ordered the house lights up, and the audience was sitting quietly.

David and the nurse started CPR, David straddling Theo, working to restart his heart, counting off the beats and pausing for the nurse to breathe for Theo. In that moment, Margot felt both powerless and vital. A life was possibly ending, two people were trying to snatch death back, and it was all being done in front of an audience who had come for a night of glib entertainment, the Bard in the park. From afar, the sound of an ambulance siren and soon the red flashing lights pulling up beside the box office. Then a gasp, a cough, and the nurse: "He's breathing."

David stopped the compressions and knelt beside Theo, who tried to sit up. She watched David take Theo's hands in his and speak, his voice low and comforting. He continued talking until the paramedics climbed up on the stage and took over. Soon they had Theo on a stretcher and ferried him off to the ambulance. David stood, picked up his sweatshirt, and looked around, seeming to notice for the first time that he was on a stage, surrounded by actors.

Margot was the first to approach him. "Thank you," she said, taking his hands. "Thank you so much." The audience around them applauded. Such a strange thing. To have people in a theater watch one man bring another back to life and honor what they'd witnessed in the most appropriate way they could think of in that moment, with a scattering of respectful applause. Nobody ever knew what happened to the nurse. They never got her name. She disappeared into the darkness of Central Park.

The four of them could also never agree on how they'd ended up at a Chinese restaurant once Theo was safely on his way to New York Hospital. Julian was certain that *he* had asked David to join them for a beer ("We owe you one."). David always insisted Margot had invited him. For Flora, everything after Theo collapsed up to the moment they were sitting in a booth in front of platters of pork fried rice and shrimp lo mein, was a blur. However it happened, Margot and David and Flora and Julian came together that night for the first time and ordered too much food and proceeded to retell the events of the evening over and over, the way you do when you know the story will be told many times—fixing the details, burnishing the best ones, eliminating the banal, accentuating the dramatic. Flora remembered David's elegant leap at the other end of Margot's hand. Julian remembered the nurse saying, "I have a pulse," and how David, working above Theo, had been dripping with sweat. "I thought we might have to revive *you*," he said to David.

"Have you ever *done* CPR?" David asked. "It's hard work."

Margot would always remember—with relief and more than a little shame—how she'd finally approached Theo when he was conscious and lying quietly. She knelt at his side and took his hand. "You're going to be okay," she said, praying it was true. He'd looked at her and pushed his oxygen mask to the side, smiled wanly, and said, "Maybe this foolish heart's had enough." She teared up as she told the story. "*Is* he going to be okay?" she asked David.

"Probably," he said, passing around the platter of lo mein. He gave them all a little lesson about the heart, how it worked, what might have felled Theo in the middle of the play. His hands were graceful and light as he sketched the aorta and various descending and ascending valves on the back of a paper place mat, indicating the places where arteries could clog and cause a heart attack. "By the looks of him," David said, a little apologetic, "I'm guessing his blood pressure and cholesterol are not the greatest. Depending on the blockage, they might have to operate—angioplasty or bypass. Both usually successful surgeries."

"What's it like," Julian said, pointing at the drawing, "to open someone's chest and see a beating heart?"

David thought for a minute, took a sip of his beer. "It's like opening up the hood of a car: you're looking for the problem. Figuring out the repair."

Julian looked skeptical. "Really? The first time you stood over a beating heart, you thought of your *car*?"

"No," David said, a slow grin. "The first time I watched someone cut open a human being and expose a beating heart, I thought, *I want to do that.*"

Julian nodded, toasted David with his bottle of beer. "Sounds more like it."

"It sounds terrifying," Flora said.

"It sounds romantic," Margot said.

The four of them were there for hours. Eating, drinking, laughing. Flora caught Margot's eye a few times, telegraphing approval. He was so nice, the doctor. Julian was explaining his theater company, and David was genuinely interested, wanting to know how they chose plays, how they decided who could join the company, how they financed the whole thing. What kind of theater? Avant-garde? Musical?

"Oh, not musical," Flora said, sounding more sour than she intended.

"Not true," Julian said, he took Flora's hand beneath the table and gave it a little squeeze. "If the right musical came along, we'd do it in a heartbeat." Flora rolled her eyes. "Hey," he said. "Musicals are a lot of work. A lot more money." He turned to David. "We mostly know each other from school or working in the city. We don't usually write our own plays because we like to find existing work looking for a home, but if somebody in the company wanted to write something, we'd help. What else?" He scraped the label of the beer bottle with his finger. "We're constantly scrounging for money. We have a small, kind of shitty space." He shrugged. "We look for good work. We look for good people."

"Is it lucrative?" David asked. Julian and Margot both burst out laughing.

"It is most definitely not lucrative," Margot said.

Julian finished his beer in one long gulp. "It's practically community service," he said.

"Then why?"

Flora and Margot and Julian looked at each other. "Because it's fun," Julian said. "Because when it works, it's the best job there is."

"Does the company have a name?"

Now Flora laughed. Julian gave an exaggerated sigh. "Not at the moment."

"I like Hester Street," Margot said, turning to David. "The new space is on Hester Street."

"I hope we're not going to be on Hester Street forever."

"He's waiting for a sign," Flora said.

"No, not a sign. I don't believe in signs. I'll know the right name when I hear it."

David finally got someone at the hospital on the phone and reported that Theo was stable. They were taking him in for angioplasty and he didn't want to make any promises, but if the surgery went well, Theo should be fine.

Around them, the restaurant's waitstaff was starting to vacuum and mop. They were putting chairs up on tables and clearing their throats. Flora picked up David's drawing and placed it on her chest, making the paper heart beat with her hand, batting her eyes at Julian. The waiters put a plate of fortune cookies down on the table, and they each grabbed one and took turns reading them aloud. David went last. He cracked open the slightly stale sugary shell and took out the tiny slip of paper and read it first to himself. "Okay"—he cleared his throat and gave a little laugh—"it says: 'You have found good company.'"

"Really?" Margot took the piece of paper from his hand. She read it and smiled and slid it across the table to Julian.

⌒

"TO GOOD COMPANY!" THEY TOASTED. "To Theo! To Shake-speare! To Central Park! To modern medicine and doctors at the Delacorte!"

Remember this, Flora thought, taking Julian's hand in hers. Remember how it feels to be with these people at this slightly sticky table on this singular night in the most remarkable city in the world, to feel so much life ahead of you, to be in love with this man. Reluctantly, they all started to gather their coats and bags.

"Hold on," David said. "How does it end?"

"How does what end?" Julian said. *"This?"* He gestured around the table.

"I hope I know how *this* ends," David said, holding Margot's gaze. Flora was sure she'd never seen Margot blush before. "I meant the play," David said. "How does the play end? Is it happy or sad?"

"Sad," Margot said.

"No, it's not," Flora said, "it's happy."

"Actually, it's neither." Julian picked up the drawing of the heart, folded it into thirds, and stuck it in his coat pocket. "Turns out it was all a dream."

TEN

David and Margot's wedding was a small but lavish affair. The ceremony was in the library of her parents' house. ("And this is the library," Margot had said, without a trace of humility, the first time Flora had visited her childhood home, gesturing around the room filled with more books than Flora had ever seen in someone's house in her life—the only twinge of envy she'd felt that day, aside from the window seat in the living room that looked out on the shimmering water of the sound; the perfect spot to read.) The reception for no more than fifty was on the back lawn under a blinding white canopy on a picture-perfect Connecticut day in May. No bridesmaids or ushers. David's niece and nephew were flower girl and ring bearer. Margot asked Flora to stay with her the night before, to help her get ready and calm her nerves, even though they both knew she was as calm as the surface of the assuringly placid Long Island Sound that day.

Weeks before the wedding, Margot had insisted on taking Flora shopping for a new dress—the first of what would turn out to be many moments where Flora confusedly stood in a small boutique while Margot casually chatted with the salespeople, pulling dresses for Flora to try, discussing Flora's figure as if she weren't there. "Flora has the most beautiful breasts, but she hides them, so let's do something about that," she would say, piling clothes into Flora's arms.

One of the dresses Margot brought into the dressing room, Flora didn't even want to try on. It was pale pink (she would stain it within minutes, and what if it was a hot day and she perspired right through?), it had a low neck (too low) and a wide belt (she was self-conscious about her middle), it was linen (wrinkles). But Margot insisted, and when Flora finally put it on and looked at herself in the mirror, she was transformed, the dress somehow making her taller and slenderer and more elegant in ways she never felt. She'd recently finished a run on Broadway, so she had her show body, lean and muscular from months of singing and dancing as a member of the ensemble (and understudy for Louisa Von Trapp) in a Tony-nominated revival of *The Sound of Music*. She'd loved every minute. She'd wept on closing night.

"That's the one," Margot said, inordinately pleased with herself. Flora stood as a woman with a multitude of straight pins in her mouth, and a pincushion strapped to her wrist, knelt in front of her and started pinning up the hem. "Just an inch," Margot instructed. "Bring it right to the bottom of her knee."

"How much is this?" Flora asked the saleslady, who handed her the price tag that had fallen off in the dressing room. It was a fortune. Flora was back auditioning and had to save every penny because who knew when the next job would come along? Margot had moved in with David and left Flora the apartment, so Flora's rent had doubled, and she didn't want to take in a

roommate—or worse, go back to word-processing legal docu-
ments at night. "I can't do this," Flora said, motioning to the
woman at her feet to cease and desist. "I can't take this dress."

"It's taken care of," Margot said. "It's my gift."

"Your gift for what?" Flora said.

"For being my pretend bridesmaid. For making me go out
with David on a second date after I thought he was too uptight.
For being the best roommate, the best friend. Please, Flora,"
Margot said, when she saw the set of Flora's face, a look she
knew so well, a combination of desire and resentment. "Please
let me buy this dress. This wedding cost me nothing. I'm wearing my mother's dress. I didn't even buy shoes; I had them. Let
me do this. It would make me so happy."

Flora looked at the saleslady and the seamstress, all smiling
at her expectantly, waiting for her decision. Lord, she wanted
the dress. She looked at herself in the mirror and she saw a
flicker of a better Flora, how she could look if she had a little
more money, if she'd had the resources to buy well-made things
designed to flatter her curves. Margot looked like a little girl,
hands clasped in front of her. *Please*, she mouthed again. *Please,
please, please.*

"It will be a loan," Flora said. "I'll pay you back as soon as I
get a new job."

"Sure," Margot said, and Flora ignored the apprehension
that she was capitulating not to a moment, but to a dynamic.
She knew she'd find reasons not to offer Margot—who didn't
need the money—the money. She knew this tiny justification
would lead to more gifts and ways of Margot slightly pressing
her advantage. If Margot's generosity had a purity to it, it also
evinced a desire for control—to be the person who knew the
just-right shop that would have the perfect dress, to offer *so*

much that a steely loyalty inevitably rose up to meet her generosity. She liked being on top, Margot. Flora knew all this and sometimes she resented it. But then she looked at herself in the mirror and thought of seeing Julian at the wedding for the first time in months while she was wearing the dress, and she surrendered.

⌒

JULIAN AND FLORA HAD BROKEN UP during the winter for what she was sure was the last time. The first two breakups had been short-lived: one a few days, the other a few weeks, but this time months had gone by and their last conversation had been rife with hurt and accusations and tears. It had been *so hard* to be a couple alongside David and Margot, who progressed as if they were on one of those motorized walkways at the airport, beating everyone else without breaking a sweat, while she and Julian struggled to keep up, burdened by heavy coats, the wrong shoes, and too much baggage. So much baggage.

When things were good with them, they were ridiculously good, and this was what Flora couldn't fathom: how they could be deliriously happy, having great sex, talking for hours on end, enjoying each other, and then something dark and nefarious would enter the room, something she never saw coming and couldn't fend off.

It would almost always start with Julian not being able to sleep. She would wake up in the night for a drink of water or to urinate or just to readjust the pillows and he would be wide awake and staring at the ceiling. At first, she believed him when he said his insomnia didn't have anything to do with her because, to her, they seemed fine and there was a lot of understandable stress in their lives. Work was unpredictable, fleeting. Auditions were a grind. Julian and Ben were always scrambling for funds for Good Company. If the space on Hester Street wasn't freezing cold, there were rodents, and if there weren't rodents, the electricity would blow, and if wasn't the electricity—the list went on and on. Once the insomnia started, it only got worse. Julian slept less and less and became uncharacteristically surly. He started to pick fights over dumb things—whether it was hot enough to turn on the air conditioner or what movie to see or whether said movie had been good or unwatchable. Flora could tell when he was itching for an argument.

"I tried to warn you this might not be easy," Margot said after the first breakup. "Has he told you about his family? His mother?"

Flora pretended to know more about his family than she did. Julian would allude to the circumstances of his childhood after a few beers, making a joke about his crazy mother or telling a funny story about her alcohol-fueled antics, but he clammed up if she asked anything too direct. He refused to introduce Flora to Constance ("I'm aware of the irony of her name"), and Flora was hurt until he said to her one night, exasperated, "Flora, I'm *protecting* you." She had to let the details unfold at his pace, and his pace of revelation was stingy. But then one night, in between breakups one and two, the floodgates opened. They were in bed, happy to be together again, maybe a little wary, but mostly grateful. She'd heard him on the phone earlier with his mother, curt and frustrated. She waited for a soft postcoital moment and asked. "Can you tell me more about Constance?"

And he did. The drinking, the pills, her eventual bipolar diagnosis that she refused to believe or treat. The volatile temper unleashed on Julian and his little sister, Violet, often late at night when they were asleep. How he would hear his mother downstairs playing the piano—"I knew it was danger-ous when it got louder and faster and stopped being anything recognizable"—and he'd go into Violet's room and wake her up and bring her into his room to keep her safe. Constance never physically hurt them—"Not from lack of trying," Julian said, "we were faster"—but she terrorized them. "But also," Julian said, "and I know this sounds nuts, but when she was good, she was great. Funny and affectionate and interesting. She just—loses her mind sometimes."

Flora had met Julian's sister once. Violet was contained, po-lite but not effusive, interested but guarded. She was a social worker in Portland, Oregon—pretty much as far away as she could go and still be in the United States. Even though Violet and Julian talked all the time, she rarely came back east, so they didn't see each other much. Violet didn't even try with Con-stance; they hadn't spoken to each other in years. Constance had never seen Violet's two sons, her only grandchildren. "And she never will," Violet said.

"Why can't you be more like Violet?" Flora had made the mistake of asking Julian once when he'd gone uptown to check on Constance and bring groceries. As usual, Constance wouldn't even let him in the house. As always, Julian would come home in a horrible mood. "She doesn't want me to see how filthy the apartment is," he said, unloading the cans of Progresso soup and boxes of Stouffer's frozen lasagna into their refrigerator. The pints of pistachio ice cream that neither of them liked. Without her children around, Constance had stopped cleaning and started to hoard.

"If she won't take help, why not leave her be?" Flora said. "Why can't you be more like Violet?"

Julian stood stock still, hands on his hips, clenching and un-clenching his jaw. She'd crossed a line. "Because," he finally said, "if I were more like Violet, Violet would have to be more like me."

After their breakups, Flora realized how enmeshed she'd become in Julian's life—willingly, *ecstatically*. She'd never be-longed to a group of friends of her choosing. All through high school it had been her and Patrick and their families—so many cousins, so many aunts and uncles, and the friends she'd had since first grade, so little room for change. She was proud of herself for how deftly she fashioned a new life after breaking her engagement and moving into Manhattan.

Her new friends liked to talk not only about theater, but about art and books and travel; they were smart and funny and ambitious and bold and *fearless*. But when Julian broke up with her, she was forced to face the truth—she hadn't fashioned a new life as much as she'd hitched her wagon to Julian's. When she wasn't auditioning or working, she had helped with Good Com-pany in any way she could. She cleaned, she organized props or wardrobe. She loved to sit in the uncomfortable folding chairs in the dingy Hester Street space and watch Julian work with actors. His concentration in those moments was fierce, but his guidance was gentle—from the careful way he steered an ac-tor's impulses and choices to the concrete advice he offered to help someone struggling to find their way into a part, including one frequent admonition she took to heart: "You have to fool yourself before you can fool the audience."

Often, while watching rehearsal, he'd turn to her and say,

"What do you think?" She was getting good at knowing her answer—seeing when an actor's reading was too hot or too cold or the pace was off. She loved that he wasn't precious about the work (that he never said *The Work*). "This is fun, it's all make-believe," he said. "It doesn't have to be torture." Julian was an ideal audience because he genuinely wanted to like things. He wanted everyone to succeed. She valued his kindness, how once when they listened to a read-through of the first (and last) play Ben wrote, Julian had given him careful, considerate notes. Walking home together later, she'd said, "But that play was awful, right?"

"It wasn't good. But sometimes my job is to make people feel okay about their place in the world."

Both Julian and Flora had accidentally been called "Florian" more than once, and the name stuck, so that when she arrived with bottles of water and snacks and a warm sweater and would take her place of pride right next to him, somebody inevitably would announce that *Florian* was in the house.

Times like those she could see them as partners, see their lives together so clearly. But then: the insomnia, the squirminess, the fights about where to eat or what to eat or what movie to see that were really all about something more significant. His irritability whenever she wanted more time or attention. Flora started to feel like she was performing an exhausting nonstop tap dance, one that required she be supportive but not demanding, entertaining but not needy.

Then one night he was late coming home, and while she sat in his living room, a voice came over the answering machine: "I must be very strong," the throaty female voice said, her mouth too close to the receiver, "to let you leave like that."

When he got home she was standing, rigid, waiting for him.

He tried to deny where he'd been at first but caved quickly. It was an actress, of course. Not someone in the company, but a woman he worked with on a *Law & Order* shoot. They both played jurors at a trial who were caught sleeping together during sequestration. She'd watched the episode, seen them kiss, seen them in the television bed, bare-shouldered, in each other's arms. The scene was only minutes long, and she knew they had nude clothing on underneath, but it was uncomfortably intimate, the emotion on-screen too real. When it was over, she said, "Congratulations. I hated it."

He'd laughed and said, "Good. Then I did my job."

After she played the answering machine message for him and he confessed, he apologized profusely but he didn't seem sorry about what he'd done; he seemed sorry he'd been caught.

The next morning, she made herself coffee and sat at his tiny kitchen table and looked around the apartment, struck by how little of herself was present in the room even though they'd been together for two years. She didn't live there, but to look around, you wouldn't even know Julian had a girlfriend unless you opened the bathroom medicine cabinet where she kept tampons and nail polish remover and a small bottle of perfume. It took her all of twenty minutes to pack her belongings—hairbrush, toothbrush, blow-dryer, robe, a few items of clothing—into two paper bags from the Food Emporium. When Julian woke up and came into the kitchen and saw her sitting at the table with her coat on, he knew. He was still sleep-ruffled, so beautiful. He looked like a twelve-year-old standing in front of her in his pajamas (he wore pajamas!), his face creased on one side from the pillow. "I don't know why I'm so ambivalent about you," he'd said to her the previous night—a searing, hurtful remark that she'd swallowed. A bitter pill that still hadn't dissolved.

"I'm tired, Julian," she said and took the slightest satisfaction in watching his shoulders slump, his face collapse a little. "I think," she said, "that we should stop making each other unhappy. I don't know how to make you happy anymore."

"Flora." He pulled up a chair and took her hands and started weeping. Of all the things she hoped would happen when she finally mustered the courage to be the one to end it, she never imagined him crying. She'd only seen him cry at the theater but that was a gentle tear and this was sobbing. "I'm sorry, Flora. I'm a mess." He said it over and over and although she wanted to comfort him, fix him, forgive him, tell him he wasn't a mess, what she thought in that moment was, *He's a mess.* Then: *Save yourself.*

⌒

FLORA WAS PROUD OF HERSELF. She made it through the wedding ceremony; she was stoic. She wanted to take in Margot and David's day, be present to what was happening without the constant awareness of Julian in the room, and she did. It felt like a good sign to her. She would get over Julian. She was going to be fine. As she headed back to the wedding tent after getting a glass of champagne from the bar inside, she bumped right into him. He smiled and she smiled, and they stood looking at each other for a minute.

"You look beautiful," he said.

"Thanks to Margot. She picked this out." Flora gestured at her dress, self-conscious.

"I wasn't talking about the dress," he said. He held his arms out and she walked toward him, and they embraced. He felt so solid and familiar. "I miss you," he said, gathering her closer, holding tight. Before she could swallow the lump in her throat and reply, before she could think of what to say, the *clink, clink, clink* of a spoon against a champagne glass. The jazz ensemble quieted, and the guests shuffled toward the front of the dance floor. Theodore Best was summoning everyone's attention; Theo, who a few years ago had collapsed on the stage at the Delacorte, setting Margot and David on their path. He looked dapper in his slightly dated suit, hair slicked back. The heart attack had scared him. He'd lost a great deal of weight and taken up walking—five, seven, ten miles a day. He was lean and leathered and looked as pleased and mischievous as Puck. Margot and David had asked him to make a wedding toast. Flora and Margot had taken bets on what he might recite— surely something from Shakespeare. *A Midsummer Night's Dream?* A sonnet? Something else? But as the guests quieted, Theo nodded to Margot and David and instead of beginning to speak, he gestured for the band to start playing and took the microphone in his hand and started to sing "My Foolish Heart."

The crowd laughed appreciatively. Everyone knew the story of the night of the Delacorte and Theo's *foolish heart.* Flora watched as David clumsily led Margot around the parquet dance floor. He would always be the perfect foil for her elegance, and Flora saw how Margot deftly took the lead, making David look nearly graceful. She thought, not for the first time, how Margot was trusting her heart to the right person, to someone who had held a heart in his hand, cut it open and understood its inner workings, if not its contradictions. Flora turned to Julian and he held out his hand. His arm encircled her waist and he pulled her close, singing lightly in her ear.

The night is like a lovely tune,
Beware my foolish heart.

As she and Julian moved to the music, Theo's pleasing voice—a light tenor, floated above the lush melody and filled the tent with romance and longing. She watched David and Margot pass through the flaps of the tent and onto the grass, framed perfectly in the gentle afternoon light, the golden hour. She watched them embrace and kiss in the riotous garden, like the beginning of a fairy tale. She couldn't help it, she wept on Julian's shoulder, quiet but fierce. "Shhhh," Julian said to her. "It's going to be all right, Flora. It's going to be all right. I know you don't believe me, but it is." She thought about walking away. She thought about giving him a little shove and turning on her heel, but all she wanted to do was kiss him. She hadn't known how good kissing could be until she was with Julian. As if he were reading her mind, he took her hand and walked her behind the tent and pulled her closer and then they were kissing. She'd never kissed anyone the way she did Julian, and standing in the wet grass, the music weaving its romantic tune between them, she kissed him as if her life depended on it, long and full-hearted, like a conversation that shouldn't end. How could she walk away? She felt like Theo was singing for her, for everyone, for all the foolish hearts. How bewilderingly hopeful she felt right then. How hurt she was willing to be. How foolish her heart.

⌒

FLORA ALMOST CALLED OFF THE WEDDING the day they bought their rings. It wasn't any *one* thing that had happened that day in April. When she thought about it—about how terrified she'd become in the jewelry shop that afternoon—she wondered if someone had cast a spell, the evil eye, a thing she'd relentlessly mocked her mother and aunts for believing in. Il Malocchio. Her relatives were all so superstitious, clutching the Italian coronet charms around their necks, made of coral or gold, brought back from Naples or Sicily by the few family members who ventured to visit the land of their ancestors.

"She's got the evil eye, that one," Flora heard so many times at family gatherings. It didn't go unnoticed that all the women Flora's aunts accused of having the evil eye—the ability to cast bad luck with an envious look—were beautiful. The mood Flora found herself in that day in the jewelry shop was so foreign and came over her so quickly it truly felt supernatural. It felt like a warning. And the message was clear—*don't get married*. Or rather, *Julian doesn't want to get married*.

"I like this one," Margot had said, pointing to a platinum band. She and David had tagged along and they were all supposed to go to lunch afterward. Flora felt dizzy, like she was going to faint. She was vaguely aware that Margot should not be picking out Julian's wedding band, but her stomach hurt, and she was clammy. She asked the saleswoman where the restroom was and went in without telling anyone. They didn't even notice she was missing. Sitting on the toilet in the tiny space, she took a few deep breaths. What was wrong with her? This was what she'd wanted forever, since practically the first night she met Julian. But did he want it? Or did he not want to lose her and so he was capitulating? Was that the same as wanting marriage?

"I wouldn't be able do it," Margot had said to her once, after the first breakup, when she'd given Julian an ultimatum, an ultimatum that didn't work. "Who wants to get engaged under duress?" This, from Margot, who could have given a tiny crook of the finger at any moment and David would have gleefully dropped to one knee.

She'd never told Margot the reason they broke up the second time. She was embarrassed. She knew Margot would not approve of their reconciliation after he slept with that actress. But when they reunited for the final time, Julian had looked her right in the eye and sworn his fidelity.

"I learned my lesson. There's nobody else for me, Flora."

"It's the one thing I won't ever forgive," she told him. "I know," he said. And then he asked her to marry him and she said yes. Of course she said yes. She chose to believe him.

"Flora? Flora?" She could hear Julian looking for her. She splashed water on her face and her wrists and fixed her hair. Oh God, were they making a mistake? She would pull him aside. She would say, *Are you absolutely sure?* She would say, *We can wait.* She would say, *I need you to be certain.*

"There she is," he said when she rounded the corner. The smile he gave her was magnificent, the world righted itself, and her brief bout of panic evaporated with a poof! He extended his hand with the ring. "What do you think of this one?" he said, pleased with himself. The band was perfect, thick and solid and gold. It made his hand look even stronger. "Do you like this one, wife?"

ELEVEN

⌇

t was Sydney.

Sydney? Flora said, not quite taking in the name. She still had the ring in her hand and was standing at the kitchen counter and had the fleeting thought that they should move to another room or go outside because she didn't want to ruin her beloved kitchen with this conversation. Outdoors, the words could dissipate in the night air, be absorbed by the vast expanse of the California sky; only the owl gently hooting out the window would bear witness. The outdoors would shed its vegetation, and next summer none of the flowers or leaves would know what she'd just found out—they wouldn't have heard her name. *Sydney Bloom?* She still thought he must mean some other Sydney, or that she was hearing the syllables wrong, because it couldn't possibly be Sydney Bloom.

"I'm so sorry."

Flora laughed. The kind of inappropriate laugh that's more of a confused bark. Sydney had always been there. Sydney had predated Flora; Sydney was at the party the night they met. She was an original company member, and had been in a few early Good Company productions until she was essentially banned for being argumentative, undermining, the all-encompassing "difficult," which sometimes was applied to women who were demanding but in Sydney's case referred to a gradual unhinging that was anathema to everything Good Company wanted to be, everything Julian believed Good Company should be: namely *good*, not only referring to the things they made, but to how people in the company were treated, how they treated others. Flora vaguely remembered a lot of drama around her being fired and that Ben had handled it because Sydney was giving Julian a particularly hard time. Julian had called her the bad penny then—"Always turning up when you think she's gone forever," he'd said, exasperated.

"Flora," he pleaded, "it was such a long time ago. It was the dumbest thing I've ever done. It's been over for a very long time."

"But I don't understand. When did it start?" He wasn't even looking at her, sitting on a bar stool at their island, his head in his hands. "It started after we were married?"

"Yes." His voice was muffled.

"After Ruby was born or before?" She didn't know why the existence of Ruby in this unfolding tale made it feel so much more worse, but it did. "After," he said, finally looking up at her. The sentences, as they trickled out, were so banal as to be boring, if they hadn't been devastating. Julian recited them like an unwelcome memorization exercise.

It hadn't gone on for long, maybe a year.
It meant nothing; it was just sex.
Always at her apartment.
He'd finally come to his senses.

"Did you care for her? Did you love her?" Flora asked.

"*Love* her? No, no—" His face contorted in an un-Julian way, an ugly way. "I can't stand her. I hated her."

"You *hated* her?" Flora could barely make sense of the words coming out of his mouth. "Why then?"

"I don't know why."

"You don't know why you started a relationship with *Sydney*?"

"It wasn't a relationship."

"Julian, please."

He sighed and leaned forward, pleading. "She just appeared one day and I don't know what happened. I don't know. She was so aggressive, and we always had this *chemistry*."

Flora felt the word—*chemistry*—scathe. The burn started in her gut and traveled like a shot up to her throat. "Chemistry?"

"Yes. And I knew her before I ever knew you and somehow—" Julian saw the look on Flora's face and stopped talking. She was as pale as he'd ever seen her, ramrod straight, livid.

"You mean she was *grandfathered* in?" Flora said. "I didn't realize that was a thing." (*Watch out for the old girlfriends*, Samantha had told her.)

Flora walked over to the cupboard and got herself a glass. "Who else?" she said.

"What do you mean?"

"I mean, who else have you fucked while we were married? Surely not only one person."

"Nobody else."

Flora breathed in slowly, exhaled. "Julian, I am begging you. *Begging.* No slow drip. I want to know everything right now."

"I know you have no reason to believe me, but I promise you, I swear to you, there was nobody else. I'm telling the truth. And Flora, it was over a *long* time ago."

"How long?"

"Years."

Years. Jesus. What was she supposed to do with *that*? Flora opened the whiskey bottle and filled her glass. It was going to be a long night.

⌒

THEY'D STAYED UP PAST THREE A.M., an endless circle of the same conversation. Flora had finally fallen asleep on the sofa and awoken with a start as the sky brightened. It took a moment for her to remember why she was downstairs, then she saw the empty bottle of whiskey and her stomach heaved and she remembered that overnight her life had become one tired, sickening cliché, starting with the cliché of the moment you wake up and can't remember the bad thing, moving straight through to *It didn't mean anything. It was just sex.*

The timeworn excuses of the previous night had come at her like a series of arrows—one to the head, then the shoulder, the waist, the neck—until she felt like a walking Saint Sebastian. Oh, and there was the next cliché: martyrdom.

After she'd fallen asleep, Julian had covered her with the afghan her mother had made as an engagement gift. She remembered how much she loved the white blanket, covered with crocheted vines and flowers, when Josephine presented it to her. As beautiful as it was, whenever she tried to display it somewhere—first in her apartment, then in Julian's—it always looked out of place, like it had dropped down from—well, from Bay Ridge. After Josephine died, right around the time Ruby moved to a big-girl bed, Flora had taken the afghan out of its plastic cover and Ruby had fallen in love with it. She wouldn't sleep with anything else. She'd sit and trace the long stitched-on vines with her finger, naming the colors of all the roses, trying to find a pattern.

Whenever the mother of one of Ruby's friends saw it, they'd want to know where it had come from, where they could find one, and it made Flora absurdly happy to say her mother had made it. Ruby had kept it on her bed until they moved to Los Angeles, then Flora had moved it to the front hall closet for naps. They all grew to believe the blanket had special powers, Josephine powers, because everyone who used it slept like the dead, including Flora, including last night. Improbably, she'd slept last night. She stood and looked out the window. How different the world looked from yesterday morning, when her worries were so much more prosaic, so manageable. Why had she gone looking for the photo? Why hadn't she waited until Julian got home? Why was she like a terrier digging at a patch of dirt when she thought of something she wanted? *Why, why, why?* Ruby would be home from Ivan's soon, and then what? She'd better make coffee.

Flora had imagined this scene before—the day Julian would come home and confess to an affair or ask for a separation or say he was unhappy. Who hadn't if you'd been with someone for any amount of time? If you had half a brain? If you had even the slightest inkling of how the world worked? You could be like Flora's friend Mona, standing in your kitchen one day, annoyed to be spreading the umpteenth batch of organic fish sticks on a battered cookie sheet, wondering how the kids could continue to love the Dr. Praeger's fish sticks, which supposedly were healthier but so much more disgusting than the unhealthy fish sticks, surreptitiously topping off a glass of white wine, and the phone could ring and it would be a complete stranger telling you to come to the hospital quickly, your marathon-running husband had been hit by a car and was near death. You could be like Nadia, whose husband keeled over on their back deck while grilling hot dogs and was dead of an aneurysm. You could be Margot and David, on top of the world, feeling secure and smug in the bubble of your success, and a tiny blood clot could swish through the chambers of a heart and cleave your life in two.

Bad things happened. The people closest to you surprised you in the most disappointing ways.

Flora *knew* this. And for so many years, she'd waited for the bad thing, the thing that would define her life, because didn't everyone have not only one, but several? But then she began to think that she was safe (oh, foolish heart) because she and Julian had had small bad things. His mother's mental illness and brief but ugly struggle with dementia before her death. Josephine's sudden devastating bout with lung cancer, her lifetime of smoking calling in its loan. Flora's miscarriages. The constant worry about money and work. And she'd told herself (would the clichés never stop?) that all this had made them stronger. A team.

The year Ruby was in kindergarten, marriages around them started crumbling, the ones that couldn't seem to survive the arrival of children and the necessary shifting of priorities. It was like an epidemic. Like everyone who had survived the toddler years looked up, caught a breath, and didn't like what they saw. She and Julian marveled. *Could you imagine? Leaving your kids? Starting to date!*

"I would send out my voice-over reel," Flora joked. "Four minutes of me talking household cleansers, tampons, toilet paper, and financial services. Call my agent for a date."

Every time she left the apartment in those days to run to

the store, Julian would say, "You're coming back, aren't you?" feigning fear. It always made her laugh and it always made her feel loved. Smug. *Her* husband wanted her back. Her husband was *afraid* of her leaving.

She and Julian hadn't inherited a kind of life; they'd built one from scratch—a beautiful, sometimes scary, mostly exhilarating existence that looked nothing like their childhoods. She thought it made them invincible, that they'd had to invent the whole thing rather than follow a well-worn template. Gradually, she'd stopped fearing the demise of her marriage, which had never been based on anything solid, just a feeling that *she'd* been the one who had lucked out. A worry that because she had pushed for marriage and Julian had capitulated, one day she might pay for her certainty about them, for her stubbornness in believing that their lives would be better together.

So here she was; here they were. Flora simultaneously felt horror and relief. Horror because how were they going to get through this? (*Sydney!* Why did it have to be someone so unworthy? It was insulting.) And she felt relief because she could stop waiting. The bad thing had arrived.

Sorry. I'm so sorry. Julian must have said it a hundred times last night, but "sorry" was his tic, his go-to response to nearly everything. It always had been. He apologized for things that had nothing to do with him, and although in her clearer moments she realized he was apologizing as a form of empathy, it also felt a little bit like a trick to disarm her—or anyone's—objections or frustrations. Now she saw all those sorries in a different light. He wasn't apologizing because she didn't book the part or because Ruby had been a complete monster all afternoon or because the pork roast had burnt while Ruby was being a monster—he was apologizing for his sins. *Sorry, sorry, sorry!* It was a dance she'd been drawn into but didn't understand. "You apologize too much," she'd sometimes say to him. Ha.

And it was terrible—how easy it was for Flora to picture Julian and Sydney together. That Julian was an object of desire both within the company and the larger world itself was something that Flora enjoyed. She recognized that he was emotionally open in a way most people weren't. He was comfortable putting an arm around someone or giving an impulsive bear hug. He was a comforter, a cheerleader. She'd watched other women—and men—flirt with Julian over the years and had always marveled at his grace, his ability to volley long enough so that the other person wasn't rejected, but not long enough to mislead. Or was she just seeing what she wanted to believe?

Sorry. *Sorry.*

She heard Julian coming down the stairs and tried to parse her feelings. She missed him; she hated him. She wanted him to go; she needed him to stay. Flora didn't realize how much she'd invested in the mythology of her marriage until it crumbled to dust last night. She'd lived her adult life with this belief: Flora and Julian met and quickly fell in love, Julian in spite of himself, Flora with the gusto of a dog chasing a shiny red ball. Julian resisted, Flora insisted, and love won. Or something like that. Their course of love hadn't been easy, but it had been true. At times, they'd struggled to find themselves at the same place with similar intentions, but they ironed out those kinks when they told the story; like good storytellers, like good actors, they whittled it down to a few symbolic moments that added up to the legend of Florian. After they were married, Flora had tired of the name; she was on the receiving end far more often than Julian, who didn't understand why the moniker got under her skin. "It's nice. Everyone sees that we're a team. Two parts of a better whole."

"No," she said, "everyone sees me as an extension of you, which is not flattering, it's diminishing." But it was a pointless conversation because Julian looked genuinely hurt when she objected and Flora was never going to win this argument, to convince him that the members of Good Company adored him and saw Flora as a perfectly fine side dish. And so they stayed *Florian*, not any couple, but the couple everyone wanted to be. The couple who had figured it out. The *real deal*, as Sam had said last night. In her softer moments she could admit the name was mostly affectionate, so she had to live with it—Florian.

But did she?

Flora realized she was feeling more than betrayal, more than grief. She felt a loosening of something she'd tamped down for a long time, and it didn't feel awful, it felt warm and liquid, and if the feeling were to take a sentient shape it would be an enormous glowing question mark.

Did she have to accept a name she hated and laugh?

Did she still love Julian?

Did she have to stay married?

Did she want to?

TWELVE

～

Why did he do it? Julian realized there was no satisfying answer to the question. None. Nothing that would make Flora feel better, nothing that would absolve him, nothing that would make any sense to her. He didn't dare tell Flora this—she was one pulsing organism, radiating rage and heartbreak; anything he said that wasn't some version of *I'm sorry* just inflamed her more—but he hadn't thought about the ring in years. Had, for all intents and purposes, forgotten that it was sitting in the bottom of the file cabinet in their garage. When he got it back all those years ago—and, oh God, they hadn't even gotten to the part last night where he got it back—he'd kept it because it was their wedding ring. What was he supposed to do with it? Throw it away?

He could hear Flora awake downstairs. He hadn't slept at all. Sitting in bed, he listened to the usual morning sounds: running water, grinding coffee, the muffled slam of the refrigerator door, the little milk frothing machine he'd bought Flora for her birthday that she loved more than it warranted.

He sat and wondered how his entire life had turned completely upside down in less than twelve hours. How could it have only been yesterday that he and Flora stood in this room on the cusp of Ruby's graduation and the world had felt laden with promise? The roll of euros from yesterday still sat on Flora's bedside table, a witness to the last conversation they'd had before Flora decided to rummage through a drawer in the garage and unwittingly excavate the past that he'd believed was long buried.

No, he corrected himself, that was not entirely true. Time to start facing the bald truth, which was that he'd always half expected Sydney's Doc Martens–clad feet to reappear on his doorstep. She was dangerous, volatile. For years her name would pop up as an incoming call on his cell phone or as an email in Good Company's inbox. He never answered. He deleted without reading. He had no idea where she was living or what she was doing. All had been quiet for the past few years and he'd allowed himself to believe she'd moved on, in one form or another. He dabbled in two competing but equally weighted fantasies about Sydney depending on his mood: The first, the more generous but infrequent daydream, was that she'd finally found someone who made her happy and so she'd forgotten about him. The second, the more frequent and to his shame more satisfying, was that she was dead. Buried. Cremated. Permanently silenced. He never bothered trying to find out if either was true. Let sleeping lies lie.

Last night had been bad, but he knew it was the amuse-bouche of rage. Flora was in shock last night. He kept waiting for her to throw plates, tear at his hair, pummel his chest, but he knew better. Flora was not a hysteric; she was a ruminator, and before she'd passed out on the sofa, she'd already started doing the math and realized that his *thing* with Sydney ran concurrently to the one year they'd been in couples therapy with Maude Langstrom. The *one year* he'd had not only the opportunity, but the *duty* to reveal what he was doing behind her back.

"Maude knew?" Flora said last night, looking dazed.

Miraculously, Ruby called at that exact moment to say she was spending the night at Ivan's house. He kept her on the phone, stalling, hiding, asking her about the run of graduation parties, if she was having fun. By the time he hung up, Flora was on the sofa, asleep. He'd covered her with Josephine's blanket and poured himself another drink and gone upstairs.

He hadn't lied to Flora last night, but he hadn't told her the whole story either. He hadn't divulged the other heartbreaking truth—that the only other person who knew about the ring, who knew about Sydney, was Margot. Her best friend.

⌒

JULIAN HAD A LONG LIST of things to blame (anything other than his own weakness), starting with that Wednesday's driving rain, the bitter cold. He was running late because Ruby had refused to wear her raincoat or boots and it had taken forever to get her out the door (Ruby was not on the list of things to blame; he couldn't go that far). Then the F train (always ripe for blame) was stopped because of a sick passenger, forcing him to take the A or C downtown. The water pouring down through the ceiling of the West Fourth Street station meant that instead of standing in his preferred spot at the far end of the platform, he stood nearer the turnstiles. When the train finally came to a stop and he stepped into the car directly in front of him and grabbed a seat and looked up after he was done wiping the rain from his foggy glasses, there she was—that familiar face, that impudent grin. Sydney Bloom.

Julian wasn't sorry to see Sydney that day on the subway, but he also wasn't exactly happy because you never knew what Sydney you were getting. She could be bright and happy or glum and anxious, loud and manic or curious and teasing. Sometimes she toggled among all those things in one brief conversation. But on this day, on the subway, she was good Sydney. Said she'd been at the same office job for some months, it was boring but the money was fine and she had health insurance, so— She was auditioning all the time, but you know how it went, having a slow year but she felt good about it picking up. She found an acting coach she loved, a woman Julian knew because they'd done a play in SoHo the previous year (enthusiastic reviews, no audience, story of his life) and Julian had only great things to say about her. Sydney asked about Ruby (not Flora, he noticed that) and he showed her a couple of photos he kept in his messenger bag and she said all the right things—she's beautiful, she has your eyes, she looks smart.

"You seem well," Julian said to her, as they disembarked. He gave her a hug and said it had been good to see her and he meant it. Sydney smiled and waved good-bye and bounded up the stairs. A promise to keep in touch. Grab coffee one of these days.

Walking across Canal Street, Julian marveled at how normal Sydney seemed. Before he met Flora, for a good two years albeit very much on and off, he and Sydney had, well, what would you call it? Dated? Slept together? Driven each other nuts? For one disastrous month, they'd tried to be boyfriend and girlfriend.

He was tending bar then, and she would continually show up to "surprise" him and sit on a stool, nursing the awful house wine, and glaring at every woman who lingered and talked to Julian. She'd show up with a roll of quarters and commandeer the jukebox for hours, singing and dancing even though it wasn't that kind of joint. She insisted on going home with him on nights when he wanted to go to sleep early and prepare for an audition the next day. She would call him, hysterical, from emergency rooms where she'd gone with a raft of imaginary symptoms. If some people at the beginning of a relationship tried to put their best-shod foot forward, it was as if Sydney needed to do the opposite: lead with her crazy and calculate exactly how far over the precipice he was willing to go with her.

And it worked at first because if there was one thing Julian's childhood had given him in spades it was the ability to manage crazy, be the emotional rescuer. Hysteria brought out the calm in him, and even though he knew it wasn't healthy, there was something about the rescue, the adrenaline brought on by tears and fake catastrophe, that felt as reassuring as a beloved ratty coat, one that smells a little musty but is too comforting to discard.

Sydney had grown up in a house almost as bad as his. It was a thing they bonded over, their disdain for everyone who'd grown up happy. The first night he met her she said, "If someone tells me her best friend is her mother, I sprint in the opposite direction." In a world where you weren't supposed to admit to the ugliness of family life, he and Sydney could say the worst. He could tell her how hard he'd wished for his mother to not come home from one of her outings; how he'd sit and watch the clock and imagine she was dead in a ditch, felled by a stroke or a heart attack or, the most likely, massive liver failure.

She could tell him how she started sleeping with a crowbar under her bed when she was thirteen so when her father turned his drunken tirades from her mother to her and her sister (another way they understood one another), she could protect them. She told him how one night she'd pummeled the wall behind her father's head, and he was so wasted he thought she'd cracked his skull and he fell to the floor sobbing, begging her to stop. "I think about it all the time," she said. "If I'm scared or nervous, I think about the feel of the iron bar in my hands and I know I can do anything."

He understood.

For the rest of the day after their brief subway reunion, Julian couldn't get her off his mind and his mind was going to dangerous places. Flashes of what had been good between them, namely sex. Sydney slowly unhooking her bra, standing in front of him brazenly cupping her breasts. Kneeling on all fours, inviting him to take her from behind. The filthy things she would say to make him come, the way she would touch herself.

He would force himself to stop and think about Flora and Ruby and all the things that made his life so good, all the wise choices he'd made. But then, as if Sydney had been reading his mind, she showed up one night at the bar on Hester Street where everyone from Good Company hung out many evenings. At first there was a crowd, but soon enough it was just he and Sydney ordering another drink. And another. Then he and Sydney in the back of a cab. Then he and Sydney in her apartment, undressed, fucking. That was the only word for what they were doing; their conversations had always been a kind of knowing foreplay. He knew full well when they got into a cab that night, what was going to happen.

Flora and Ruby were long asleep when he got home and he

sat in their living room and stewed in his bad behavior. He swore he would never do it again, but while he was berating himself, he was also thinking about how when they got to Sydney's apartment she'd pushed him down on the bed, whipped her shirt off, and lazily circled her nipples with her fingers and how he wanted to watch her do it again.

Sydney's zeal cancelled out his reluctance. When he left Good Company, she would be waiting for him across the street, sitting in the window of a diner. Some nights he was able to ignore her, go home, be true. Some nights they would go back to her apartment. He never stayed long and swore every single damn time that it was the last.

That same spring, couples therapy swept through the playgrounds of the West Village like a particularly virulent strain of pink eye. It seemed to Julian that Flora came home every day with a fresh story of yet another marriage in trouble. First it was Lexy Garcia, who wheeled her double stroller into the playground one morning and announced that the previous evening, after her husband, Harry, read *Good Night, Gorilla* to their daughters four times and carried each child to bed while clomping down the hall and grunting like a gorilla (a moment, Lexy said, when she'd thought to herself, *I married a good man, a good father*), he'd poured himself a glass of expensive red ("A Châteauneuf-du-Pape—I should have known then it was something very good or very bad") and announced he couldn't be married anymore.

"Just like that," Flora told Julian, her cheeks red with indignation. "He said, 'Lex, I don't think I want to be married to you anymore.' Can you imagine? Like he was opting out of his Costco membership."

Only days later, their downstairs neighbors Nick and Billie

were in peril because, as Flora reported, Billie could not handle another single second of Nick spending every goddamn living moment on his BlackBerry—even when he was supposedly watching his three children, "not only in charge of feeding them or playing with them, but *keeping them alive.*" Billie said the BlackBerry was like a mistress and for all she knew it *was* connecting him to a mistress because who wouldn't be more alluring than a woman who was home all day with twin three-year-olds who still didn't sleep in their own beds all night and would only eat food that was yellow?

Then a woman from Music Together discovered her husband was sending flowers to his assistant. Then it was Ruby's teacher, Lill, which hit all the mothers particularly hard because Lill had been their mainstay for that first bit of all-day school separation, the sage giver of advice, the neighborhood guru who repeatedly told them to stop beating themselves up over too much sugar or after-dinner television or missing a bath because: "This stuff is hard, moms. You have to get through it however you can." So when Lill stood at the classroom door one morning looking, as Flora said, like she'd been on a week-long bender and told everyone at drop-off that her husband had packed up and moved out on Friday night, the *moms* were shocked. And it turned out that Lill had one extremely foul mouth when betrayed, because more than a few kids had come home saying, "Shit-goddammit!"

"*Everyone* is in therapy," Flora said to Julian one night.

"We live in New York City."

"I'm not in therapy."

"Do you want to go to therapy?" Julian asked, not expecting Flora to say yes. In the equation that was their marriage, Julian was the one who needed therapy. He was the one with the bruising childhood and the emotionally demanding job of herding a bunch of fragile egos. Flora was steady, solid as a rock. She didn't look up to answer, continued scrubbing the pot encrusted with macaroni and cheese a little too hard. After a minute or two, long enough so Julian assumed her nonanswer was an answer, she'd turned to him and said, "We can't afford it. It's a lot of money, not counting the babysitter."

"That's not what I asked. Do you *want* to?"

She wiped her hands on a dish towel and walked over to the living room sofa and sat and stared out the window. The days were getting longer, and it was still a little light after dinner, that uplifting tilt of the earth. Now she sounded sheepish, a little embarrassed. "With Ruby in pre-K, I do feel kind of lonely sometimes. A little adrift. Am I really going to be the voice of toilet paper for the rest of my life?"

Julian resisted saying, *I hope so!* The Soft'n'Tuff television spots promising sanitary goodness had been keeping them afloat while he developed a promising new work for Good Company, a play that was attracting genuine funding and producers with impressive track records and verifiably exciting actors. They'd snagged a coveted residency. Things felt like they were falling into place for once.

"I feel blue sometimes," Flora said. "I'm not sure why."

"Honey, you miss your mother."

Flora noticed he didn't bring up missing her work. "Yes, I know. But I can deal with that sadness. I'm talking about something else. And how I feel like we're on separate planets sometimes."

Julian watched Flora, sitting on their worn-out sofa, now carefully folding Ruby's clothes, matching the socks and making them into little balls in a way he could never quite get right. Flora was sad? How had he not seen that she was sad? But looking at her now he could see the smudges of fatigue under her eyes, her tired posture. "I don't want to come home one night and have you say you can't be married to me anymore."

"That's never going to happen," he said, while a tiny sliver of fear embedded itself in his heart. Was he responsible for Flora being sad?

One night, lying in Sydney's bed, Julian calculating how long he'd have to linger so as not to insult her, trigger her temper, she'd taken his hand into hers and played with his wedding ring. He queasily let her twist the ring on his finger, pretended not to care even though the sight of her touching his wedding ring somehow felt like a bigger violation than sex. When he left that night, he vowed (again) never to return and although he broke that promise to himself, he did start removing his ring and slipping it into his back pocket before he entered her apartment, because the ring brought Flora into the room with him, and that was a line he couldn't cross. A paltry consideration, but one he enforced.

⌒

HEADING DOWNSTAIRS, he wondered if Flora would let him stay in the house. Explaining what he'd done to Ruby was unthinkable, as was the idea of packing his bags and leaving.

Flora was sitting on a stool at the kitchen island. The ring was still where she'd left it last night. Her eyes were swollen, pink at the lids. A wave of sorrow moved through him. He walked in the room and went straight to her, took her in his arms, and she was too tired, too confused to resist.

"I'm going to make this right," he said. "I won't lose you, Flora."

She disentangled herself and gave him a wan smile. "It's not up to you, though, is it?" She poured two mugs of coffee. She picked up the ring. "Why don't we start with this?"

THIRTEEN

⁓

I f Margot had known what Donna was about to tell her, she never would have taken the call. To begin with, she was sitting in the enormous trailer that housed hair and makeup—the *vanities*, as they were called on certain sets, usually by the old-timers. Every actor's relationship with the vanities was complex. A vulnerability that wasn't chosen but imposed. Margot didn't think David was as familiar with the contours and peculiarities of her face as the makeup team at *Cedar*. They knew if a person had been crying or not sleeping or drinking too much or drinking at work or forgetting sunscreen. In one notable instance of set lore, Gwyneth, the head of the makeup department, told one of the actors to get a tiny spot on the back of his neck checked out by a doctor and it turned out to be a melanoma caught at an early stage, no doubt saving the man's life. And because the vanities were practiced at being quiet to the point of almost being invisible, they overheard things others didn't. Hair and makeup could pretty much piece together the social dynamics of the show at any given time: who was arguing, who was happy, who was threatening to leave, who was sabotaging their coworkers, who was sleeping with whom. The world of *Cedar* behind the scenes was nearly as melodramatic as the show. Someone was always wanting more money. Someone was always wanting more screen time. The producers were watching the bottom line and keeping the story "digestible." Actors were never satisfied.

"What's the opposite of prestige TV?" Kelsey, who played Dr. Cat's sister, had said to Margot a few weeks ago, which made her bristle. Kelsey was a season-seven addition to the cast, and when she showed up for her first day of work, Margot couldn't believe her eyes. She understood the logic of finding someone who resembled her to play her sister, but did she have to look so much like Margot? And be so much younger? The resemblance was unnerving, and Kelsey didn't help things by toting around a ten-year-old picture of Margot from *People* magazine and holding it next to her face and saying, "Isn't this insane?"

So Margot found herself jumping to defend *Cedar* whenever Kelsey complained, which was a lot. Margot didn't think *Cedar* was *that* bad. They weren't the *opposite* of prestige television, they were just working in a different register. True, characters were good or bad, smart choices trumped selfish ones, and love almost always prevailed, but they'd had some interesting story lines and had tackled difficult subjects: date-rape and surrogacy and AIDS and euthanasia and depression and addiction.

Margot had asked her friends on other shows if the vanities were the fulcrum of gossip, an ill-meaning coven, and although the answer varied by degrees everyone agreed on one thing: they couldn't be messed with; they were responsible for how you looked. Gwyneth ("*not* named after Paltrow," she'd take pains to say to anyone who would listen. "My mother had never even *heard* of Gwyneth Paltrow when I was born," which was blatantly untrue; makeup Gwyneth was born the year Spielberg cast actress Gwyneth as young Wendy in *Hook*) gave Margot an earful of gossip almost every day. An eerily accurate earful. "I think Nikki and her husband are having problems," she'd said a few weeks ago, lowering her voice even though they were the only two in the trailer, feigning caution. "Every time she's on the phone with him lately it's all *uh-uh, okay, fine, see you later, whatever*, and it used to be *Love you! Miss you! Bye sweetheart!* And twice she got a call from an attorney's office and stepped outside to take it."

"How do you know it was an attorney?"

Gwyneth gestured for Margot to look up and started layering mascara on her lashes and shrugged. "She keeps her phone on the little table over there and I could see when the name flashed. Same place my mom used." When Nikki announced her divorce in the press a few weeks later, Gwyneth was practically ecstatic. "Told you so, told you so." She sang a little song and danced in a circle around Margot, like one of the witches from *Macbeth*.

So Margot had a rule about not taking phone calls in front of the vanities because you never knew what they might overhear, but on the day that would soon live in infamy, when Margot saw Donna's number on the phone she made an incorrect assumption and answered. When it was bad news, Donna usually emailed first. Margot cheerily picked up on the second ring.

"Are you sitting down," Donna said, her voice loud enough for Gwyneth to hear, which Margot knew because Gwyneth's impeccably shaped and tinted eyebrows shot up her forehead and she mouthed, *Uh-oh.*

"I'm in makeup. Should we talk later?"

"They want to kill you," Donna said, plowing ahead.

"About the money?" Margot said, throwing discretion to the wind. Everyone asked for more money all the time; that was hardly news.

"No. I mean they are literally going to kill you." Margot was briefly perplexed because whenever Donna said *literally* she meant the opposite. "I'm sorry, babe. But Cat Newhall is toast."

"Hold on," Margot said to Gwyneth, whose eyes had that purposefully blank *I'm not listening* glaze that she'd seen her turn on and off like a light switch.

"You're good to go!" Gwyneth said, a little too eager, snatching the protective paper bib off Margot and waving her away. "Have a great one!" She picked up her phone before Margot was even out the door.

"Thanks," Margot said, stepping out of the trailer, wondering who Gwyneth was texting first. "Donna, what the fuck?"

"I know. Listen, I'm not supposed to tell you. Bess is calling soon, but I wanted to give you a heads-up. You have to pretend to be shocked."

"I *am* shocked."

"Well, hang on to that feeling, because I really need you to act surprised."

"I assure you I'm surprised. I don't understand. When?"

"Soon, I think. You're getting the script soon and maybe you have two or three more episodes. Maybe an accident or something. Bess wasn't specific. You know better than I do how they kill people off."

Margot stood leaning against the trailer, stunned. A bunch of extras passed by, all wearing lavender scrubs, the uniform for everyone at *Cedar*. In season one the scrubs were all dark burgundy, but Brooke Reed, who played the head of hospital and was number one on the call sheet, complained so vociferously to Bess about the color "washing her out" that they'd changed to lavender. A few of the extras waved to her. This particular group came back a lot, they were the background characters to the ER. She wanly waved back. "I just— Are they allowed to do this? It's because I asked for more money, right?"

"Bess didn't say anything about the money. I mean, who knows, but I didn't get that impression. And yes, they are allowed to do anything they want. Unless you're pregnant. Are you pregnant?"

"I'm *forty-eight*."

"Entirely irrelevant these days."

This was true, Margot thought, but how many times had she and Donna talked about how grateful they were not to have children—how lucky they were to have not *wanted* children? "No, I'm not pregnant. I—I wasn't expecting this."

"It happens," Donna said, back to her insouciant self. Margot could hear her typing away on her computer, the bad news dispatched with, thinking of the next thing already, moving right along.

"She didn't give *any* reason?"

"You can ask her, but it sounds like the usual—she needs a ratings boost."

Margot was quiet for a minute. Her ire rising. "Remember when they brought Kelsey in and I told you they were paving the way for me to leave? Bringing in a younger me who didn't require as much makeup and corrective lighting? I was right."

"Margot, I know this is a bummer." Margot bit her tongue. *A bummer?* "But last negotiation, if you'll recall, you wanted out entirely."

"Right. And they wouldn't let me go."

"So let's think of this as belatedly getting the thing you wanted two years ago. Let's have lunch this week. Talk through next steps. You're going to be fine."

"I am?"

"Of course you are. You're Margot Letta. This is an *opportunity*. Start thinking about what you'd like next. Where to go from here."

Margot checked the time. One hour until she had to be on set. "One last question," she said, involuntarily calling up Mia, the interviewer from last week. "Does Charles know about this?"

"I don't know," Donna said, "good question."

Margot threw on one of the many cardigan sweaters she kept in her trailer because it was always freezing on set and a pullover would mess with her hair. For a pediatrician, Dr. Cat sure loved her long coiffure, which was both annoying and inconvenient. She couldn't sleep between her scenes for fear of ruining the back of her hair and needing an unscheduled redo and incurring the wrath of the hair department. If she was tired, she had to prop herself up with enough pillows so her hair could hang over the edge of her sofa. She'd cross her arms over her chest, like a corpse, and try to doze. She went looking for Charles. Friday meant special lunch buffet, and he might be there, not eating but holding court. Charles was the most obsessive person on set about his weight. Or rather, he was the person on set who was not shy about his obsessiveness about his weight, which as a man was allowed. All the women were equally as controlling but pretended they weren't. They didn't eat because they weren't hungry—had "just eaten" or had "a big breakfast" or they'd take two bites and be "stuffed" or they'd load a plate of food, bring it back to their trailer, and throw it away—or, in some cases, vomit it away. Like Lauren, who played a radiologist and was notoriously bulimic. Everyone knew not to use a restroom after her unless you enjoyed the faint aroma of vomit.

"Have you ever asked her about it?" Margot said to Bess once, back when they used to hang out in Bess's office and drink tequila and gossip and talk about the show, back when they both tried to take the job more seriously.

"Ask her? You mean like write it into an episode?"

"No. Like maybe to help her? Offer treatment?"

"Not cool. I don't meddle in anyone's personal life," Bess said. Margot held back a laugh because Bess was happy to dig into anyone's personal life for plotlines and equally happy to ignore the troubling ones when she didn't want to be inconvenienced.

Margot was lucky. She'd always been able to eat pretty much whatever she wanted, although lately she'd noticed her skirts getting a little tighter. A little uncomfortable. She knew it wasn't beyond Mavis, the wardrobe mistress, to surreptitiously take someone's clothes in a little if she thought they weren't being careful enough around food. Mavis ran a tight ship, forthright and terse. She had an entire language made up of sighs—a veritable symphony. She kept an eye on the craft services table and didn't hesitate to stand behind an actress piling a plate for lunch and say, "Huh? Bread *and* pasta salad?"

As she approached the buffet, Charles was standing over a table of untouched mini sliders, and the moment he saw her she knew he knew. She and Charles had been close once, but they didn't hang out off the lot anymore. He had a family now, two kids with his partner, who was the stay-at-home dad. But they'd played husband and wife for almost ten years and they had been through some stuff. They had their shorthand; they (mostly) had each other's backs. Margot was one of Charles's "bridesmaids" when he married Nathaniel and she gave the baby shower when they adopted their first child. He drew her into a hug now, patting her back a little in an attempt at comfort or distraction, she couldn't tell. At least he wasn't pretending. "Let's go to your trailer," she said, noticing people were already watching.

⌣

"HOW LONG HAVE YOU KNOWN?" she asked, sitting down in Charles's trailer.

"A few hours. If it helps, she sounded terrible, genuinely upset."

"Bess called *you?*"

"This morning."

"She hasn't called *me*. Donna told me."

"She's a coward. She doesn't like delivering bad news. At least she didn't let you find out by reading the script." The previous month another actor, a woman who played a physical therapist, had gotten her script delivered late one night only to discover she'd be shot by a former client breaking into her house to steal opiates. The next day would be her last. But that had been Bess's punishment for the young woman, who had complained to *Entertainment Weekly* that she wished the show would be a little less soap opera and a little more authentic—a little more life-and-death. "She wants more life and death?" Margot had heard Bess say, tossing the magazine into a trash can. "Done."

"What did you say to her?" Margot asked Charles.

"You know Bess. It wasn't like she gave me any opening to talk. *This is good for the story, blah, blah, nothing personal.*"

Nothing personal. Of course it was personal. "Did you—object?"

"Margot. Of course I objected."

"Lightly object or *really* object?"

He sat down across from her and gave her a hard look, a chief-of-surgery-daring-his-subordinate-to-continue-with-the-same-line-of-questioning look. "I strenuously objected, for what it was worth, which was nothing. Since when do you and I have any power here?"

"I know." She wanted to stop herself, but she couldn't. "I just think if the shoe were on the other foot, maybe I would make a fuss. For you. Stand my ground."

"Really?"

"Really. I would."

"Really you wouldn't. Bess would say she was sorry and then you would be sitting here telling me that you couldn't do anything. And that would be the truth."

Charles stood and started making them tea; he had a well-stocked pantry. His trailer was so much homier than hers. Family photos, a pretty vase of roses that looked like they were from his yard, the ubiquitous scented candle. After season five, she'd stopped bringing in anything personal except books. Her trailer was the set lending library, especially for the younger actors. Just last week Kelsey had come in to borrow a book. Margot was excited—maybe there was more to Kelsey than she'd thought—but then Kelsey said, "I can return it tomorrow. I have an interview this afternoon."

"You want it as a prop?" Margot said.

"Why not? Everybody does it. To, you know, look well-read."

She picked up a slim paperback. "How about this?" She held up *To the Lighthouse*. "I love Maine."

"That's not even set in the United States, Kelsey."

Kelsey read the back of the book. "Okay, cool. I like Scotland, too."

"Then be my guest," Margot said, hoping beyond hope that the interviewer was a Virginia Woolf scholar and would ask Kelsey to describe her favorite part.

Charles handed her a little pot of Darjeeling and a tiny crock of honey with a tiny spoon, all on a wicker tray. What occurred to her in that moment was how embedded Charles was, how present. His trailer was a perfect reflection of his taste; he brought things here he loved. What occurred to her was that as much as they both complained—about Bess, the hours, the plots, the coworkers—Charles was happy here. They sipped their tea and Margot told herself to let it go. Be gracious. But then something else occurred to her: the likely reason for Charles's equanimity. She put her cup and saucer down, and he quickly slid a coaster beneath them, protecting the coffee table that wasn't even his. "This is going to be good for you," she said.

"How?"

"Come on, Charles. You lose your beloved wife, Cat? Surgical chief is a widower and single dad? You are getting *episodes* out of this, not only a few great scenes. It's going to be your arc for the entire season. A good arc."

"So what are you saying? I should have *quit*?"

The phone in Margot's pocket rang; she let it go to voicemail. She sat there and briefly contemplated making a stink. Debated storming out and giving the door a good melodramatic slam, but she just sighed and slumped in her seat. She didn't even have the energy for that. Charles put down his tea and moved to sit next to her. "I know it sucks to be fired. Killed. Whatever. But Margot, be honest with yourself: you've had one foot out the door for years. I have a family to support. So. You know."

Walking back to her trailer, she thought about what Charles said. Was it true? It was sort of true. She had eagerly said yes to the pilot, never imagining the show would get picked up. Another hospital drama? It would be the third one on the air at the same time and the most conventional one to boot. It had truly never occurred to her that she was signing herself up for a decade or longer. When they'd first come out to Los Angeles all those years ago, when David was struggling, she thought they were escaping for a few months. She thought they'd be back in the city for Labor Day and life would resume.

Here she was, ten years later. Not ten unhappy years, not entirely, but not the ten years she'd expected. Maybe this was a good thing. Maybe she would have opportunities now she didn't have a decade ago, when she was dewy with youth, bright with possibility, but also hadn't earned the stripes of middle age, hadn't been *seasoned*, to use a word she loathed that most certainly had to have been invented by men, with their love of aged beef and barbecue and martinis and *seasonings*.

Bummer.

Her phone rang again, and she fished it out of her pocket and answered, expecting to hear Bess on the other end. But it wasn't Bess. It was Julian.

"Margot? We need to talk."

FOURTEEN

⌒

Ruby was sitting by herself in the enormous breakfast room of the fancy hotel in the center of Madrid. The breakfast room was an open courtyard off the lobby with a glossy marble floor and mosaic-top tables surrounded with elegant wrought-iron chairs. Tiny songbirds flew freely through the space and hopped from empty plate to empty plate, hunting for leftover crumbs. She was drinking the most sublime orange juice she'd ever tasted, full of pulp and frothy and bright. It was ambrosia, *ambrosiac*, she thought, wondering if that was a word. If it wasn't, it should be.

She was eating alone because like every morning so far in what was turning out to be the longest vacation of her life, the rest of Ivan's family—and Ivan—were still asleep at ten a.m. In spite of the nice hotels and the superlative orange juice, traveling with Ivan was making her crazy and they weren't even halfway through the trip. She and Ivan were bickering all day, and she was aware that the tension between them was putting everyone else on edge, and she felt terrible about it but powerless to stop. So many things irritated her! Getting up early and eating by herself, in peace, was an attempt to tamp down her burgeoning dislike of her boyfriend and was leagues better than lying in bed in the hotel room watching Ivan sleep and becoming increasingly furious with him because they were wasting the nicest part of the day. July in Spain. It was *hot*. Ruby hated the heat. She'd tried everything to ameliorate its effects—hats, wider-brimmed hats, long-sleeved blouses, hydration—but by midafternoon she was sweaty and miserable. Anyone with half a brain, as she had unfortunately blurted out to Ivan in front of his parents a few days ago, would get up early and see the sights before the heat of the day became unbearable.

"Nobody is stopping you from getting up early," he'd said, more hurt than mad. That he always answered her impatience with patience just made her angrier. But she'd done it: she'd started getting up early and going out with her new camera, her gift from Margot, and exploring in the early morning hours. Ivan would text her when he and his parents and sister were ready to meet and start their day.

"Here's our early bird!" his mother would sing when they met at the designated place. Ruby would try her best to be cheerful and pliant and grateful and to be—as her mother had admonished her as she'd climbed into the taxi to the airport—a good guest. But, *God*.

She shouldn't have come. She should have known better. She'd been losing patience with Ivan for months. She'd hoped the romance of Madrid and Seville and Barcelona would carry her through the trip. (And if his mother said *BarTHHHelona*—dragging out the theta as if she were making the most hilarious joke in the world—one more time, Ruby was going to pop her one.) Her irritation with Ivan had started almost the minute their plane rose from the runway at LAX, stretching out over the Pacific for a bit then banking to the right, turning back east and heading to Europe, a thing that she'd only done three times in her life (was *only* the right word? She wasn't even nineteen. But compared to her schoolmates who spent every spring and summer in Europe or Australia or Tahiti or South Africa, *three* seemed hardly anything). Leaving Los Angeles for a trip ordinarily gave her a thrill, but sitting next to Ivan, his hand possessively clutching hers, made the back of her throat itch, the way it did when she'd accidentally eaten a walnut.

He started pointing out all the Los Angeles landmarks they were flying over, as if she didn't know. The oil fields near the airport with the pumps that resembled those glass ostriches constantly dipping their beaks into water, the small rise of Baldwin Hills, the long spine of the Santa Monica mountains, the Griffith Observatory near her house. Trying to summon her affection for him, which seemingly had expired the second she was handed her diploma, she told him how when she was little and they flew back to New York after visiting Margot and David her father would bring her to the window as they were approaching Manhattan and ask what she saw and how she would always say what he'd taught her to say: "I see the greatest city in the world."

Ivan pretended he hadn't heard the story before, which she appreciated, but then he said, "We'll see how you feel about New York City after four years of living there."

She extricated her hand from his and turned more aggressively toward the window. She'd told him over and over that she wasn't going to school *in* the city. But he was obstinate in his refusal to learn the geography of the small upstate town that would be her home for the next four years. He would be safely ensconced at Stanford, his dream school, and he'd hinted more than once his belief that after a brutal northeast winter, Ruby would want to transfer back to California. Ivan loved California. She loved it, too! But she wanted an adventure, an experience that would be a clear demarcation from home. She knew Ivan's insistence was about their future and his refusal to face what to her was splinteringly obvious: they were going to break up soon, possibly the minute the trip was over, because Ivan was flying back to LAX and she was flying into New York City (take *that*, Ivan!) and going to Stoneham to join her family for the summer production of *The Cherry Orchard*.

He would be someone she eventually referred to, fondly, as her high school boyfriend. *Ivan*, she would tell people in some unidentifiable future when she was living in whatever New York borough young transplants were flocking to by then, probably Queens, and probably she would have taken up smoking and be able to stand firm in the face of a couple of martinis— *Can you see me with an Ivan?* she'd say and laugh her by-then captivating laugh and stub out her cigarette and shake her head and say, *He was sweet, though. A good starter guy, Ivan was.*

Ruby finished her juice and stood up from the small corner table. Even though this was their third day in Madrid and she'd been told twice that breakfast was included and she didn't have to pay or sign anything or leave a tip, she still walked out of the room waiting to be accosted by someone who worked there accusing her of dining and dashing.

Today they were going to the Prado, and Ivan had promised they wouldn't race through, the way his family liked to— like it was a contest to see who could finish first. She liked Ivan's sister, Rachel, but Rachel only liked to shop. She and Ruby did bond over their hatred of the heat, though; Rachel was fair-skinned and freckled and claimed she was allergic to the sun and was also allergic to any sunscreen except one that her mother specially ordered from a pharmacy in Paris and that Rachel had forgotten to pack. They had to stop at every *farmacia* and look for the French brand. Ruby had researched it online and there was nothing special about the formulation. "Look," Ruby would say, handing her a tube of lotion and comparing the ingredients to the computer printout she'd tucked into her purse, "it's the same."

"Noooo," Rachel would say, mournful. "That's not the one." She wouldn't wear a hat because hats made her forehead break out. It was too hot for long sleeves. Rachel and her mother would shop, darting down the street between storefronts like a couple of albino mice, and when they'd accumulated enough packages they'd return to the hotel to sit poolside, under an umbrella, their long legs covered with layers of beach towels, reading magazines.

Ruby knew she was being a baby. She was embarrassed by her own petulance. She *did* appreciate Ivan's parents' generosity. She did. The first-class travel, the beautiful hotels, the long lunches with carafes of rosé and platters of fried fish, but she missed her parents. She missed Margot and David. She'd never spent so much time embedded with another family and although the Kozlovs were kind, she couldn't adapt to their rhythms. Ivan's parents constantly bickered in a way that stunned her.

"That's just the way they talk," Ivan said, brushing away her concern. "They've been married for twenty-five years; it's how they communicate, registering disapproval."

She didn't say that her parents had been married forever, too, and they would never speak to one another the way Ivan's did. She couldn't imagine her father biting off Flora's head because she took the wrong turn on a street or misread a sign in traffic. She couldn't imagine Flora criticizing Julian for wanting dessert or another glass of wine or an afternoon nap. It seemed like the Kozlovs disliked each other. But Ivan pooh-poohed that observation, too. "People show their feelings in different ways."

Was that true?

THEIR FINAL NIGHT IN MADRID. Tomorrow Barcelona (*Barthhhh-elona*, she couldn't help thinking). At dinner, Mr. Koslov got into an argument with the maître d' because he wanted to move to a different table and when he was told that table had been reserved, he threw a tantrum. He stormed outside to have a cigarette. Mrs. Koslov had sat, grim, watching her husband's back, the smoke rising above his head. As they were leaving Ruby saw her slip a wad of cash into the waiter's hand and apologize. They'd all walked back to the hotel in silence. Ruby had never been so uncomfortable, so happy to be back in her room with Ivan, who was taking a shower—his second of the day—before bed because he liked to keep the sheets nice and clean.

He was such a weirdo.

Ruby couldn't fall asleep because something was going on at home. Or rather, something was going on up at Stoneham, where her parents had decided to go a few weeks early, just the two of them. This alone was suspicious because it wasn't the original plan. She'd felt a tension in the house starting on graduation night. At first she tried to tell herself that it was because high school was over and she'd be heading to college soon and they were all on edge. But several times she'd heard her parents speaking in harsh voices and when she'd walk into the kitchen they'd abruptly stop talking and turn to her with smiles so forced they were ghoulish.

"I wish you would tell me what's wrong," she'd said to her mother one afternoon when they were sorting through her clothes, deciding what she should bring to Spain.

"What do you mean?" Flora had said in a believable voice, but she hadn't turned to look at Ruby—a dead giveaway.

"Mom. I know something's going on."

"Nothing's *going on*. As usual, we're grappling with logistics and timing and we might head up to Stoneham a few weeks early. We'll be away longer, so there's a lot to do."

"I'm not dumb, Mom."

Flora had turned then, exasperated. "Ruby, believe it or not, not everything that goes on in this house is your business."

"*Fine.*" Ruby hadn't let on how much Flora's comment stung. And she was probably being paranoid—she told herself as much—but it had almost seemed like they were eager for her to leave for Spain. She was also positive that a couple of times when she'd FaceTimed her mother, her mother looked as if she'd been crying. "Crying? What do I have to cry about except that you're not here?" Flora joked. "You know me, it's allergies. The jacaranda are killing me." But the jacaranda weren't still in bloom.

Also, Margot was being unusually remote. She was back at work, and Ruby knew she was busy, working long hours, but Margot had always found time to answer Ruby's texts and her responses had been perfunctory since she left. When Ruby mentioned this to her mother, Flora had laughed and it felt genuine. "Darling, I'm flattered you are this interested in what we're all doing, but truly we're running around, as usual. If you were here, it wouldn't feel strange. And I wish you were here. I really miss you."

But did she? The thing that worried Ruby most was that her mother was telling the truth: nothing was wrong. This was the new normal. Out of sight, out of mind. She'd wanted so badly to leave Los Angeles, her high school, her same old group of friends who she'd been with since eighth grade, *Ivan*, and get away and start fresh in a place that looked completely different, would smell completely different. Snowy weekends and rainy mornings and muggy afternoons. She was starting to understand how tethered she was to home and how unpleasant it would feel to be outside the goings-on of the group of people who constituted her family.

Ruby knew she was overreacting. Except she didn't think she was overreacting. In the bed next to her, Ivan started to stir. He rolled over and flung an arm around her waist, mumbled something. She stayed still, debating whether or not she wanted to turn to him, initiate something. The thing she would miss about Ivan, the thing that had kept her with him for so long, was how attentive and loving he was in bed. She knew she didn't have much to compare him to, but she suspected she was right. The only other boy she slept with was her friend Will, who had turned his parents' garage into a kind of music studio and after making her listen to more than two hours of his original compositions, mostly composed of found sounds—"Can you tell what this is?" he'd say every four minutes, and when she'd say, "Noooo," he would grin like he'd pulled something over on her. "It's a spoon against a rock!" "It's a squirrel chewing a nut!"—had pounced on her on the uncomfortable sofa along the garage wall. She was a little stoned and thought, *Why not?* and afterward had the useful realization that if someone was both boring and self-obsessed in daily life they were probably not worth getting naked for.

The second time—and all the times after that—were with Ivan.

"What time is it?" he mumbled into her neck.

"Midnight," she said.

"Good." He wrapped both arms around her and pulled her tight and she gave in to the feeling of comfort. She relaxed.

Seven more days. Seven more days until she said good-bye to Ivan and his family. Maybe she would break up with Ivan at the airport. Maybe that would be the *kindest* thing to do before she flew to New York to join her parents.

"I can hear your brain, Ruby. What's churning away up there? What's on the Ruby itinerary?"

This was another thing she would miss about Ivan. He was always tuned to her frequency, and that was nice. He made her feel understood, sometimes uncomfortably so. "Nothing," she said, not wanting to get into it with him; she'd be with her parents soon enough. She moved her hands to his waist, slipping her fingers under his boxer briefs, feeling the warmth of his skin, his immediate eagerness. *Might as well.* "Nothing for you to worry about."

FIFTEEN

M argot was called to Bess's office right after she got off the call with Julian (Julian. She was going to *kill him*, but she couldn't think about that right now).

"Come here, you," Bess said when Margot walked into her office. The last thing Margot wanted to do was hug Bess, but she realized this wasn't her scene, it was Bess's. She let herself be enveloped by Bess and her soft, freckled skin, her distinctive scent that always reminded Margot of a church—musty wooden pews, burning candles, myopic narcissism. Bess was a massive human being, tall and strong. Her arms were sinewy and solid from the Pilates instructor who came to her office four times a week. She rocked Margot a little, and Margot breathed slowly through her mouth to stop herself from pushing Bess clear across the room and out the window.

"This is a dark day," Bess said, releasing Margot. "I am beyond—" She broke off, as if the next word were obvious.

Beyond: *Sad? Guilty? Relieved?* Margot didn't care. "I know," she said, signifying nothing.

"Tequila?"

"Sure."

During the first year of *Cedar*, Bess had been a nervous wreck. *Cedar* was her first shot at running a show, and she knew she wouldn't get a second if she didn't do a good job, deliver the well-received series the network was expecting in a reasonable time frame and on budget. During those early months, Margot and Bess had grown a real friendship, one separate from work. So many late nights in Bess's office with a bottle of Don Julio 1492 and leftovers from the refrigerator down the hall that serviced a conference room. She and Bess would pick the meat out from the middle of a spinach wrap or a ciabatta roll (God forbid they ingested flour!) and wash down the dry turkey, wilted lettuce, and pallid tomato with tequila. She remembered when Bess had cared enough about each episode to be on set all the time, to gather the cast and crew before the start of a technically difficult scene—or even, especially in the earlier days, something more emotional—and give a little pep talk. She thought about how the first time Dr. Cat had to deliver the *not what we hoped for* speech about an ill child, Bess had pulled her aside and told her she was being too clinical.

"This isn't about telling the parents how sick their child is; it's telling two people they are going to outlive their child. Imagine how you would feel."

Margot had her process, and sometimes it involved a specific memory from her life and sometimes she borrowed one from someone else's. That day, she'd thought of Ruby. A terrible thought? A generous one? Both, she suspected. Starting that day and for the rest of her years on *Cedar* whenever she had to give parents gut-wrenching news, she would imagine having to tell Flora and Julian something awful about Ruby. It worked like a dream.

"I hoped we weren't going to have to go in this direction," Bess said, pouring them both generous splashes of tequila. "I want you to know that we considered other scenarios, but here's the thing: the ratings are bad, Margot. Worse than we've let on. I need something to keep eyes on the show. I need to kill a character the audience cares about."

"People care about Charles's character," Margot said, only half-joking. "Or how about our darling twins? You could kill off one of the twins."

Bess stared at her. "We don't kill off children."

"Unless they have cancer."

"Exactly." Bess sighed and looked out the window. Margot could tell she was already bored with the conversation, with her brief moment of regret. "I'm giving you a kick-ass death. It's going to be so good everyone will clamor to hire you. I promise."

"Can I ask one favor?"

"Sure."

"Not cancer. Please, no bald cap. No bad makeup? Can I go out looking okay?"

Bess rapidly tapped a pencil on top of a pile of scripts on her desk, and Margot could tell cancer for Dr. Cat was already in the works. She knew how Bess's mind worked. The oncologist getting cancer would be her very first thought. Bess loved "a circle." Closure on *Cedar* was always an event foretold. "I need three or four episodes," Bess said. "No aneurysm. No death-on-impact car accident."

Margot shrugged. "Lots of ways to die that won't fuck up my face. Internal injuries?"

"Okay." Bess stood up and hugged Margot again. "I can do internal injuries. I'll figure it out this afternoon. No bald cap for my favorite. Plus," she said, patting Margot's head, "this hair is too good."

Margot left Bess's office and went back to set like the pro she was; nobody would have known what was going on with her. But the minute she was finished with her scenes, she fled. Tonight, everyone would get this week's script and by tomorrow morning her on-set world would completely change and all-too-soon she'd be dead doctor walking. She got in her car and left the lot and instead of heading home, decided to go to David's office to pay a long-overdue in-person visit. She was going to have to tell him not only about the demise of Dr. Cat, but about Flora and Julian and that damn wedding ring. He had to find out from her first.

Any regrets? Everything had gone wrong since the day with Mia-the-journalist, and although she knew it was irrational, she somehow blamed her for unknowingly poking at the embers of long-buried things, for unleashing dormant demons and everything the past week had wrought. What a mess. But Margot had survived the last decade or more by refusing to traffic in regret. She was steely. She put her head down and put one foot in front of the other, never looking further than a few steps ahead, far enough to keep moving, and these little blips were going to be no exception. But *regrets*? She had a few.

⌒

WHEN DAVID FIRST JOINED his younger brother's practice and they opened the stroke clinic, she used to visit all the time. The office was so clean and reassuring, with its reception desk, the rows of patient rooms, the fan of magazines on the table in the waiting area. Whenever she felt a pang of regret over leaving New York, she would drive to the Pearlman Family Neurological Practice and Stroke Center at Cedars-Sinai and count her blessings. Thank the gods for David's family, who had made sure he'd have a place where he felt useful and needed and was able to forget, most of the time, his earlier incarnation as a cardiac surgeon.

As Margot waited for the elevator in the lobby, she remembered how her face confused people who recognized her. She was familiar, and on some level they recognized her as a doctor, but how? She put her sunglasses back on and kept her head down. When she got to the offices, the receptionist was someone new.

"Where's Jacob?" she asked.

"He left, like, over a year ago," the young girl said, looking up as Margot took off her glasses. Had David told her Jacob left? She'd loved Jacob; she couldn't believe she wouldn't have gone to his going-away party, bought him a gift. The first few years of the center, he'd been a stalwart.

"I'm Natalie," the new receptionist said, blatantly gawking.

"Hi, Natalie. I'm Margot. Could you tell Dr. Pearlman his wife is here?"

Natalie was momentarily dumbstruck. "I'm sorry," she said, blinking rapidly, "I'm kind of freaking out right now. I love your show and I watch it all the time and *Cedar* is one of the reasons I'm working here at, you know, *Cedars*-Sinai."

"Great," Margot said cheerily, aware of the room behind her listening in. "You like it? The job's good?"

"I like it. It's fine. I mean, it's better than fine. It's good. It's not like the television show. It's a little more—"

"Like life?"

"Yeah, I guess." Natalie laughed, sheepish. "So"—she leaned in closer to Margot—"if you ever need an assistant or anything. I can run errands, pick up dry cleaning. Take care of your cats!"

"I don't have any cats," Margot said, breaking the spell. Dr. Cat loved cats; Margot was deeply allergic. The one season Bess had tried to make cats a part of Dr. Cat's *Cedar* life—because she didn't believe Margot was allergic—they'd had to reschedule shooting twice due to hives. "I'm heading back, if you'd be good enough to let Dr. Pearlman know."

David's office was pristine, as always. A few photos of her on the desk. One from their wedding day. One from Flora and Julian's. A candid of Ruby from a few years ago. Margot looked out the enormous windows that faced Third Street—not the most interesting view, but it was expansive. Down below, Amarosa's, the small Italian restaurant where they would meet all the time for dinner when they first moved to Los Angeles and David was regaining his footing. Same red-and-mustard-yellow tablecloths. Same awning. Those first months were so hard that any place they frequented during that time became a place she avoided once he was doing better. Her memory of Amarosa's was getting there a good half hour before she was supposed to meet David, so she could have a drink or two, take the edge off.

She'd choose a table in the front so he wouldn't have to navigate through the room with his cane. She knew by the look on his face, his posture when he walked through the door, whether he was having a good day or a bad day. Whether he was physically struggling or mentally and emotionally grappling with the past. The worst of many horrible days after the stroke was when his memory was coming back and she had to tell him about Abbie Jensen. He'd been devastated, of course. Even though the baby's issues were horrifically complex, not only one congenital heart defect but a cluster; even though an alert nurse had noticed that something was happening to David immediately, and a resident in the operating theater had stabilized the situation until another doctor could scrub in and successfully finish the procedure; even though Abbie Jensen had lived for ten days postsurgery—nobody could assure the Jensens (nobody would try) that Abbie's outcome wasn't affected by David's midprocedure stroke.

The stroke had not only taken him out of the operating room and into an office job but had wiped away his swagger, his easy confidence. Margot missed it.

The door to his office opened. "What a great surprise," he said, closing the door behind him. "You're done early."

"I am," she said and laughed. "In more ways than one."

He sat at his desk and barreled ahead, talking about an upcoming fundraiser they were both speaking at for another stroke clinic down in San Diego. "They called about the auction. I told them from the get-go that you weren't giving away visits to the set or lunch with Margot Letta anymore, but they keep pestering me."

She had *hated* filling those auction requests. The VIP tour of the set, the meet-and-greet, the inevitable request about a daughter-friend-cousin-neighbor who "wanted to get into the business."

"Even if I wanted to offer a set visit, I couldn't." She sat on the sofa. He moved over to sit next to her while she told him about Donna's call, her meeting with Bess; she gave a strong performance.

"I'm sorry," he said, taking her hand.

"I keep waiting to feel outrage. Or anger. Or regret. Or something. But I don't. It's strange."

"Maybe this is a good thing, then."

"Maybe." She motioned for him to come closer. He had a bit of dried egg yolk right on the front of his tie. Something that would have mortified the old David. She scraped it off with her fingernail.

"Didn't notice that," he said, chagrined.

Margot stood and went back to the window. "Can I ask you something?"

"Always."

"Are you sorry about not having children?" She didn't turn around to look because she didn't want to see his immediate reaction. Post-stroke David didn't have any kind of poker face, and the truth was *they* didn't choose not to have children, she did. Margot had told David early on that children weren't in her future, not given her work. She saw what happened to women in the theater when they had kids: most of them left, like Flora. Or they worked every few years or only in the summer, like her mother. "I won't change my mind," she'd told him, "so you have to be sure." He disappeared for two weeks, the longest weeks of her life. She went to work and came home at night and checked her answering machine messages hoping for his voice and tried to imagine calling him and saying, *Okay, maybe just one.* But she couldn't because she didn't mean it. The day he knocked on her door and stood there with a bunch of daffodils and a box holding an antique emerald engagement ring, was—in spite of his hesitation; *because* of his hesitation—one of the happiest of her life.

"No," he finally said.

She turned around and saw what she feared. Not only regret, but sorrow. Grief etched on his face, plain as day. She walked over to him and wrapped her arms around his waist. For all that had changed between them over the years, this hadn't. How comforting his presence was. She felt his long release of breath. He smelled like he always smelled, bright and herby. "I'm sorry," she said.

He pulled away a little too abruptly. "Don't be." He picked up a bright yellow stress ball and gave it a series of hard squeezes. "So how are they doing it? The demise of Dr. Cat?"

"It's going to be quick, Doc," she said, choosing to be grateful for the change of subject, surrendering to her more cowardly impulses. "Four episodes and I'm off to the great beyond. It's a big secret, of course. I can't tell anyone until the episodes air in September, and then I'll have to do press for a bit. So that's annoying."

"You'll have the summer."

"I guess I will. For the first time in a decade. That's something."

"I can take some time off. Let's plan a trip. Spain. Morocco. Greece. We can go anywhere you want."

"You'd do that?"

"Of course."

She hadn't had the time to think about having the summer free or how good it would be to get away. "There is one place that comes to mind. Somewhere I'd love to go *back*."

"Okay. I'm listening."

"Good. Because first I have a story to tell you."

SIXTEEN

⌒

When Ben dropped out of Juilliard to join a soap opera, everyone thought he was nuts. A casting director saw his performance as Iago in the school's production of *Othello* and wanted him to audition to play twin brothers—one good, one evil. He got the job. "Just for a couple of years," he told his friends about the part he'd play for seventeen years, until the daytime drama went off the air, "just to get some money in the bank."

By then, he and Julian already had their plan in place to create a small theater company. Ben's soap opera money and his willingness to help fund the company was the only reason they were able to get the whole venture up and running. Six years in, Good Company on its feet (wobbly but walking), and Ben's parents retired and living in Florida, Ben was eager to give his idea a try: one night of summer theater up at Stoneham, a play from the canon. He wanted to put the entire property into service, to create the kind of production where if a character said they were going for a swim, the actor playing that character would jump in the pond and swim.

Flora still remembered the day she first laid eyes on their friend's property with crystal clarity, the kind of clarity brought on by raising a kid in a five-hundred-square-foot apartment in the West Village with one rickety fire escape out back.

"You *own* this?" she'd said to Ben, standing next to the old Farmhouse originally occupied by Ben's great-grandparents, taking in the Little House (only little in relation to the sprawling Farmhouse) at the bottom of the long sloping lawn that also led down to a pond big enough to have a floating wooden dock in the center. To the side of the pond was a derelict barn. It had been red once.

"I own it with my sisters," Ben said, "but they don't live close by and hardly ever visit. You can't see it from here, but there's a little cemetery up behind the barn." He rocked on his heels a bit, inordinately pleased. *"A cemetery."*

"We're not doing *Our Town*, dude," Julian had said, kind of joking, kind of not.

Their first summer production—*Cat on a Hot Tin Roof*—was, to put it mildly, chaotic, starting with prolonged negotiations about where everyone would sleep (some combination of the Farmhouse and the Little House and a bunch of tents on the lawn borrowed from generous neighbors) and who would manage provisions (Flora, as it turned out; Ruby was five months old, and Flora was happy to be with her most of the day, shopping for sandwiches and takeout pizza, taking walks, dipping a toe in the pond).

Ben assigned roles before everyone arrived and his only rule was to be off book before the week of rehearsals began. Everyone from Good Company who wasn't working came up, along with a dozen others and somehow during the course of the week it all came together. Furniture was dragged out onto porches and lawns to create sets. A team of people with carpentry skills built a wooden platform next to the Farmhouse as an additional stage. The musicians took over the barn, composing their own interstitial tunes. Ben erected a small canopy out back where everyone gathered for rehearsal, meetings, food, and drink.

The day of the show, the inaugural audience comprised a bunch of friends from the city and a handful of curious neighbors. The town's mayor brought her five kids. The acoustics were tough. The grills they'd borrowed for the intermission barbecue wouldn't stay lit. When the sun set, the mosquitoes descended. It was grueling and a little ragged, but it was also exhilarating, unlike anything Flora had seen or experienced before. It was community theater as Ben had described and imagined and he fairly levitated all night. Nobody wanted to leave when it was over. The singing and dancing and eating and drinking went into the early hours of the morning. "I don't think he'll do *that* again," Flora said to Julian as they crawled into bed, tired, bug-bitten, tipsy.

Early the next morning, up with Ruby, Flora saw Ben on the porch of the Farmhouse, sitting at a table with a legal pad in front of him. "Making notes," he told her. "Next year is going to be much easier."

By the fifth summer—the summer of the photograph—Stoneham consumed Ben year-round, to Julian's great annoyance. Good Company was no longer as reliant on Ben's funds as it had been because they finally had a good team in place, including an excellent grant writer with a magic touch. Julian had successfully wined and dined a few retired actors who wrote checks when needed and all they asked in return was to be plied with champagne on opening night, introduced to the cast, exuberantly thanked. It wasn't Ben's money Julian missed as much as his partnership, his interest.

So when Ben suggested that Flora and Julian take the Little House for the entire summer—not only two weeks—it was an attempt to ameliorate the tension. Whatever the reason, Flora was ecstatic. She and Julian sat and did the math. Julian would have to go back to the city for auditions and on occasion for Good Company, but he had a good stretch of time off. Flora had booked her first national voice-over commercial that spring. She caught her voice on television almost weekly: *Aren't you tired of constantly changing the paper roll? Try Soft'n'Tuff! Durable, gentle, and long-lasting.*

"Flora, that was great," the advertising copywriter had said to her from the control booth after her first take, "but how about one that's not so—*Heroic* Mom?"

They wanted *choices*; she gave them choices. Frazzled Mom ("aren't you tired of *constantly* changing the paper roll?"). Exhausted Mom ("aren't you *tired* of constantly—"). Grateful Mom ("It's durable, *gentle*, and—*long*-lasting").

"Does Dad ever change the paper roll?" she'd joked at one point, to no effect. She must have given them twenty takes, and she swore they'd used the very first one: Toilet Roll Hero. But she'd say *durable, gentle, and long-lasting* a hundred times if it gave her more time with Ruby. If they were extremely careful with money (who knew how long the commercial would run), she could take the summer off for the first time in her life.

She'd been so conflicted about her shift to voice-over work. Conflicted because it broke her heart a little to just stop—stop auditioning, stop singing, stop performing in front of an audience. Conflicted because how to argue with a job that was keeping them afloat, keeping them in health insurance, gave her time with Ruby, and now was going to give them the entire summer?

A summer in Stoneham would be paradise for Ruby, yes, but she and Julian also needed a place to spread out and breathe. The last few years had been *hard*. Julian's mother had died, then Flora's. They'd barely had a chance to process their grief—hers profound, his complicated—with all the work that was cleaning out and vacating two apartments, one a literal pigsty. They were both executors of the respective "estates," and the business of death was all-consuming. (The only positive: Julian's mother had—completely unexpectedly—left an insurance policy that, when split with Violet, meant they had a decent college fund for Ruby. Just like that, one enormous cause of insomnia lifted.) Between funerals and paperwork (my God, the paperwork) and hiring help to clear out and dispose of the furniture and belongings nobody wanted, they were both spent. As a result of all of it—grief, exhaustion, worry—Flora could feel how she and Julian had drifted into their own separate corners—hers Ruby, his Good Company.

Julian teased her about how much she loved therapy with Maude Langstrom, but she did! It helped. It was a relief to have someone help her process her grief over Josephine and the sad fact that no matter how terrible Julian's mother, Ruby had lost the only grandparents she'd ever have. And when Maude asked if Flora would like Julian to come to a session, she eagerly said yes, even though they just ended up talking about Good Company the whole time. It was okay, he needed support, too. How was it, she often wondered, that this person who was barely cared for as a child had created a world where he cared for so many? Lately, she felt she came last, right behind everyone at Good Company and Ruby.

When Margot heard about their summer plans, she asked if she and David could come along, too, because the Little House had three bedrooms and wouldn't it be a blast? She was taking a break after her latest play and David could come up on his days off. Flora hesitated.

"But we haven't seen them in so long," Julian said, which was true. When Ruby was nearly one, David and Margot had moved to London for what was supposed to be one year but stretched into three. David was teaching a new procedure his mentor had pioneered for infant valve repair. And because Margot was Margot, she booked a show on the West End that happened to run concurrently to David's visit, a show that won the Olivier.

"I would have stayed forever," she told anyone who would listen. She'd loved her work and the flat in Mayfair and the shopping and the proximity to Europe, and even the food, she said, was so much better now than it used to be, even though Flora didn't think Margot had been to London since she was a kid. She told them all this over dinner recently, while eating Continental-style, knife in her right hand, fork in the left, tines down, acting as a tiny spear. She and Margot used to joke about their friends who ate like that, how they were broadcasting their semester abroad. "Don't knock it," she said, noticing Flora eyeing her. "It's easier this way."

"I was looking forward to the three of us," Flora told Julian.

"Me, too," Julian said. "But we'll still have time alone and they'd come up for the show anyway. Margot's in it." He shrugged. "It's up to you, but I think it'd be nice. I miss them."

And that was how, on an unseasonably cool Saturday in June,

the two families packed themselves into a rental minivan along with a classroom goldfish named Gryffindor that Ruby was in charge of keeping alive until September. ("Not *really*," Ruby's teacher told Flora, pulling her aside and lowering her voice. "Nobody will notice if you bring back a new fish. They all look alike. Just hold on to the castle." She pointed to a neon blue many-turreted plastic castle at the bottom of the bowl that the fish would hide in, probably to escape the insistent *tap-tap-tap* of eighteen five-year-olds.) As they left the city, the mood in the van was giddy. David and Julian up front, Margot and Flora in the back with Ruby between them in her booster seat, eating fistfuls of cheddar goldfish crackers, their vile smell permeating the inside of the vehicle, roping them all into playing a series of games. *I spy with my little eye something green!*

Seeing how taken Margot and David were with Ruby, Flora was grateful she hadn't resisted their company. Ruby's arrival changed things for the couples, as babies do. Flora and Julian had tried so hard for Ruby, three almosts, so much heartache, that they closed ranks the first year of her life. When they weren't working, they hunkered down and indulged falling in love with Ruby Josephine Fletcher. Everything she did was fascinating, every sound she made enchanting. She was a good baby. They couldn't get enough of her, the whirlpool swirl of her double crown on the back of her head, her delicately arched brows, her smile, her laugh.

Flora secretly loved complaining about the things she'd listened to everyone complain about for years: the lack of sleep, nursing until her nipples stung, sitting in a dark apartment at three a.m. holding a wailing infant and wondering if she was the only person awake in New York City. She tried to remember every minute because she and Julian agreed their family was complete. They wouldn't try for another baby. Wouldn't put themselves through it all again—the thermometers, the ovulation chart, the lost pregnancies, the obligatory sex tinged with desperation.

Racing up the New York State Thruway, Flora faced another, reluctant truth: they had drifted because Margot and David's lives were progressing in a way that made Flora feel resentful, left behind. Her relationship with Margot—who seemed to move through life so effortlessly—had always been marked by imbalance, but the crevasse had widened and it was sometimes physically painful to be around Margot, who was working all the time—good work, desirable work. She'd come back from London and immediately landed in a small off-Broadway production that got her rave reviews in the *New York Times*.

But sitting in the van with Margot on the other side of Ruby, Flora felt nothing but joy. Julian was telling Margot about a new play he'd read, one written by her old boyfriend Quinn, who was a hot new playwright ("He wasn't my *boyfriend*," she said, her nose wrinkling in disapproval). Julian was trying to convince Margot to read the play. "The lead is perfect for you. It probably *is* you, now that I think about it."

"No thanks. I'm doing fine playing other people. Not really interested in playing dumber *me*."

"It's a good part! He's taking it to Seattle in the winter. Six weeks."

"Wow, you sure know how to sell a girl. *Quinn*. Seattle in the winter." She laughed. "Is this a Good Company thing?"

"No, but not because it's not a good play. The timing was off for us."

"I'll take a look," Margot said, "but I doubt it."

⌣

ONE AFTERNOON, while Ruby had fallen asleep in the living room in front of an episode of *Arthur*, Margot and Flora made lemonade and went out to the front porch. Their days had taken on a lovely shape: quiet mornings, long lunches with wine, naps, ambitious dinners with more wine, maybe one of the movies piled in the living room next to a VCR. It was the week before everyone would start to arrive from the city for *The Crucible*. All four of them were dreading the intrusion to their idyllic sojourn. Flora and Margot were sitting on opposite ends of the saggy wicker sofa on the porch, facing each other, toes touching, the pitcher of lemonade on the floor between them. A perfect summer afternoon.

"So tell me what happened," Margot said. Flora didn't have to ask Margot what she was asking about.

"I was tired," Flora said. "I was only home to put Ruby to bed on Sundays and Mondays. You know what eight shows a week is like—it's your life. The problem with that is I have an entire *other* life in my life, and it was excruciating—to be away from her so much."

"People make it work," Margot said. "You know how hard it is to get back in, once you leave for too long."

"I do know. But can I remind you I was playing a set of measuring spoons in *Beauty and the Beast*? It wasn't *Into the Woods* or *Wicked*. It wasn't even *Mary Poppins*, and I'm not being a snob." Margot raised a brow. "I'm not! I loved doing the show—most of the time. I was incredibly grateful for the work. But when I weighed it all"—she spread her hands wide, mimicking a scale—"measuring spoons or Ruby? It wasn't much of a contest.

The show has been running for twelve years. God only knows how many people had the part before me. It was a job, but it wasn't exactly a career move."

What Flora didn't want to admit to Margot was that she'd gotten close with *Wicked*. They "loved her but were looking for someone with a little more height." She'd been called back four times for *Into the Woods* and they thought she was "terrific but went with someone a little younger." She had cried on the subway all the way home that day because she knew her agent was being kind—those excuses weren't the truth. It wasn't height or age—not for those shows—it was Flora; she wasn't making the cut. How many years did she have left in her—the auditions, the rejection? When to accept that her career wasn't still a work in progress—all potential—but near its finish line? She'd been thrilled to be cast in the ensemble for *Beauty*, but it was grueling work. The part stretched her dance abilities to their outer limits. The spoon costume was punishing, heavy and hot and unwieldy. She had to go to physical therapy for her neck and back every Monday—her only day off. Two matinees a week, where she said good-bye to Ruby before lunch.

"You know Gerry Walters, right?" Flora asked Margot.

"Yes, he's awful."

"Take Gerry Walters being awful on a regular day. Now imagine him as an enchanted candelabra with a costume that has tiny propane tanks strapped to his arms so he can light up his hands with real flames while singing and dancing." Flora loved Margot's snicker, low and full of glee. "Oh, he must have been a nightmare," Margot said.

"A total nightmare. Before his hands were shoved into the propane tanks, he'd dance around pinching the bottoms of the women in the ensemble and saying, *Ooh-la-la! Ooh-la-la!* Someone finally complained to the dance captain and he was told to stop, which made him nastier. One night, as we made our entrance to sing 'Be Our Guest' for the millionth time, Gerry moved the right candle a little too close to his left sleeve." Margot sat up straighter, wide-eyed. "And just like that"—Flora snapped her fingers—"his left sleeve was on fire."

"Oh no," Margot said, covering her mouth and laughing harder.

"The costume is flameproof—still, he was *on fire*. So I sort of two-stepped closer to catch his eye and I'm singing and doing my awkward dance steps, but I'm also trying to point with my arm-spoons toward his flaming sleeve. I could tell some of the people in the front rows had noticed. Finally, after glaring at me for being out of place, he understood. He put out the flame and made it into a little piece of stage business and the audience applauded. All good, right? We came offstage and I turned to see if he was okay and he came after me like a rabid dog. I screwed up his timing. I wasn't on my mark. I put everyone in danger by being a fool. He missed part of his song because of me. He called me the C-word."

"Flora, that's unforgivable."

"Unforgivable yes, but also so *clarifying*. I looked at that guy—what is he, sixty-five? Dressed as a candelabra, screaming at me, red in the face, dripping sweat, and he has *lit torches* in place of hands, and I thought, *That's it. I'm done.* I gave my notice the following morning."

They sat on the porch quietly for a few minutes, sipping lemonade. "I'm sorry," Margot said. "I'm sorry you can't do both. Broadway and Ruby."

"But the thing is, I don't *want* to do both."

And as she said it, Flora was surprised to feel herself believe

it. Because the decision had been harder than she let on. She'd
been one of the lucky ones who worked regularly and sometimes understudied the bigger roles and went on when an actor called in sick or was on vacation. Flora never thought she'd
be the star, but she thought she'd be the trusty sidekick. She
imagined herself as Miss Adelaide in *Guys and Dolls* or Fantine
in *Les Misérables* or even Penelope Pennywise in *Urinetown*. A
supporting part with a knockout number. She thought she'd
get out of the ensemble, be more than a set of kitchen spoons,
but no. Her knees ached all the time. Her feet hurt. She had no
energy left for Ruby on her days off, and it wasn't as if she was
making a ton of money. By the time they paid their babysitter and her physical therapy and Maude—God, Maude was a
fortune—she netted so little. After two years, she was making
more doing voice-overs than working on Broadway. Still not
enough, but more.

"I love voice-over," she told Margot.

"You do."

"I do. It's so *pure*. No wardrobe or makeup. No blocking. I
stand in front of the microphone, and I act. I can hear myself
and make adjustments until it's exactly right. I have all the takes
I need. It's satisfying. It's a good life."

"I'm glad," Margot said. "I might be envious." She poured
them both more lemonade. Stood up. "Here comes Julian."

Flora turned to see Julian walking across the lawn. He'd just
come back from a few days of auditioning in the city, and had
gone straight to the pond to cool off. His hair was slicked back
from his swim, towel slung around his neck. He was tan and
muscled from running the rural roads the last few weeks. He
was so handsome and she was pierced with longing for him even

though he was right there. She waved. He waved back. From inside she could hear Ruby awaken. "Mommy? Mommy!"

"I hate when she naps these days; she wakes up so cranky," Flora said.

"I'll go get her." Margot went inside, letting the screen door slam behind her.

"Hey," Julian said, walking up the porch steps.

"How was your swim?"

"The swim was great. But look." He held up his hand and pointed to his empty ring finger, his eyes troubled.

"Oh no. What happened?" she said.

⌣

BEFORE DINNER, they all traipsed over to the pond to look for the ring, half-heartedly poking around in the grass, knowing it was futile.

"I'm really sorry," Julian said to Flora. "It slipped off in the water somehow."

"It's okay," Flora said. "We'll get a new one when we can."

"I feel terrible."

"Hey," she said, putting a hand on the side of his face. "It's a *thing*. It's fine."

"Who wants ice cream?" David said. "I'll make us sundaes."

"Me!" Ruby said.

Margot took Ruby's hand as they made their way back to the Little House, arms swinging. The thing they never really talked about whenever they talked about the summer of the photograph, was how they'd all fallen in love with each other again, with the constellation of Julian and Flora and Margot and David. The foursome reknit themselves with Ruby at the center, and had she ever been more essentially Ruby than that summer? The halo of curls that were bleached blond by the end of August, the topknot she insisted on every morning, the endless cascade of castaway wands and tiaras and lengths of tulle wrapped around her waist.

Ruby looked up at Margot and Flora heard her say, her high-pitched voice a little tentative, "Are you my friend?" Did Flora imagine that Margot was choked up when she leaned down to Ruby and said, "I am your best friend, Ruby. The absolute best"?

Ruby cheered, "Hooray!"

Flora braided her fingers through Julian's and felt where the ring should have been. *Oh well.*

Later, they would all agree: that summer, the summer of the photo, had been the sweetest.

SEVENTEEN

Sydney hadn't planned on taking Julian's dumb ring. She'd slept with enough married men not to be bothered by a slender band of gold or silver or platinum or whatever precious metal went into their precious marital medals. Julian's mistake was being obvious. Disrespectful. She didn't have any illusions (delusions) about what they were. She understood the two of them were like damaged birds tossed from separate but equal nests and somehow they'd found each other and recognized their similar wounds. They both harbored the same hollowness and she was able to fill it with sex, yes, but also with the satisfaction she got from summoning him. She could ride that high for days, the knowledge that she could make him come to her and abase himself. Julian the mensch. Julian the devoted husband. He exposed himself to her, bared the damage, and she made him squirm and groan and want her. He *wanted* her. Even though he didn't linger, even though he sometimes showered before he left so he wouldn't slip into the marital bed smelling of her, she still felt like a feral cat lazily extending its paws in satisfaction every time he timidly knocked on her door, looking vaguely sheepish and amused.

But then one night, when they were done and he was in the bathroom washing his hands, his face, his mouth, his dick, she picked up his jeans from the floor and his wedding ring fell out of the pocket and rolled clear across the room, hitting the leg of a chair and landing in front of the bowl of cat food. She realized he must have taken off the ring before he entered her apartment, and something in her combusted. When he came out, all soaped and shampooed and purified, she said, "Why don't you stay tonight?"

"You know I can't do that," he said. She reclined on the bed, unbuttoned her shirt. It usually worked. But that night, he'd grabbed his pants and his belt and dressed more quickly than usual, avoiding looking at her. She was lonely. She wanted to talk about things couples talked about, like what they were doing that weekend or if they should see a movie or order takeout or go to the Chinese restaurant down the block. All she'd gotten out of him in a vulnerable moment was the most anemic sentence: "I can't deny our connection." Still, the sentiment thrilled, because talking about feelings was usually off-limits, unless it was anger. They were allowed to poke and argue and accuse and fuck and make up. Rinse and repeat. "I think about you all the time," he'd said one night, running his hands over her body, undressing her. "I tell myself every day I'm not going to and then I hear your voice and you drive me crazy—"

She replayed that conversation in her head because it was one of the few times he'd shown his hand. "Why can't you stay?" she asked. She tried not to sound needy, but it was hard. She needed.

"A lot of reasons," he said. He looked at his watch, and she knew he was about to say he had to go. This was another thing she hated: how his presence in the apartment was anchored by the slenderest of threads; anything could break his concentration and she could feel his attention start to float away back to his other life, his real life.

Her impulse didn't solidify until the next day, when he called and asked if she'd found a ring. He was heading back to Stoneham, the cult she was never allowed to join.

"Ring?" she said. "What kind of ring?"

"Come on, Sydney. I lost my ring. Did you find it?"

"You weren't wearing a ring yesterday." (True!)

She knew she had an expiration date. She could see it on him lately, his eagerness to be done with her. She didn't know what she would do with the ring, but it might come in handy. If nothing else, a souvenir. Why shouldn't she get to keep it?

⌣

HAD IT ONLY BEEN FIVE months after David's stroke? To Margot, it felt like years. She should have been used to how her world could occupy one shape, so sharp and certain, then, with no or little warning completely dissolve, leaving her with a nauseating, untethered drift, wondering if this was *it*, if the drift was a permanent condition rather than an in-between. She'd learned to tolerate that uncertainty in her work—that brand of tolerance was required to survive—but when David's stroke started to unravel her home life, too, she ran. She wasn't proud of it, but she'd needed to leave.

She never got to audition for the play she was hoping to read for the day of David's stroke. Despairing and scared, she agreed to the out-of-town run in Seattle for Quinn's play, even though it brought his particular brand of toxicity back into her life, because she was a more solid person when he asked, firmly affixed to David, who kept her heart beating to the right tune. Or at least, he had. He would again, she was sure. He'd only been home from the rehab facility for a few weeks. He was still struggling; she was struggling. She offered to stay home, but David insisted she go and, truthfully, she hadn't required any convincing. She hired a home health aide and a physical therapist to come in every day. Flora promised to go every afternoon with Ruby and call Margot to let her know how his day had been.

The whole production in Seattle was one long, dreary, rain-soaked cluster-fuck. The play had landed with a thud, to the worst reviews Margot—all of them—would ever get. None of the critics cut anyone a break: the play was disappointing and trite; the cast didn't seem to understand the tone and the entire evening dragged; the staging was tired; the lighting left Margot in an unfortunate shadow at a critical moment; it went on and on.

What she always wondered about that time was why none of them had seen it coming. Nobody thought the play was a masterpiece; it needed work—that's what an out-of-town run was for, getting it out of workshop and in front of an audience and seeing, *feeling*, what worked and what didn't, but none of them had thought it was an unmitigated disaster until they started reading about it in the papers. After the reviews in Seattle, ticket sales came to a grinding halt. The producers papered the audience with students and old folks who were often listless during the performance and sometimes genuinely pissed.

Margot barely left her room during the day. She stopped

socializing; no more lunches or after-show drinks. She counted off the days. In dreary Seattle. In February. The morning she found Julian's ring, she'd been sitting sullenly in her obnoxiously bright apartment in a run-down Victorian in a just-okay neighborhood in Seattle. Someone had made an effort with her room, painting the walls in contrasting tropical colors, sunset pink, tangerine orange, Kool-Aid green, and lemon yellow, but the room ended up looking like an exotic fruit bowl in the wrong locale. A Gauguin in Cleveland. A Bonnard in Buffalo. All the colors did was throw into stark relief the unrelenting gray outside. She was waiting for Sydney Bloom to finish showering in the bathroom they shared, a situation she had objected to vociferously to no avail. Out-of-town arrangements were always iffy, and nobody cared that she was the female lead. All the housing was practically the same. Plus, her rooms could be much worse. One summer on the Cape she'd been in a run-down inn with six rooms to one tiny bathroom they all shared with a healthy mouse population. But tonight was their last performance. The end of the misery.

She heard the shower turn off and the low drone of Sydney's hair dryer. It took Sydney forever to get ready in the morning, and Margot took a petty satisfaction in knowing that Sydney's casual, natural look was carefully cultivated and took, based on the cosmetics in the room, a surfeit of expensive products and at least an hour, while Margot showered and let her hair dry naturally and maybe bothered with moisturizer.

Margot had worked with Sydney a couple of times before—in the early Good Company days—and never understood her appeal, not as a person or an actor. She was a little bit manic, hard to read. Ben and Julian had let her loose from Good Company years ago, but Quinn still cast her (Margot had a good guess as to why). Even though her part in this production was small, she still managed to be a distraction every night. She was too loud or she wasn't loud enough. She was heavy-footed on the stage. Sometimes she ran up on her lines. She couldn't give three clean performances in a row.

Margot finally heard Sydney vacate the bathroom. She'd had to pee from the minute she woke up. She grabbed her towel and headed into the bathroom. She was brushing her teeth when she noticed a piece of jewelry on the floor beneath the sink. She would play it over and over again in her mind, whether Sydney—even unconsciously—had wanted her to see the necklace, the ring threaded onto a slender chain. But there was no way Sydney could have known that one of the few people on earth who would see that ring as familiar was Margot. She picked up the necklace, telling herself she wasn't seeing what she thought she was seeing—the flat gold ring with the double milgrain, a little beat-up now. She slid the ring off the chain and held it up to the flickering fluorescent light that needed to be replaced, and looked inside: J AND F. She'd been at Stoneham when Julian said he lost the ring. She'd gone down to the pond and poked around in the mud with everyone else. She slipped the ring and the chain in her robe pocket. Quickly dressed and left.

Back in New York the following week, she met Julian for a drink. "Still looking for this?" she'd said, slamming the ring on the table.

"Where did you find that?" he said, looking at the ring on the table in front of him. He'd gone a shade of green.

"In my bathroom in Seattle. The bathroom I shared with Sydney Bloom, and she, apparently, has been wearing your wedding ring on a chain around her neck like you are both in high school and she is going steady with the star of the school play."

"Oh God," he said.

"What is going on, Julian?" Margot sat and motioned to the bartender for a drink.

"Nothing. Nothing, I swear," he said. His entire posture belied the words; he slunk into himself in a way Margot had never seen.

"Why does she have your wedding ring?"

"She took it."

Margot sighed and did a quick calculation. How much did she want to know? Because if she knew the sordid details how could she not tell Flora? How could she not hate Julian for whatever he was doing?

"Margot—" Julian started. She put up her hand to stop him.

"Is it over?" she asked. "Whatever it was?"

"Yes."

"Does Flora know?" A curt no from Julian.

She didn't want to think of what had happened that had the ring sitting on the table in the bar between them. Oh, who was she kidding? He'd fucked Sydney. She was and wasn't surprised. Nothing surprised her anymore, but Julian? She was so disappointed. "Are you planning on telling Flora?"

"No. No!"

"Good." They sat for a few minutes, quietly sipping their whiskeys neat. "She couldn't take it, Julian. She's given up a lot for you, and if you tell her—"

"Margot." His face was set, eyes blazing. "I don't need the lecture."

"I hope you're right." She slid the ring across the slab of

highly varnished wood. "I don't ever want to talk about it again. But I promise you that if I have the slightest inkling that you're cheating on Flora, I will tell her. God, Julian. Sydney?"

He sighed and looked heavenward, as if some clarification was written on the wall amid the college sports pennants and bottles of booze. "I—"

"I don't want to know," she said. "What are you going to do with it? You can't wear it." He already had a replacement ring, an exact replica of the first one. She knew, because Flora told her, that he'd gone out and bought it himself. He said he wanted to surprise her, but Flora was disappointed they hadn't done it together.

"I know," he said. He took the ring off the table and put it in his jacket pocket. "I'll take care of it."

EIGHTEEN

⁓

Flora woke up to the smell of coffee wafting up from the kitchen. She and Julian had been at Stoneham for almost three weeks; they'd left home as soon as Ruby took off for Spain, and though Flora was in no mood to cede anything to him—not even an *idea*—she could grudgingly admit that the relocation had been a good one. She'd forgotten how well she always slept in "their" bedroom, the room beneath the eaves at the front of the house, even these days, when Julian was relegated to the downstairs bedroom, even these nights, when her brain fought sleep like it was some kind of death.

The Little House was a comfort; nothing ever changed. The flimsy rocking chair she'd purchased one early summer at a garage sale was still in front of the window. When Ruby was small and woke from a nap, she loved to be rocked. If Flora closed her eyes, she could feel the weight of groggy Ruby against her, the slightly sweaty head, her intoxicating toddler smell—apple juice, shampoo, dirt. All the board games they'd bought over the years—Clue and Monopoly and Yahtzee—were still downstairs. The refrigerator still hummed too loudly. The gas burners still needed to be lit by a match. The front porch with its wicker love seats and saggy cushions was still one of her favorite places on earth to sit and read or nap—or, it used to be one of her favorite places. It reminded her too much of Margot right now. The mornings with mugs of coffee out there, the evenings with mugs of wine.

When Margot found out about the reappearance of the ring, she had called Flora daily, sometimes hourly. Flora ignored all the calls but one, and the conversation had been brief, painful, and pointless, with Margot apologizing over and over and Flora barely listening. She hung up on Margot midsentence. Texted Margot not to contact her again.

Julian had told Flora about Margot leaving *Cedar*, and though Flora tried to summon some kind of emotion, she couldn't. She didn't know what to feel about Margot. Betrayal—yes. Anger, sure. All the things she felt toward Julian. When she tried to unravel the morass of emotion around Margot and think of what she wanted to say to her, she got confused, and her mind would go fuzzy and blank. No reception.

She got out of bed, wondering what Julian was making for breakfast. He'd turned into some kind of overly attentive nurse. Bringing her coffee in bed, fluffing pillows, fretting over her needs and moods and wants. It was, by turns, impressive and irritating. Today was the last Sunday in July; soon everyone would start to arrive for rehearsals.

As Flora pulled on a pair of leggings and a Juilliard sweatshirt that she must have left in the closet over a decade ago, she engaged in her new morning ritual: figuring out how she felt. How was she today? The shocking thing about the past few weeks—or, *one* shocking thing in a series of tremors—was how removed she could be from her heartache. The anger she could keep closer. Anger was satisfying and actionable. She had a whole new series of gestures that popped into her head like stage directions in a script. She *slammed* and *banged* and *stomped*. One night, as she was interrogating Julian and he was apologizing in a way that was making it worse—("I never went out with her," he pleaded. "I didn't take her *anywhere*." "That's supposed to make me feel *better*?" she'd said. "I'm starting to take *her* side.")—she eyed the glass of red wine in her hand and thought, *Flora throws the wine on Julian's shirt*. And then she did.

On the bedroom dresser, her phone buzzed. She ignored it and sat in the rocking chair, looking out the window. In the wake of finding the ring and all that followed, Flora initially told Julian he was going to have to go to Stoneham alone. "But what will we tell Ruby?" he said.

"I'm sure you'll figure it out," she said. "I'm sure your massive ability to make shit up will come in handy." But as cavalier as she was in conversation, she didn't know what to do about Ruby, either. She didn't know what to do about herself. She vacillated between sorrow and fury and seemed incapable of finding some middle ground, just kept being buffeted between the two.

"We need to get away. It will be good for us," Julian had persisted. He was still charming, her husband. He was still persuasive. "Come away with me, Flora. Please."

She agreed to go. She agreed to give it a try. She did not agree to be amiable, to stay for the whole production, to put herself in the position of having to pretend in front of cast and crew that everything was okay. "I don't know how long I'll stay," she told him.

"I can live with that. It's a start."

On the bedroom dresser, her phone buzzed again and again. Someone was calling. She picked up the phone and looked at the string of missed calls, four of them, all from Margot. She'd left a voicemail, too. Flora didn't want to listen, but she couldn't ignore Margot forever. Or could she?

"The only way through is through" was a thing she used to blithely say to people who were facing a rough spot. What terrible advice! She didn't want to go through; she wanted to turn back, put herself in the garage that day, and end the scene without finding the ring.

She pressed play on the voicemail.

Flora, it's me. Hi. I, uh, I know you don't want to hear from me, but please don't hang up. Disconnect. Whatever. I miss you and I feel so awful and . . . Margot paused here, and Flora felt her throat tighten, the tears build, the sadness she'd worked so hard to contain rise up and make her feel like she was on a boat listing to one side. She could hear Margot take a shaky breath. *I'm on my way to work. Today is my last day taping, Flora. The big death scene. I wish you were here. Maybe they'd let you pull the plug. Ha ha. It just hit me, how inconceivable it is that you and Julian won't be in the studio today watching. I'm such a wreck and—*

Flora hit end and sent the voicemail to trash. The call wasn't about Flora, it was about Margot wanting everything to be the same for her, for her big finale.

Fuck her.

Out the window, the hemlocks they'd planted the summer of the photograph had grown past the second story of the house. The lights they'd strung with Ruby were still on the tree, and Ben had added more on the lower branches. In the distance, Flora could see Ben on the front porch of the main house, surveying his domain. Someone was with him—his lady du jour.

Ben dated a series of frighteningly competent women, all toned and beautiful without an artsy bone in their taut bodies. She could also see his daughter, Tess, poking around the hydrangea plants that were in full bloom around the porch. Ben must have her for the summer. Ruby would be glad Tess was there; she loved playing big sister.

Ruby. What were they going to do about Ruby?

"Do you even like it here, Mom?" Ruby had asked Flora one of the last summers they went to Stoneham. She had to have been twelve or thirteen. Flora weighed a few responses. "Why?" she finally said.

"I don't think it's fun anymore."

Improbably, of all of them, Flora had continued to love Stoneham the most. Partly it was the joy of getting out of the city. Partly it was because voice work could be solitary. At Stoneham she could pitch in where needed. She worked with the musicians sometimes. Sometimes she cooked or sewed or helped with props.

But that last summer, the summer before they headed west, she could see Julian pulling away from the whole enterprise. Ben had invited a documentary crew that year, and they overran the place. The presence of cameras changed the vibe of the entire week of rehearsal and the performance. "I'm not driving two hours north for the kind of scene I manage to avoid in Manhattan," Julian had said that summer. As always, she capitulated to what she told herself was his discernment. But was it discernment or resentment? Julian could be so generous and encouraging and supportive when he approved of the cause, when it met his litmus test for good, and so quick to dismiss when it fell short.

She couldn't help but tally all the things she missed because they weren't Julian's "scene." When they first started dating, she'd stopped singing in—or even attending—church because Julian was so dismissive ("Time for the magic show?" he'd ask when she was getting ready to leave the house on Sundays). She'd given up musical theater (but that was for Ruby; she couldn't deny that). Every vacation they took, every break they had, was dictated by the demands of Good Company. The list went on. She knew this line of thinking wasn't fruitful or even fair. Before Ruby complicated life, she'd had nothing but admiration for the way Julian moved through the world—his certainty, his choices, his loyalties. She'd fallen in love with all of it. She was proud of it.

And even when she questioned his priorities, she accepted them because she thought she and Julian were a team, both playing by the same rules. How to incorporate this information into the story of her life? How to accept that she'd been lied to so grievously, fooled so completely? How to decide if her life—as she'd always thought—had been a series of carefully considered choices or, in light of this new information, a series of unfair accommodations?

She went downstairs to the kitchen and poured herself some coffee. From the window, she could see Julian on the front lawn talking to Ben. She wondered if Ben had picked up on anything in the week since he'd arrived. She didn't think so. She went out to the front porch, and at the sound of the screen door, Ben and Julian looked up. Ben looked pleased; Julian looked worried. What now?

"Hey," she said. "What's up?"

"Very exciting developments," Ben said, rubbing his hands together. "It's supposed to be a surprise, but I figured I could tell you guys. To be honest, I thought you already knew. I hope I didn't spoil anything."

"Knew what?"

"About the return of the one and only Margot Letta! She'll be here by the end of the week. Exciting, right? Gang's all here?"

"Super exciting," Flora deadpanned. She turned and went back inside and straight upstairs. Leave it to Margot to launch some kind of surprise attack, to descend on whatever shaky truce she and Julian had managed to put in place for three weeks. Although, to be fair, that could have been what the voicemail was about.

Back at the upstairs window, she watched Ben and Julian make their way up to the Farmhouse. Rehearsals would begin in a few days, and she was certain that Julian would welcome the distraction. He was probably dying for everyone to arrive and get to work, be in his element, have a reason to avoid Flora, her anger, and her sadness.

Flora wasn't a saint. She'd been guilty of false pride. She had genuinely, truly believed her marriage was better than anyone else's. "You never know what goes on behind a closed front door," Julian liked to say. But she knew what went on behind her door; she knew! It had been a defining truth of her life, that she and Julian were the real deal.

The hemlock directly outside the window, Ruby's tree, was sickly. The needles were yellowing, and the bark was covered with something that looked like white mold. Earlier in the week, Ben had brought out a local arborist to take a look. Before he even got all the way down the hill, he'd diagnosed the disease. A parasite was affecting all the hemlocks in the area.

"It's a shame," he said. "These trees used to be real reliable, but now they're all suffering."

Doing the new math of her life, the constant, exhausting recalibration, she realized when Julian planted the tree, he'd been in the throes of an affair with Sydney. She asked him if he'd made one of his many now-understandable trips to Manhattan that summer to see Sydney with dirt under his fingernails from planting Ruby's tree.

"Flora, please," he'd said, covering his face with his hands. "I don't know. I don't remember."

"Poor thing," the arborist had said, putting a gentle hand on the tree's trunk. "It's being eaten away from the inside."

She knew how it felt. She had to get out of there.

NINETEEN

‿

So, it was going to be a bike.

Dr. Cathryn Newhall would be pedaling happily down a fictional street in the fictional town of *Cedar* after a long fictional shift and in a light fictional rain. She'd be wearing headphones and listening to music (Bess was ingenious about incorporating what Margot thought of as op-ed details into story lines—the headphones on a bike, the improperly worn helmet) and coming in the opposite direction would be a big, bad SUV that would take a curve too quickly, skid on the slick roads, and—the episode would end with the sound of the crash and the very *Cedar*-like close-up of the front wheel of the bike, ominously spinning in the dark, to some incongruous upbeat indie-pop tune trickling out from Dr. Cat's EarPods.

Margot was relieved when she got the script because, regardless of what Bess had promised, Dr. Cat could have perished on a plane or in a car crash off scene and her final episode would be a closed casket with a huge blown-up photo of Margot on top. But Bess had come through on her promise to give Margot a "good death." It would happen over four episodes, and Margot tried not to care that she would spend most of the four episodes in a hospital bed. At least she wouldn't have to worry about her hair.

Driving to the studio on her last day of shooting, she tried to focus on the day ahead and block out everything that was going on with her and Flora and Julian. It was a complete shit show, and she was livid that Flora refused to talk to her. Margot tried to sit down and compose an email to Flora, but that felt cowardly and also Margot didn't know what to say, how to make Flora understand that she'd been trying to *help*. Or how to say it in a way that Flora would believe. Margot wanted to tell Flora first that she and David were thinking of returning to Stoneham, but if Flora wasn't going to talk to her, she wasn't going to wait around. She called Ben directly and told him she was available for *The Cherry Orchard*. Chekhov wasn't her favorite, but she loved that play and she knew it and, as she'd hoped, Ben was thrilled to have her, even at the last minute. "I'll have to bump someone," he'd said, "but fuck it. This is great news." She'd left a voicemail on Flora's phone—in spite of Flora's request not to call her—and had to hope Flora would listen.

After Margot found Julian's ring in Seattle, she considered telling Flora, but the thought barely landed before she batted it away. She kept waiting for Flora to discover Julian's affair herself. She kept waiting for Julian, in a fit of conscience, to confess—that seemed the most likely scenario—but the months went by and nothing. Eventually, she was able to tuck the knowledge of the affair and her complicity in covering it up in the deep recesses of her mind, a place where she stored everything she didn't want to confront: who Julian was versus what she believed; what her marriage was versus what she'd imagined; what her career was versus what she'd dreamed and trained for.

Whenever Flora and Margot sat around dissecting the relationships of their friends—who was solid, who was on thin ice, who never should have married in the first place—Julian liked to finger wag, saying that no one ever really knew what went on behind closed doors and that people's marriages took on a different hue when they had an audience. Like Meg and Marta, who bickered nonstop in front of company, but Julian had once observed them in the back of the theater talking privately and was stunned to see how loving and kind they were with each other. Or Gabe and Charlene, who were saccharinely polite when in mixed company, but after they divorced, Charlene confided all the horrible things Gabe would say to her in private, how he would berate her, accuse her of flirting with other men, being dumb, having no manners.

"You can't tell," he'd say.

"We're not adjudicating," Flora would say, "just gossiping. It's fun to speculate."

Margot would train her eyes on a fixed spot during those conversations, terrified of catching Julian's eye, terrified of them inadvertently exchanging a meaningful glance that Flora or David would see. Margot was certain she'd made the right decision. Sydney Bloom. My God. It wasn't like Julian had fallen in love with another woman. It wasn't like he was a serial cheater, although she supposed he could be—how would she know? But she believed Julian when he told her it was a single, horrifying mistake. She saw the look on his face when she handed him the ring, the shame and the relief. She saw how he was with Flora *after* the ring. Something in him had shifted for the better.

In her more truthful moments, she could admit that she

needed Julian and Flora to stay together. She needed them. She wouldn't have survived the year after the stroke without their companionship and help. She knew what happened when friends divorced—no matter what anyone said, no matter how hard everyone tried, if the divorce was anything less than perfectly amicable, you had to choose a side. She would choose Flora. No question. Not because she loved her more, but because Flora would need her more, and because Flora would have Ruby most of the time and Margot would choose them. And where would that leave David? Margot and David were better together when they were with Flora and Julian. Spending time as a foursome was invigorating, vital. She wasn't going to ruin it all. Not for Sydney Bloom.

Margot didn't regret taking the ring from Sydney. She stood by that decision. She believed in the power of objects, and she believed Sydney was dark in the heart and that if Sydney had Julian's ring to fixate on, threaten him with, she would have found a way to continually work herself back into his life— blackmail via ring. It would have never ended because Sydney didn't want anything *from* Julian, she wanted Julian. She wanted to be the object of his attention—good or bad, like a recalcitrant toddler. What Margot *did* regret was returning the ring to Julian, because that had been the selfish part of the act. She could have disposed of the ring. Pretended she'd never seen it. Instead, she'd nearly thrown it at him, triumphant and accusing, enjoying both the prop and the staging. "Looking for this?" she'd said that day all those years ago, practically spitting, slamming it down on the table in front of him. She'd thrown herself into it, enjoyed the performance, and had relished the look on his face, the complete shock. She never imagined Julian would do something as dumb as stashing the ring away where

Flora might find it. "I'll take care of it," he'd said back then, but he hadn't. What an idiot.

⌐

MARGOT HAD BEEN ON SET for a lot of "last days." There was a ritual to the departure of someone who had been part of *la famiglia*. No matter who was leaving (unless they were leaving on bad terms), all negative feelings were tabled for the final scene. The longer a person had been there—and Margot had been there from the beginning—the more extravagant the moment. For Margot—and she was genuinely moved by this—a huge crowd gathered, even actors who didn't have to be on set that day. Two directors who no longer worked for the show, but who happened to be on the lot, had also stopped by to watch.

Her final scene was Dr. Cat's actual final scene. It didn't always happen that way. Sometimes the last scene taped was a throwaway and felt anticlimactic. But today, Dr. Cat would be in intensive care. Both she and Charles know she isn't going to make it. She tells him she loves him; she asks him to take care of their children. She reminds him of the first moment she saw him, that first day in the corridor. How she looked at him and thought, *If I can have that, everything in my life will be good. I'll be safe.* And how it was true and she didn't regret a thing. Blah, blah, blah. Long, slow breath, brief flutter of eyelids, and *ciao*, Dr. Cat. The scene was *Cedar* corny, but she and Charles hadn't worked together so long for nothing.

While she was in makeup, she sat and thought about all the years and all the ridiculous story lines and all the times she and Charles had bickered and made up. She thought about the night early on, before Charles had come out to her, when they'd gone out drinking, wanting to create more of an ease with each other. It was at the end of a long day of shooting, the day of Cat and Charles's first kiss. It happened in the rain, of course—everything happened in the rain because Cedar was some combination of Seattle and Portland. In the scene, they'd been fighting over an objection Charles raised to a decision she'd made about a patient, and the fight—as it so often did on television—turned to heat and the heat turned to passion and the passion became a kiss. As always on Bess's set, there was no rehearsal, and she and Charles were just getting to know one another. They'd had to do the scene a lot—a dozen times?

A thing Margot could never admit to David was how much she loved kissing another actor if the person was a good kisser, and she'd been lucky with Charles. He was a romantic. He'd been with lots of women—and men—before he met Nate, before he'd fallen in love for good. Kissing Charles was the opposite of kissing David, who was gentle and considerate and slow and lovely, but—kissing Charles was *hot*. Kissing Charles was new-relationship kissing, when you can't get enough, when you feel like you might devour the other person. And that night after the dozen or more camera kisses, each take better than the one before, more believable, sultrier, they were feeling each other. Giddy, they went to a bar, and when Marvin Gaye came on the jukebox, she grabbed Charles's hand and led him to the tiny dance floor. She felt a kind of permission she knew she didn't really have because of how they'd spent their day, firing each other up. She kissed him for real that night and he kissed her back and they grabbed their coats and walked to their cars and the kissing continued. He put his hands up her shirt and she was ready right then and there, Charles's mouth on her nipple, to undress and fuck him. She was so ready, and she was so lonely. She and David were inching their way back to intimacy post-stroke, and it was often fine but always tentative and not nearly often enough and here was Charles and he was beautiful and his mouth was on her and she could feel that he was hard and all she wanted was for someone to tear open her blouse and fuck her brains out on the hood of her car, like a horny, desperate teen.

He was the one who had pulled back that night. He was the one who had stopped them and told her how beautiful she was and, God, so sexy and but and but and but. He'd opened the car door and she'd gotten behind the wheel, and he'd cupped one side of her face and said, "I'll see you tomorrow." He said, "I love you."

"I love you, too," she said, and they both meant it and they both understood what kind of love they were talking about. A collegial love. He came to her trailer the next morning and told her about Nathaniel. About leaving his first wife, about knowing he was bisexual for so long, about being terrified of being found out.

"So last night?" she'd said.

"If I weren't in a relationship? If you weren't married?" He'd shrugged then. A *who knows?* shrug. She was nothing but grateful afterward that she hadn't made that easiest and dumbest of mistakes—sleeping with her costar. And they'd navigated that little bump with aplomb. It had in many ways brought them closer, and whatever little frisson of romance lingered made them a better couple at work.

She was going to miss him.

When they were doing his close-up on her final scene, she did something nobody was allowed to do on *Cedar* without asking Bess first. She improvised. She looked up at him from her hospital bed and said, "Remember that first night? The night outside the bar? The first time you told me you loved me?"

It worked. He was surprised, in a great way, and Charles was a pro. "I do," he said. "I'll never forget. The tequila, Marvin Gaye telling us to *get it on*, that navy raincoat I unbuttoned in the parking lot." Then he cried and held her hand to his face. Then she cried. And it was beautiful. They did it three more times and Bess called, "Cut!" and she was done.

She climbed out of the hospital bed as the room erupted in applause. A few stagehands rushed forward to remove the taped-on wires and tubes. She pulled a big terry-cloth robe over her hospital gown. Bess hugged her and took her hand and led her to the center of the soundstage, where so many people she'd known for longer than she ever expected were standing and waiting—lining the halls of the fake ICU, lining the staircase of the fake hospital lobby, milling about beyond the sets, among the cameras and craft services tables. "Ladies and gentlemen"—Bess had a bullhorn (as if she needed one)—"this is a series wrap on Cathryn Newhall. Margot Letta, everyone." Bess raised one of Margot's arms high in the air, as if she'd just won the big fight. "Margot Letta!"

Margot had been on the other side of a cast member's departure. Politely standing in the freezing studio, waiting for the big good-bye, wondering why she had to take time out of her day. But now that it was her, it was surprisingly emotional, surprisingly lovely. She looked around the room at everyone applauding—Gwyneth weeping, Charles whistling, all the ER nurses cheering, Kelsey beaming (she knew she was ascendant), the crew stepping forward and ostentatiously bowing to her (she'd always been good to her crew), a production assistant rolling forward a table with a huge cake that had a picture of her wearing the dreaded lavender scrubs on top.

Off to the side, her agent, Donna, was standing with David, and next to them, an empty space rebuking her. If this had happened a month ago, Julian and Flora would be there, too; they wouldn't have missed it for the world. As she made her way through the crowd and to the cake, which was illogically lit with candles, someone at the back of the cavernous soundstage opened one of the massive elephant doors. Funny, it had been ages since she'd been on set when those doors were open. She always hurried back to her trailer when she was done for the day. As always, the California sun shone bright outside the walls of the studio and as the stagehands rolled back the heavy wooden doors, a blade of light sliced straight through the stale darkness that was the world of *Cedar*, her old world, and lit a path in front of her, one she'd never noticed before. A new way out.

TWENTY

~

Flora hadn't been on the Upper West Side since they left New York City for Los Angeles. She didn't recognize a single shop or restaurant on Columbus Avenue. Gone was the Indian restaurant where she'd had dinner during one of her and Julian's breakups, and her date spent the entire evening checking himself out in the mirror on the wall behind Flora. No more Tap-a-Keg East and West, her favorite dive bars. The cheap Italian with enormous bowls of just-okay pasta where she treated herself on payday was gone, as was the little downstairs Chinese place at the end of her old block where she and Margot would meet once a week after Margot had moved in with David and share orders of shrimp with walnuts and garlic string beans. All her haunts, vanished; it was the story of the city. What was more boring than hearing people's recitations of what used to be their New York from block to block? Unless the story was your own, then the mourning was real and the remembering a necessary comfort, a way of reasserting and fact-checking memories, of staking a place to a certain time—

for Flora, a time when everyone wanted frozen yogurt and a bar with a pool table and cheap Italian restaurants with butcher paper and crayons.

Flora had fled Stoneham and was staying at a friend's apartment and she didn't know what she was doing. *She didn't know what she was doing.* It ran through her head like a disturbing mantra and always in the third person. She was vaguely aware that she was wandering closer and closer to the street where their old therapist, Maude, used to live and work. Flora had *loved* Maude. She loved that Maude wasn't cloaked in mystery or withholding about her personal life. Maude frequently talked about her own husband and their son, Jason, and the difficulties and compromises of being a working wife and mother. She loved Maude's office on the garden floor of her home—an entire brownstone!—and how when Maude's husband—also a therapist—came home from his office down the street after picking their son up from school, Flora could hear them upstairs, stomping around in what she assumed was the kitchen, and Maude would roll her eyes and say, "The barbarians have landed."

But what was she doing on Maude's street? What was she going to do? Confront her? Ring the doorbell and accuse her of being two-faced, unethical, a bad person? Scream *Malfeasance!* like Mr. Potter from *It's a Wonderful Life*?

Maude probably wouldn't even remember her. Flora had stopped therapy before Julian, who had continued to see Maude until they moved to California. She'd probably ring the doorbell and stand on Maude's stoop and have to explain—as she did so often—who she was. "I'm Julian's wife?" was a thing she said more times than she could count. Or worse, Maude would remember her as the idiot who had sat through couples therapy without ever learning that her husband was having an affair. She didn't know if Maude still practiced from the basement of her townhouse or if she'd left the city or if she was even alive. Maude couldn't have been *that* much older than Flora, but she'd seemed decades older, with a son in middle school and a thriving practice and enviable real estate.

Before she knew it, she was standing across the street from Maude's house. What was she doing? Then, as if summoned, across the street and pulling a grocery cart: Maude Langstrom. Flora recognized her immediately. She was a little heavier, a little grayer, but her posture was exactly the same; she had the same haircut, short and sensible and not very flattering. Flora's heart started racing, and before she could second-guess herself, she waved and called out her name.

"Maude!" She waited for a few cars to pass and crossed the street. Maude stopped and was looking at Flora, confused. "Maude!" Flora was a little winded when she caught up to her. "Hi, sorry. I didn't expect to see you right out on the street. I wasn't even sure if you still lived here and—here you are!"

"Flora?" Maude took a step back, blinked as if she wasn't sure who she was seeing. Smiled and opened her arms wide and gave Flora a welcoming hug. "Flora, how wonderful to see you. Are you back? Living in New York?"

"No, no. Just here for a little bit. A visit."

"So you're still out west?"

"For now, yes." Flora had imagined confronting Maude for so many hours and days; now she had the chance, and she was tongue-tied. She did not want to exchange pleasantries, but what else could she do?

"And you're well? Julian's well? Ruby?"

"Everyone is pretty good," she said, noticing that Maude

was almost entirely gray now and it suited her. She was like a
character straight from central casting for an Upper West Side
woman of a certain age. The Aerosoles black loafer, an Eileen
Fisher skirt that had seen better days, and a long wool sweater
with bulging pockets. She had a colorful scarf around her neck,
probably purchased at the Seventy Seventh Street flea market,
assuming that still existed. Maude was watching Flora pleasantly.

"I swear I remember that," Flora said, gesturing to a clunky
turquoise necklace that looked like an adept kindergartener
had made it.

"I'm sure you do," Maude said. "Like everything, I've had
it forever. I like to imagine that with this flash of color around
my neck, nobody is noticing that my hair isn't—shall we say—
fresh today."

They both laughed. Maude was rearranging herself, getting
ready to continue on. Flora cast about, trying to think of an
opening line. "Mind if I walk with you a little?" she finally said.

"Please do. How is Ruby? I still think of her and the stories Julian would tell about her, the things she'd say. Is she still
funny?"

"She thinks she is. She's pretty sure she's the funniest person
in the house."

"Sounds about right. How old is she now? Seventeen?"

"Eighteen. She's off to college next month."

Maude shook her head, amused. "I won't bother with time
flies, et cetera." She waved her right hand. "And you and Julian?
Things are good?"

Flora was both surprised and not surprised to feel herself
welling up. "Things right now are complicated, to be honest."

"Hmmm." Maude resumed walking, and they moved along the sidewalk quietly for a few minutes. Maude turned and smiled at Flora. "So—how long have you been standing here waiting for me to leave the house?" She laughed, and though the laugh was friendly, it was also knowing.

"I'm not a stalker. I swear. I'm wandering—sentimentally wandering. But if you hadn't come out when you did, maybe I would have hung around, maybe I would have rung the doorbell or called you. I don't know." Flora shrugged. "I realize this is highly unorthodox and possibly alarming!" She forced a laugh, but it came out more like a sob. "I'm sorry. I'm not as crazy as I seem right now, although I am a little—addled."

Maude moved into professional mode, her voice evening. "Would you like to make an appointment? I probably have some time open next week. Today's my day off," she said, gesturing to the shopping cart.

"I don't know how long I'm going to be here. I—"

"We could make a phone appointment if that's easier."

"Okay." Flora nodded, unsure of her next move. She looked at Maude, who stole a glance at her watch. She decided to plow ahead. "So, I found out a few weeks ago that when Julian and I were seeing you—during couples therapy, and after—he was having an affair and neither of you bothered letting me in on that slightly important detail and I was wondering"—Flora could feel herself gathering steam, her anger combatting her chagrin—"I was wondering if that was a typical way to treat couples in therapy. If it's ethical." Flora stopped and took a shaky breath. She hoped her face wasn't as red as it felt. Maude was composed. She looked up at the sky, a beautiful cloudless July morning, and sighed. "Okay." Maude turned her cart around with two crisp movements, planting it back in the opposite direction, signaling some kind of decision. "I hate grocery shopping, anyway. I have a few minutes. Let's go inside."

Nothing in Maude's office had changed except the color of the couch, the same Crate & Barrel microsuede model, only navy now instead of beige. Flora remembered the first time she sat on the sofa how she'd admired its girth, the sturdy way it held her and left room for at least two more adults; she'd wondered if she and Julian would ever be able to buy something as comfortable and good-looking for their place and get rid of the lumpy flowered thing she had inherited from Margot, who had inherited it from an aunt in Connecticut, where chintz sprouted like dandelions.

Everything else was the same, too. Maude's rolltop desk—Flora could see now that it was a cheap reproduction—the low table in the corner for kids with some Legos and a small sand garden. That table used to make her so sad, imagining little kids acting out things they didn't have the words to say. The woven cream macramé wall hanging straight from 1972. She pointed at it. "Those are all over Los Angeles now, you know. You could probably sell it on eBay."

"Really?" Maude looked back at the wall. "I don't even notice that anymore. My mother made it for me for my first office. A tiny room in a big building further west." She turned back toward Flora. "So, Flora. What can I do for you?"

Flora had a brief sense of herself from outside the room, outside the window, looking in as she sat in Maude's office. What was she doing? "I'm sorry," she said. "You must think I've lost my mind."

"No," Maude said.

"I *am* angry."

"I gathered from the question about my ethics." Maude smiled gently.

Flora widened her hands. "I'm feeling a little lost, Maude."

"I have to tell you, Flora, I'm not sure I remember what you're talking about. With Julian. It's been a long time."

Flora was immediately incensed. She bit the inside of her lip to keep herself from screaming. Not remember? This was Maude, who never took a note, never wrote anything down, and always remembered everything from week to week. Flora had asked her about it once and she'd shrugged it off. "I don't need notes. It all somehow sticks." It had reassured Flora then, made her feel as if she'd picked the best therapist in New York City, one whose connection to her patients was so finely tuned, one whose memory was so unassailable, that she didn't even need a written record.

"You remember that you were seeing Julian and me together." Flora regulated her voice as if she were at work.

"Yes, of course. I remember the round robin. First you, then you and Julian, then just Julian." Maude smiled indulgently. "You graduated."

"But I *didn't* graduate. That's the thing. You told me I was done, that I didn't need therapy anymore." Flora flinched hearing herself. She sounded like an aggrieved Ruby; all that was missing was a *Mom!* at the end of the sentence. She took a deep breath. "I'm sorry," she said. "I'm not here to yell at you."

"It's okay if you are," Maude said. "You wouldn't be the first. Occupational hazard. What can I *do* for you, Flora? What do you need?"

Good question, Flora thought. What could Maude do for her? Apologize? Explain? Offer some new bit of information that would make her choice clearer? "I wish I knew the answer to that," Flora said. "I guess I wonder if you ever considered telling me what I didn't know—since I came to you because I felt a little adrift, not connected to Julian. I was struggling. We were struggling."

Maude sat a little straighter in her chair, clasped her hands. "If Julian told me something in confidence, in the privacy of my treatment with him, then no, I wouldn't have considered telling you. That's how I work with every couple, and I would be surprised if I didn't make that clear from the start."

"Okay, but then—as far as I can piece together—once Julian told you he was in another relationship, sleeping with someone else, you terminated our one-on-one therapy."

"I don't remember that specifically, and I'm not disagreeing with your timeline, but Flora, I wouldn't have suggested terminating therapy if I didn't think it was a good idea, apart from what was going on with Julian."

"Well, I think that's what happened, though. I think you couldn't continue to see me knowing that Julian was lying to me and—"

"Okay," Maude said. "Let me save us some time here. As I think you suspect—and you're correct—I can't talk to you about what Julian and I discussed in his sessions, even if I could remember the specifics, and I'm sorry to say that all the ginkgo biloba on Seventy-Second Street—and that's a lot—wouldn't help me there. So how *can* I help you, given what I can't talk about?"

"Was it a conflict for you to be treating me when you knew Julian was lying to me?" Flora leaned back in her chair, relieved to have thought of something sensible to say. Straightforward and clear.

"No," Maude said.

"No?"

"No, not for me. If my assessment of the situation was that I could help you both? Then no."

"But you knew something I didn't!"

"I hope that's why I have a thriving business." Maude laughed. "The value of couples therapy is that I'm not getting *one* side of the story. The whole point of treating couples separately is that people can work out things with me they are afraid to talk about in front of their partner. Sometimes those issues come out in joint sessions; sometimes they don't. It's how it works! I understand your umbrage, Flora, I do. You're hurt. But my job is to ferret out what lurks in the shadows and try to bring both couples, each in their own way and often on separate timelines, into the light, into a better place, toward what we sometimes call a breakthrough." Maude stood up and poured them two glasses of water. "Julian lied to you, and I understand how your feelings for me have become tangled in that knot. I'm sorry for that."

"I feel like you kicked me out of therapy before I was ready."

Maude moved from her chair and sat next to Flora on the sofa. "Flora"—she put a hand on Flora's wrist—"I wouldn't have done that. I promise you: I didn't *choose* Julian over you."

Flora deflated in the chair like a party balloon losing its last bit of air. She'd been so angry with Maude, *so angry*. For weeks, she stoked her anger like it was a bonfire she alone was in charge of tending. Of all the things Flora thought she needed to hear from Maude—that Julian was wrong, that Julian had wronged her; that Maude was wrong, that Maude had wronged her; that Maude was sorry and had often thought of how she'd screwed up and now was so relieved to have the chance to apologize. Of all of the ways she imagined this conversation going— aggrieved, agitated, recriminatory—she had never once imagined Maude's kindness. She hadn't imagined Maude's hand on her wrist, that simple declarative statement, "I didn't choose Julian over you." She couldn't stop herself; the floodgates opened and she wept and wept. Maude sat next to her quietly, handed her a box of Kleenex, and let Flora sob. "Go ahead," she said, patting Flora's back. "Go ahead." She sat until Flora straightened, blew her nose, and smiled at Maude, weakly, gratefully.

⌐

MAUDE STOOD IN THE GARDEN window of her office, watching Flora make her way down the street. The children from next door were zooming up and down the uneven sidewalk on shiny metal scooters. She hated those scooters. Hadn't they gone away years ago? Why were they back? She walked upstairs to brew some tea, thinking about Flora. She'd had patients throw tantrums in her office, give her a hard time about whatever she was reflecting back at them, but she'd never had anyone reappear from the past to accuse her of wrongdoing.

Flora and Julian. Ah, it had been a tricky situation, that one. Not the affair—those revelations happened all the time in couples therapy—but juggling Flora and Julian and their respective needs. She'd liked them both—smart, intuitive, selfaware, the kind of patient she was pleased to see walk through her door. She was wracking her brain to try to remember more of Flora's story. It had been long enough that their files were probably in storage, but she was pretty sure that Flora's issues were nothing special, for lack of a better phrase. Lots of talk about trying to juggle work and parenting and identity and desire. Not easy stuff, but not unusual.

But Julian? Julian, she remembered very clearly. And she supposed Flora was a little bit right—Maude *had* chosen Julian, not because she liked him better or didn't like Flora enough, but because he was the one she thought she could help, the one who needed more help. She'd never forget the session where he unloaded his tumultuous, violent childhood. Some of her patients with that background were permanent victims, some prickly survivors—both had a penchant for self-sabotage.

She was genuinely sorry to discover that Flora and Julian were struggling. Back then, she believed they were a good couple in a bad spot. She remembered how she and Julian had worked on his penchant for secrets, also common with adults who had grown up having to take the temperature of the room every minute of every day—they got good at lying to survive the unpredictable tides. She warned Julian about the danger of secrets, how they were tiny cracks that compromised the tensile strength of a relationship. But that was the other thing about patients who had to keep their home lives hidden, cloaked in shame—secrets felt safe. The truth was much scarier. What a terrible thing to do to a child: weaponize the truth.

She sat and made some notes about her conversation with Flora. She'd told Flora to stay in touch. Maybe someday she'd write a book, and though she'd have to get permissions, couch all the identifying patient details, *this* was an interesting story, a good case. She wondered how it would end.

TWENTY-ONE

⁓

Julian should have seen the request coming, but he didn't. By the time Flora suggested he join her for a therapy session, he'd nearly managed to convince himself that whatever was bothering her had nothing to do with what he was doing late at night. He was vaguely aware of the ridiculous ways he was spinning his justifications, the biggest one being that his time with Sydney was less egregious because he knew Flora and Ruby were asleep, oblivious, and that he'd be there in the morning when they woke, showering them with the fullness of his regret.

Still, he was taken by surprise when Flora asked if he would join her. "Maude thinks it might be helpful to come in together."

Julian could have come clean right then. He could have taken Flora's hand and said six of the most disturbing words in the English language: *I have something to tell you.* He could have put an end to all of it: the affair, the lying. But before they married, she had been clear: "There's one thing I will never forgive. If you ever cheat on me, that will be the end. I won't go through what my mother went through. I won't do it." And nothing that had happened since had led him to believe in any other possibility.

When she found out a friend had been unfaithful, a drawbridge closed fast in her heart. And it happened all the time—good God, they were surrounded by actors; lines were constantly being crossed. Sometimes what happened in rehearsal or on stage or in front of a camera seeped into life; it was inevitable. The lines between life and work could be blurry. By necessity, actors held their emotions closer to the surface than most people, and though he'd never tell Flora this, it was fun—to fall in love with someone for a month, a week, an afternoon. The reconstructing of boundaries didn't happen in a flash; sometimes those lines were *never* redrawn, to the delight of tabloid journalism. But Flora would brook no betrayal, not even a Jimmy Carter–like lust of the heart. She'd made that clear from the beginning: he could do whatever he needed to do to play a part, he could even enjoy it, but he couldn't bring it home and he couldn't talk to her about it. She set her terms.

And he'd done something so much worse than a brief on-set fling. He was sure confessing would be the end of them. So he went to therapy with Flora and lied. And then one day Maude said, "We haven't talked about your sex life yet. How is it?"

"It's good," Flora said, a little too quickly.

"Julian?"

"It's good." Maude let the *good*s sit there, acquire a little heft. "Good is—*good*, I guess," she said. "Could it be better?"

"Yes," Julian said, willing to press a little in the moment. "I think it could be better."

"Well, sure," Flora said curtly, eyes widening. She understood they'd never managed to find their way back to pre-trying-to-get-pregnant sex. It was hard. "It could always be better. Julian could get home before I'm asleep. He could wake up earlier. He could help a little more when he is home. We could have an apartment where Ruby isn't sleeping on the other side of a piece of particleboard. Our apartment is *tiny*. The list goes on." And there it was: Flora and her defensiveness. He thought Maude shot him a sympathetic glance. "If tiny apartments prevented sex, hardly anyone in New York City would be having it," Maude said. "Julian? You're awfully quiet."

God help him. God forgive him. All he could think about in that moment was Sydney Bloom, pushing him back on her bed, unzipping his pants, and slowly climbing on top of him.

"Julian? Where did you go just then?"

"Sorry," he said to Maude, mortified. "Nowhere. I'm sorry."

"We were talking about sex, how it is with you and Flora."

He looked at Flora biting her lower lip, her worried eyes, his wife. "It's mostly good," he said. "It's good."

He couldn't remember when he started seeing Maude alone or even how it ended up that way. He thought money was part of it, and that Flora felt she was done. "I graduated," he remembered her saying. He remembered her saying they could manage it if he wanted to keep seeing Maude, and he did because it *was* helpful to sift through the debris of his childhood. He liked having a person who was perfectly happy to listen to him talk for an hour straight about Good Company and its many conflicting personalities and all his worries and frustrations. But he was biding time; he suspected Maude knew he was biding time.

One afternoon, Maude casually asked why he wasn't wearing a wedding ring. "I seem to recall you wore a ring before the summer. I tend to notice that stuff in couples therapy," she said coolly. "Not that it's a big deal. Many people don't wear rings. Unless it *is* a big deal."

"I lost it," he said. "We keep talking about getting a new one, but other expenses—including this, to be frank—seem to get in the way."

Maude nodded. He looked out the window. A heavy spring rain, and people were rushing past, angling umbrellas in front of them to fight the wind. He thought of the missing ring and the certainty that Sydney had taken it in spite of her insistence that she hadn't. He told himself it was why he kept going back, that he was hoping to get the ring from her. But that hardly explained what he did when he got there. He put his head in his hands. "I have something to tell you," he said to Maude.

They went round and round for weeks after he finally confessed what he was doing. How sex with Sydney was electric and intense. Dangerous but a welcome release from the pressures of life, from the ways he thought he was failing everyone—the company, Flora, himself.

"Sure," Maude said. "Forbidden sex, by its very definition, is more interesting than married sex. I guess what I'm wondering, Julian, is what's your endgame here?"

⌒

MONTHS LATER, one brilliant fall day, Julian left Good Company early to be home for dinner. He'd started doing it once or twice a week, and in addition to making Flora happy, it completely elevated his mood—getting out of the work space, out of his own head for a few hours, sitting down with his family. He walked uptown via Broadway, and before he knew it he was at Washington Square Park, a few blocks from home, at the most perfect time of day, just as the sun was setting, the autumn leaves ablaze with color. The golden hour. The park was so romantic, the light so lovely, he felt for a moment that he'd moved back in time and if he squinted, across the park, a character from a Henry James novel would appear on one of the stoops, ready to hop in a horse-drawn carriage to pay some late-afternoon social visits.

He sat down for a minute on a bench near the big kids' playground, which was emptying out as darkness started to fall, enjoying the crisp fall air, the hustle and bustle of people making their way home from work. The light was fading, and then he heard Ruby's voice: "Mama! Mama! Watch me!"

He realized then that the only two people left in the playground were Flora and Ruby. His family. Of course Flora was the last to leave. She liked keeping Ruby outside until the last possible minute, and next week it would be dark an hour earlier and everyone's outdoor time would contract. He stood, unobserved, watching them. Ruby was on the little swaying rope bridge, and Flora was holding her hand, helping her balance. Ruby got to the other side and stopped with a flourish—a jump and a little "Ta-da!" She and Flora laughed. Flora opened her arms, and although Ruby was too big to jump, she leaned over and let Flora lift her down and Ruby wrapped her legs around Flora's waist, her arms around her neck. Flora hugged Ruby tight, swaying a little, whispering into Ruby's ear, and Julian knew without hearing that Flora was singing to her.

He felt something inside him shift. For months Maude had been talking to him about the barrier he'd built between himself and Flora and Ruby. He'd argued with Maude. What *barrier?* He loved those two more than anything, more than he even thought it was possible to love other human beings.

"I'm not talking about love," Maude said. "I believe you love them. I'm talking about vulnerability. I'm talking about opening yourself to Flora all the way, because you haven't done that yet. You've closed off a little part of yourself. You are so good at compartmentalization. You've even constructed a secret that keeps you separate. A secret, I have to say, you don't seem to enjoy that much."

He would admit that sometimes he felt that Ruby and Flora were a universe of two. Some nights when he came home from work, the current between them was so strong he couldn't find his way in. They would be midsentence, midsong, midproject, or sometimes none of the above, they would be midthought but in tandem. Sometimes it felt like they had their own weather system. Sometimes he resented it, hated how Ruby wouldn't let him pour her orange juice or bowl of cereal. He'd storm into the bedroom to rouse a sleeping Flora. "She won't let me give her breakfast."

"Oh, for God's sake," Flora had said the last time he'd awakened her on her one day to sleep in.

"Well, what can I do?" he'd complained. "She won't let me."

"She's *five*," Flora had said. "What's your excuse?"

Flora angrily poured the cereal, splashed the milk into a bowl while Ruby watched her, sheepish. "Sorry, Mama," she said.

"Next time," Flora said, walking back to bed, voice raised, "you two figure it out."

Julian watched Flora gather their belongings and take Ruby's hand. Now, he felt as if he'd moved *forward* in time and he wasn't part of his family anymore. He could feel what it would be like to be the divorced husband, the part-time father, not *of* his family but outside of it, all because of his own foolish behavior. All at once, he was flooded with terror. Sure that somehow Flora knew what was going on, knew he was talking to Maude about how to vanquish his ill-gotten mistress from his life, just biding her time until she decided to kick him out.

"People walk out of their sad marriages all the time," Sydney had said to him some weeks ago, preening in front of her mirror. "What are *you* afraid of?"

He hadn't answered her. He never had any intention of leaving Flora for Sydney, for anyone—it had never even once occurred to him, not even as a passing thought, so what *was* he doing?

Flora and Ruby were exiting the playground. Flora had Ruby's little pink backpack over her shoulder and was holding Ruby's hand. As they started to cut through the park, he hurried to catch up but found himself following them, listening. What were they talking about? How did they never exhaust their conversations? As he got closer, he could hear Ruby explaining some game at school, something involving dolls and Pokémon cards and pieces of licorice.

"You have licorice in the classroom?" Flora asked.

"No, not *real* licorice. Toy licorice. So if two people get *three* cards and both dolls move, the licorice breaks the tie."

Flora laughed. "You made that game up yourself?"

"Not all of it," Ruby said, always fair and square. "But I figured out most of the rules."

"Clever girl," Flora said. She stopped and leaned down to kiss Ruby on the head. She kissed her three times. "The cleverest girl."

And that was that. Whatever spell Sydney had cast over him, whatever weakness or deprivation he'd leaned into ever since the night she'd shown up at that bar, when Flora leaned over and kissed Ruby, the spell was broken.

"We have affairs because we think they're going to make us feel more like ourselves," Maude had said to him the previous week. "So how does this relationship make you feel?"

The answer was lonely. It made him feel lonely and disgraced, like the worst possible version of himself. Like a fool.

He heard the question again: *What are you afraid of?*

This, he thought, watching his wife and daughter, holding hands, arms swinging, heading home without him. He was afraid of losing them.

TWENTY-TWO

Where's Mom?
Julian knew those were going to be the first words out of Ruby's mouth when she saw him standing in the vast terminal at JFK by himself. *Where's Mom?* Good fucking question, was what he would like to say. He'd left for the airport early, hoping that on the drive down he could formulate some neat and believable explanation for Ruby as to why her mother not only wasn't at the airport but had decamped from Stoneham entirely. Julian felt like he had to explain the origin of the world or the meaning of life or prove Fermat's theorem, that was how inexplicable the situation would be for Ruby.

He had more than an hour to kill before Ruby's flight arrived, and he aimlessly wandered the arrivals terminal. He sat with a too-strong iced coffee on an uncomfortable metal bench and watched the crowd. Next to him a woman with a sign in Spanish decorated with flowers. On the other side, a family welcoming home a son from Japan. He thought of that dumb movie Flora and Ruby loved, the one that began with people in an airport, the one they made him watch every Christmas. Sitting there, he realized the beginning was quite ingenious. All the faces around him were in play, their emotions bared: boredom, nervousness, eagerness, dread. When a person walked through those doors and saw someone after an absence, that first glimpse would carry in it a thousand words, the unvarnished truth. What would Ruby see when she looked at his face? What would he let her see?

Relief, for one. He'd been lonely. He missed her. Anger? He would try not to look angry, but he was furious with Flora for leaving him to deal with Ruby's return alone. Whatever he'd done, they needed to parent together, not for his sake—he was willing to fall on his sword if that's what it took—but to cushion the blow for Ruby. But what was the blow? He felt like Flora had set a trap for him, one he'd have to craftily navigate. Whatever he told Ruby might be recast by whatever Flora eventually decided to tell Ruby. Flora said she'd be back for *The Cherry Orchard*, but he didn't know what to believe anymore. He would try to conceal his anger from Ruby, his frustration, but he was also hurt. He knew he had no claim to being hurt, but he never thought Flora would hang him out to dry so brutally.

He'd spent weeks berating himself for his stupidity, starting with keeping the ring when Margot gave it back to him. He'd considered throwing it away but couldn't bring himself to do it, so he stuck the ring in an envelope and put the envelope inside a folder and buried the folder at the bottom of the file cabinet, where he thought nobody ever went. And then there was the story about losing the ring in the pond. Driving up to Stoneham from Manhattan that day, ringless, he knew he needed a plausible explanation, one that wouldn't have Flora insisting that he keep searching for the ring. He panicked and became the dramaturg of his own life, making the general (the ring is lost) more specific (the ring is in the pond). Sitting in the airport, waiting for Ruby, he recognized these broodings for what they were, of course—distractions from his original sin, his first terrible decision, the affair.

He spotted Ruby coming through the arrivals terminal from a good forty yards away. He recognized her walk, the set of her shoulders. She was dragging her duffel behind her, the one with wheels he'd insisted on getting against her objections and was absurdly satisfied to see her rolling the huge bag. She was tan, and her long curly hair was a few shades lighter. Ruby had always looked more like Flora than like him. She had his sometimes-brown, sometimes-green eyes, but her face was all Flora: round and cherubic, wide eyes that made her look more innocent than she was, pert nose, pointed chin. Seeing her coming toward him, seeing Flora in her face, physically pained him, a sharp cramp somewhere under his ribs. While the three of them had been apart, he'd been able to put off the possibility of their separation taking on some permanent form. With Ruby walking toward him, nervously scanning the crowd, comeuppance was a closening shadow. He swallowed hard and started to wave, and she finally spotted him and quickened her pace.

As she approached, her face looked tight, worried. (*Where's Mom?*) The closer she got, the deeper her frown, until he could feel himself frowning in response. "Rubes?" he said, holding out his arms.

"Dad." She practically threw herself at him, dropping her bag to the ground, holding on to him tightly. He sighed and enveloped her and breathed her in. She smelled like sun and the drugstore moisturizer she used and wintergreen Life Savers and home. Ruby smelled like home. He squeezed his eyes tight;

he would not cry. "Honey," he said into the side of her face; she wasn't letting go and neither was he. "Are you okay?"

"Dad," she said, bursting into a full-out sob.

He held her at arm's length. "Ruby, what's wrong?"

"Dad, Ivan broke up with me."

"Oh, baby." He suppressed a smile but welcomed the tiny burst of joy that released in his heavy heart. Good riddance to Ivan. Ruby deserved someone with more personality and glee. Also, he was ashamed to think, what a reprieve. An eighteen-year-old with a broken heart was not necessarily going to be on the lookout for trouble at home; her tuning fork might be a little muddled. "Aw, honey," he said. "I'm sorry."

She wiped her face with the back of her hand. He opened his backpack and took out a packet of tissues, handed them to her. He took the handle of her suitcase and they started to walk as she blew her nose. "He's a real shit, Dad. Wait until you hear the things he said. Just wait."

"Did he break up with you during the trip? Why didn't you call?"

"No!" she said, indignant. "He broke up with me at the airport in Madrid. *At the airport*, Dad! I had to think about all the things he said the entire flight home."

"I'm sorry. You must be exhausted."

"I am." Ruby nodded fiercely. "I mean, I had some wine." Julian raised a brow at her. "Dad, I drank every night in Spain. It's *fine*. I had two glasses, maybe three. I watched a movie and passed out for most of the flight, but still—" She stopped abruptly. Staring down the long arrivals hall. Looking confused.

Here it comes, Julian thought.

"Mommy!" Ruby picked up her pace and was heading toward someone, and Julian took off after her, to stop her from

approaching a stranger, but then he saw her. Flora. Holding
her arms open now, laughing as if she didn't have a care in the
world. He hurried along, wheeling the duffel while Flora held
Ruby in an embrace. She didn't look Julian in the eye.

"Mom, you're not going to believe what Ivan did. He
dumped me."

"He didn't. In Spain?"

"At the *airport.*"

"Oh, honey. That's terrible." Flora roped her arm through
Ruby's, and they started walking toward the exit, Julian behind
them, the family sherpa. "Tell me what he did. Start at the beginning."

TWENTY-THREE

When Flora left Stoneham, she went straight to her friend Michael's studio apartment on Barrow Street. He'd recently moved in with his new boyfriend, but was keeping the place as an office—*Or maybe as insurance*, Michael said when she'd emailed him to ask if he knew of anyone who had space available. Michael was one of the first Good Company recruits and one of her all-time favorites. Funny, talented, kind, and discreet.

"I need a little time alone," she said, trying to sound upbeat and vague. "Ruby's in Spain, and you know what it's like up at Stoneham when the masses arrive, and I miss the city."

"Makes perfect sense," Michael said, handing her the keys. "I changed the sheets and put out clean towels and stocked the fridge."

"I didn't want you to go to all that trouble."

"Flora, do you remember how many nights you fed me back in the day? I would have stocked it with Dom Pérignon if I could."

She had fed him and so many other young members of Good Company from her tiny kitchen only a few blocks away. It had been her joy to offer the platters of spaghetti and meatballs, trays of lasagna and baked ziti, and the house favorite: her famous homemade sausage rolls. She'd loved channeling the women who had taught her to cook and whom she missed so much.

At first she wasn't sure she wanted to stay back in her old neighborhood, and it did give her a kind of vertigo. She felt both back where she belonged and a little bit lost, sometimes literally. She was constantly taking the wrong train, misremembering connections, walking in the wrong direction when she emerged from the subway. She thought she remembered everything perfectly, but it turned out that she remembered ribbons of things but not the way those ribbons connected. She remembered all the storefronts on Bleecker Street even though the residents were different, but couldn't remember whether Greenwich Street came before Washington Street or where Seventh Avenue became Varick.

Walking around, she kept thinking she recognized someone approaching only to have them come closer and realize she didn't know them at all. It happened time and again until she realized she was recognizing *herself.* All the women with dark clothes and dark glasses and dark curly hair, rushing about with their tote bags and sensible sandals and aggravated expressions. It was like looking in a mirror. It was comforting.

One day, ambling along, she came upon a bunch of clear recycling bags on the curb, full of empty bottles of expensive champagne and wine. She recognized some of the labels from Margot's house and remembered what it was like all those years ago to push Ruby's stroller on garbage days in the West Vil-

lage and how she'd eye her neighbor's castoffs, often with envy.
Even the garbage in New York was aspirational. At least in Los
Angeles it was all concealed in a huge plastic bin. Those banal
thoughts occupied her the day she looked up and realized with a
start that she had turned onto the street where Good Company
lived. She ducked into the fancy coffee shop on the corner of
Hester Street that hadn't been there when they left and got a
good, strong espresso and continued down the block.

She didn't believe it was an accident that she was standing
in front of the familiar deep green door with the gold letter-
ing saying GOOD COMPANY. Once there, she couldn't think of
why or what she was hoping to see. A portal back through time
where she could observe Julian and Sydney? Stop the forward
trajectory of their relationship? She put both hands on the old
wooden door that she'd restored right after she and Julian were
married. She'd spent days sanding and patching and painting,
until the door looked almost new. She was relieved to see that
someone was keeping it in excellent condition. Even though
they were faint, the voices behind the door were raised and
pitched in a way that she could tell someone was reading lines.
The wood, warmed from the morning sun, felt solid and satisfying beneath her hands. She stood for a moment, communing
with her past, then turned and walked away.

For the ten days she was in the city, Flora spent almost every night at the theater. She called old friends, who offered her
house seats. She went to the box offices of all the small theaters
she (and Julian) had loved to see what was available. Sometimes
she'd go to a matinee in the afternoon and see a different show
in the evening. She saw the big jukebox musical about a pop
singer. She endured the too-young movie star playing Hedda
Gabler. She saw a rollicking performance about a girl band in

Ireland in the '70s that was so clever, so well-done, so musically engaging that she had a keening in her chest for days after. She tried to sit through a gentle, spare two-hander about a well-known writer mourning his wife, but she left at intermission; she was crying too hard.

She thought it would be painful—spending so much time in the audience—but it wasn't. Not a bit. She loved everything about going to the theater in New York City. She loved the terse nod acknowledging her seatmates and the ensuing polite (or not) negotiation of the tiny armrest. She loved how when one of her seat partners was a solo woman (it was almost always a woman), they could strike up a companionable back-and-forth about *what they were seeing.* She loved it when the lights started to dim and everyone around her would resettle in their seats, close their playbill, clear their throats, try (unsuccessfully) to expel all coughs. She loved how one night a teenager in front of her opened a bag of candy the minute the lights went down and before the curtain even rose an elderly woman behind her leaned forward with a vicious *Shhhhh!* at the crackling cellophane. Oh, New York. It didn't cut you any breaks. Mostly, she loved how everyone in the room existed in that moment in time together and the tacit agreement that they were all a little better, a little luckier, than everyone out on the sidewalks pursuing less interesting New York attractions.

Her friend Michael was in a Classic Stage revival of *The Lion in Winter*, playing Geoffrey, Henry II's conniving middle son. He was outstanding and the entire production, which could easily have been tired or trite, was instead fresh and biting. She saw it twice. Hanging out backstage with him the second night, she expected to feel her loss more acutely, and she did—a baseline tremor in her bones, but it was a gentle hum, not a clamor. She could live with it.

That night, she went out with Michael and some other members of the cast. He'd also invited a few Good Company friends—anyone who wasn't already on their way to Stoneham—to join them. Unlike her Los Angeles life, where she felt like a supporting player to Margot or Julian, everyone at this table was interested in *her*. "Tell us about your work, Flora," Michael said.

Her work. When had she stopped thinking of it as her work and started thinking of it as her *job*. She described *Griffith* and the part she played and how an advertising executive she'd met once on a toilet paper commercial, of all things, had created and written the show and had remembered Flora and asked her to be the lioness—the character who ruled over all the animals in the park.

"I know that show!" the actress who played Eleanor of Aquitaine said. "I watch it with my kids. We love Leona. Flora, you're very funny."

"I love doing it. It's great to be singing again—it's been a while."

"Voice work is the purest form of acting," the actor playing Henry II said, a little too unctous, a little too Barrymore. She and Michael exchanged an amused smile. She ate it up, though. She'd said the same to Margot. "I agree," she said.

"But don't you miss it, Flora?" Michael finally asked. "Being in front of an audience? New York? Good Company? All of it?"

The table got quiet, and she looked around and recognized how much they needed her to say yes. Yes, she'd made a terrible mistake. Yes, Los Angeles was vapid and empty. Yes, the theater was worth the sacrifice. Yes, if she could do it all over again, she'd do it differently.

Years earlier, when they decided to leave New York, Flora had asked Julian why he was ready to give up Good Company, hand it over to someone else. "You know, it's funny," he'd said, "we started it to have a family, our own theater family. I guess it never occurred to me that we'd end up being *a family*, with all the complications and frustrations of a family." He rubbed the side of his whiskered face with his palm and frowned. He was tired after another middling production. Not eager to start reading new plays again. "I don't want to be a lifer," he said. "I don't want to be the person who stays so long they look up one day and realize they *can't* leave."

Around the table, Flora could see all variations of what Julian was talking about—the lucky few, those who got regular work; the people who booked enough work to manage, but never enough to change their lives in any tangible way; the people who were holding on to the company because if they let go, they'd have nothing and no one. How could she tell them how little she missed it all?

"I miss my people," she said, raising a glass. "I miss all of you."

Her last night in Manhattan: the Delacorte. Michael was a member of the Public and offered her one of his season tickets. Still her mother's daughter; lines were not for her. She walked through the park on a sultry summer night and settled in to watch *Twelfth Night*.

Funny, the memories that hit hard and the ones that didn't. Sitting on the bleachers, only lightly paying attention to the show, she remembered waiting for her entrance in those heavy fairy wings—how they secured with a harness under her dress that gave her a rash. She remembered smelling of bug spray and makeup and hoping the glitter on her face wouldn't run into her eyes on hot nights. She remembered the nights she would stand in the wings to watch Margot deliver her monologue. She loved watching her friend transform. Margot's voice became stronger, her back straighter, her neck extended; she experimented with words and rhythm in ways that would only be noticeable to someone who observed so closely. She loved how Margot would come offstage and see Flora and frown a little and say, "How was it?" As if it were ever anything less than great.

Only twenty minutes into the show, a clap of thunder and the blinding flash of lightning over the ball fields. The actors carried on; the regulars groaned—they knew what was coming. The show would proceed through rain, but not through lightning and thunder. Sure enough, within minutes the production stopped, the skies opened, and everyone rushed for the exits. In front of her was a mother running with a young girl by her side, both of them holding sweaters over their heads. "How will we ever know how it ends?" the girl whined to her mother, who laughed. "We have the book, silly. We can go home and read it."

Riding the subway downtown, wet from the rain, chilly in the air-conditioned car, Flora thought about aborted endings, the theme of the summer. She'd been evading her own. Stalling.

Sometimes Flora thought she was overreacting or being deliberately obstinate or dramatic, but deep down she didn't think any of those things about herself. Her heart was broken, and how to take part in a relationship with the person who was responsible for her pain?

She'd lost her husband and her best friend and couldn't figure out which one she wanted back first—if she wanted them back at all. Here was the rub: to have been chosen—first by Margot, then Julian—to have been plucked from her life into theirs, it had been the greatest fortune of her life; it had *given* her a life with more texture and intellect and art and curiosity and companionship than she ever imagined deserving when she was just a girl in Bay Ridge trying to find her way across the river into a different kind of life.

What she wanted more than anything was to be with Margot right now. They'd open a bottle of wine and she would tell Margot what Julian had done and Margot would say all the right things. She would be incensed. She would offer measured advice. She would ask what Flora needed. She would hug her and say, *I'm so sorry. He's a prick.*

What she wanted more than anything was to be with Julian right now. They'd open a bottle of wine and she would tell Julian about the horrible secret Margot had kept from her. How she'd betrayed her trust, their friendship. Julian would say all the right things. He'd be incensed, tell her how disappointed he was in Margot. What had she been thinking? He would take her in his arms and say, *You didn't deserve that.*

The thing was—she kept saying this to herself, *the thing is,* as if she were arguing her case to a jury—how to get beyond her husband's betrayal without her best friend? How to get beyond her best friend's betrayal without her husband? And, oh, she felt like a fool! Whenever she felt herself inching toward some kind of understanding, a fleeting softness, for Julian, she thought of Margot and her heart snapped shut like a poked oyster.

Flora hadn't planned on going to the airport to meet Ruby. She'd planned on a text, a phone call, an explanation as to why she'd wasn't at Stoneham, but the night before Ruby arrived,

Flora woke up in a panic, almost as if the moment Ruby's plane ascended into the air, it exerted a gravitational pull on Flora in the little apartment on Barrow Street. When she closed her eyes, she could see the plane's path in her head, as if she were watching its journey on a screen, as if she were in the plane with Ruby herself.

"What do I tell Ruby?" Flora had asked on the day she barged into Maude's life, a frantic harried voice from the past looking, she was sure, like a cartoon character who'd stuck a finger in an electric socket.

"Depends," Maude said. "If you and Julian work it out and stay together, I recommend saying nothing. If you're not staying together, obviously you'll have to decide how much you're going to tell her. Keep the conversation general and focused on how much you both love her. Ruby isn't a child."

Was that true? She wasn't a little girl, but she was still a child who wanted her parents to be together, who wanted her small family to remain fierce and intact. Flora had imagined the conversation so many times in her head (*Nothing to do with you. We've grown apart. Best for everyone.*), but Ruby wouldn't swallow any fable, no matter how pretty they tried to make it.

"She'll blame me," Flora said to Maude.

"Why do you say that?" Maude asked.

"Because I'm her mother," Flora said, managing a tired laugh. "And because in her eyes, Julian can do no wrong."

"Except he can," Maude said, "like all of us."

Flora had groaned then. "And Margot. I haven't even dealt with Margot."

"Margot is a thorny complication, but your immediate concern needs to be Julian and Ruby. Then you can decide where Margot fits in all this."

"This mess."

"This life."

"Ruby will blame me for not forgiving Julian."

"Even if you do decide you want to separate, you are not re-quired to tell Ruby exactly what happened, assuming you and Julian can agree on what to tell her."

"But if I don't tell her, she'll be so mystified. She's grown up in a happy family. Witnessing a *good* marriage." Maude was quiet, and when Maude was quiet, Flora always felt she'd said some-thing wrong—or significant. "I know what you're going to say."

"I can't wait to hear," Maude said.

"You're going to say that maybe it is—*was*—a good mar-riage."

"Was it?"

"Yes! But it was a lie. I didn't know a huge part of the story."

"Now you do know. Now you have to incorporate that in-formation into the bigger story. It doesn't negate it, Flora, it changes it."

"So you think I should forgive Julian?"

"I didn't say that. Only you can know if you can, if you *want* to. But I think you should keep in mind that forgiveness is a choice. It doesn't arrive on fairy wings; it doesn't descend from the sky for you to take or leave. Forgiveness is an action."

Flora shook her head, annoyed, and sat up a little straighter on Maude's sofa. Why did it come down to her having to grant forgiveness? "I felt so lucky," she finally said.

"How?"

"To be chosen. I can't imagine what my life would be if I hadn't met Margot, if I hadn't gone to Julian's party all those years ago. It's embarrassing, how grateful I felt that they chose me. *Me.*"

Maude's face softened. She had the kindest eyes, creased and knowing. "They chose you for a reason, Flora. Not because you happened to walk through the door. They chose you because you enlivened their world, too. And here's the thing: now it's your turn to decide if you take them back. You get to choose."

TWENTY-FOUR

⁓

S itting on the porch of the Farmhouse at Stoneham, where Ben had kindly given Margot and David one of the nicer bedrooms, Margot surveyed the scene. For so long Stoneham had been a thorn in her well-manicured paw. So many summers she imagined going back, making some kind of triumphant return. In spite of Ben's initial enthusiasm and promise of a role for her, it hadn't materialized. He'd called her back to haltingly explain why he couldn't fire someone to fit her in. "As much as I'd love to, it wouldn't be cool." He insisted he needed her there in other ways, to advise with the production, be a kind of assistant director and acting coach. "Or screw it all! Just come and have fun."

Five days in and she couldn't square the Stoneham she was experiencing with her memory of the place. She knew it had changed, of course—she'd seen photos, and Flora and Julian had talked about it enough (she never watched the documentary; she couldn't)—but she hadn't viscerally understood how big the production had become. From her perch on the porch, the property the day before the show resembled a small Roman village preparing for the annual bacchanal.

On one side on the lawn, actors rehearsed a scene from *The Cherry Orchard*. At some point over the years, the original, modest stage next to the Farmhouse had been replaced by something sturdier and larger, and a group of at least a dozen actors were practicing a dance that appeared to be a nod to the traditional Russian Cossack dance merged with hip-hop. The musicians had been kicked out of the barn years ago, but now had their own bandstand down by the pond, where they were composing, practicing, making a general ruckus. The barn had been claimed by set and wardrobe. People went in and out all day with buckets of paints and rolled tarps and lengths of lumber and piles of clothing.

A crew of limber young folk were dragging all the furniture out of Ben's living room and onto the lawn to create the drawing room of the play. Down the hill, the porch of the Little House was being transformed into a nursery. On the day of the show, the audience would traipse around from scene to scene with their blankets and lawn chairs.

Behind the Farmhouse, the small canopy of yore had been replaced by a huge wedding tent where people met and rehearsed and ate and drank. The inside of the tent was also elaborately (insanely?) decorated. Vintage chandeliers and empty birdcages hung from wires run between poles that were artfully draped with lengths of red and black silk. Candelabras and samovars were scattered here and there on the long rented tables. String lights overhead. The bar at one end of the tent was overflowing with bottles of booze and wine and coolers of beer and soft drinks. "Who pays for all this?" Margot had asked Ben. He couldn't be funding everything; that would be ridiculous.

"I cover a fair amount, but everyone who can gives money, people donate stuff and it accumulates from year to year. We don't throw anything away; everything is recycled. Somehow it all works out."

Each night a different group of people were in charge of dinner, and the meal had taken on the vibe of a competitive sport. Last night, the dinner team had covered all the candelabras and chandeliers with fake cobwebs. Baskets and bowls of ripened fruits and vegetables lined the centers of the long tables. The entire tent was lit with votives. As if the table staging wasn't enough, a dozen people wearing elaborate animal masks from some prior production marched the serving platters from the kitchen into the tent. It looked like a Kubrick hallucination of Miss Havisham's buffet.

It's not that Margot hadn't expected change. Ben had been putting on a show for eighteen years, and it was not an exaggeration to say it had taken on the sheen of legend. Or, as she started to think of it within hours of arriving, a whiff of pretention. Stoneham had always been a little precious, but had it always been so in love with itself?

Part of her discomfort, she recognized, was that she wasn't used to being around theater people anymore, and she'd forgotten about the *drama*. Like how last night someone mentioned *American Buffalo* and within seconds anyone who'd ever been in the play—approximately 90 percent of the men on site— jumped to their feet and started firing off lines to each other, getting increasingly louder and more strident, until everyone laughed and applauded, as if it were the most hilarious thing they'd ever seen.

She'd spent so many years cloistered in the world of *Cedar*, away from auditions and the New York theater world, she forgot how all conversations led back to the same place: recent accomplishments and the new fall season and who was auditioning for what and which plays were in workshop—all with the sole purpose of charting the filament of the Stoneham universe. Where was your star? How bright did it shine? She forgot how snobbish everyone was about television. She didn't expect them to watch *Cedar*, but half of the people she spoke to pretended they had no idea where she'd been or what she'd been doing for ten years. "Sorry, I don't watch TV" was a lie she heard at least twice a day.

But then last night, the actress playing Madame Ranevskaya, the female lead of *The Cherry Orchard*, had cornered Margot. Margot didn't know Hadley Yates very well, but she'd seen her in a couple of shows back in the day and admired her. "I'll be frank," Hadley said, taking a long drag off her cigarette (so that's how she got that amazing gravelly voice), "I'd love to get some television work. We bought a second home not too far from here last year. I'm free at the moment and I could use some real money. How hard is it to get a good season arc? If I came out to Los Angeles?"

"I'm sure lots of shows would be happy to have you," Margot said, not having any idea if that was true. It was tricky, using someone like Hadley on television. Theater actors often didn't know how to turn down their performance to fit the screen. The same way so many television actors were lost on a stage, ineffective. Not many people could toggle back and forth. Margot wasn't allowed to tell anyone she was leaving *Cedar*, which was fine with her because that information would only lead to questions about what was next. Questions she didn't know how to answer.

"The work is easy, right? Compared to a play?" Hadley said.

"I wouldn't mind a few lazy weeks in sunny California in November."

"It's harder than you think," Margot said, trying not to sound annoyed. "I'm happy for the break. I'm ready for a change, to be honest."

"What kind of change?" Hadley's eyes narrowed and looked Margot up and down.

"Something creatively satisfying. I miss New York. I'd love to get back on the stage. Money isn't everything, right?"

Hadley's laugh could only be described as a cackle. "If you say so." She downed the rest of her whiskey, patted Margot's arm. "Let's stay in touch."

Margot knew she was being peevish. And envious. And slightly bitter. She'd woken up to an email from Donna with a promising subject line: *JOB OFFER*. She was still in bed when she read the email. She'd groaned and covered her face with a pillow. The longest-running courtroom drama on television was offering her a season arc as a judge. The cosmic joke of it was too much. How many times had she and Charles joked about being put out to pasture as a judge? "Overruled!" they'd take turns saying in ever more dramatic voices, pretending to bang a fake gavel. It was as if she'd conjured the offer all those years ago by mocking it and the universe had kept it in its back pocket, waiting to spring it on her at her lowest moment. She hadn't replied yet.

She thought she could see someone moving around in the Little House. Were Flora and Ruby here? She could walk down there, but she'd promised Flora not to be in touch, never mind knock on their screen door. But David hadn't promised anything. Maybe David could be her emissary, take the temperature of the house, see what was going on.

Just as she was thinking of him, he appeared, coming back from the pond, where'd he gone for a swim. He was in excellent shape for someone in his midfifties because he worked at it. Still slender and strong. But she couldn't help but notice now, watching him from a good distance, that his body was softening. His limp was more pronounced than usual. It was always worse when he was walking uphill, fighting gravity. And he was tired. He wasn't sleeping great in the antique bed that was too short for him. They should have stayed in town at one of the inns that hadn't existed when they first came to Stoneham. She had almost asked David to stay back in Los Angeles, because part of her wanted to make this trip alone. She was relieved now that he'd come. As he came closer, she wondered briefly if she could make a joke about whether he'd found Julian's ring in the pond. When she'd told him the whole story that day in his office—finding the ring, returning it to Julian, keeping it quiet—he was mostly confused as to why she wouldn't confide in him. "I didn't want to implicate you," she said. "Didn't want to give you information that you wouldn't want, that *I* didn't want." He'd been hurt. She was pretty sure they weren't at the joking stage yet.

"What's up?" he said, approaching the porch steps.

"Ruminating. Wondering if this place was always so annoying."

He laughed. "I don't know. I like it. Look at all this." He gestured and took in the whole panorama. "It's pretty impressive."

"I guess," she said. The stroke had also wiped away his sarcasm. She'd never get used to it. "I'm just being bitchy."

He sat down on the porch swing and patted the seat next to him. "Come on over here."

"How was your swim?" she asked, settling in beside him.

"Spectacular. I saw Ruby," he said.

"You did? Where?"

"At the pond. She came down for a dip."

Margot stopped herself from saying, *Did she ask about me?* "What did you two talk about?" she said.

"Her trip."

"Was it fun?"

"Ivan broke up with her."

"Oh no. In Spain?"

"Apparently. She was pretty sanguine about the whole thing, to be honest. She told me about all the places she went. She *loves* her camera, said she used it all the time. She can't wait to show us the pictures." Margot leaned into David, relieved. Ruby wanted to show her pictures! "We talked about the Prado," he said.

"Did she love *Las Meninas*?"

"She loved *Las Meninas*."

"Of course she did. And the Goyas?"

"She loved *some* but not *all* of the Goyas."

"Fair. It's a lot of Goya." Margot's sneakered toe pushed the swing gently back and forth. "I don't suppose you talked about—"

"Nope."

They sat listening to the creak of the swing for a moment.

"She was worried about the necklace I gave her," he said.

"Worried? Why?"

"Because she realized in Spain she doesn't want to be a doctor." He turned to Margot and smiled, and they laughed. "Oh, poor thing," Margot said. "She'll want to be five other things before graduation. What did you say to her?"

"I reminded her of when she was little, the last summer you and I were here. Remember? When she memorized your lines?"

"How could I forget? Sitting with her dolls right on that porch down there. 'It were a cold house I kept!' Flora and I nearly keeled over. Did she remember?"

"She did. Then you taught her bits of other monologues."

"She was so good at memorizing, such a perfect little mimic, performing at dinner every night."

"And she hated it."

Margot stopped the motion of the swing and turned her whole body to look at David. "She did not hate it."

"She did."

"I don't remember that *at all*. I remember her standing on a chair, under the tent, saying with her tiny lisp"—Margot made her voice high, clasped her hands in front of her—"'Wherefore art thou Romeo? Deny thy father and refuse thy name.' She was perfect. So sweet and funny."

"Right. And the next night she didn't want to do it."

Margot thought for a minute, and now she remembered. Her gently coaxing Ruby and Ruby bursting into tears. "Right. Well, she was tired, I think. And we didn't *make* her do it."

"No, just lathered her with attention and applause and cupcakes when she did."

Margot sighed. "I get it. I'm a monster."

"Not what I'm saying. It *was* funny and sweet, but she got tired of it. I took her back to the Little House that night—the night she cried—and I told her that just because she was *good* at something, it didn't mean she had to do that thing to make other people happy."

"You did?"

"I did."

Margot took David's hand. "So what did you tell her about being a doctor?"

"Same thing. I told her the necklace was for graduation, for what she'd already done. And, you know, that premed majors aren't the only people who have hearts."

Margot shook her head. "You're so *annoying* sometimes. You're too good, David Pearlman. Too good for the likes of me, anyway." Margot resumed pushing the swing.

"Ruby said she'd be up soon. She's *dying* to see you."

Margot stood and walked to the edge of the porch looked down at the Little House, nervously willing Ruby to appear. "How much do you think she knows?" she said.

"Honestly? Nothing. But I guess we're about to find out."

lora and Julian had struck an amiable peace for the sake of Ruby, but not an intimate one. During dinner the previous night, they'd tried so hard not to telegraph anything negative to Ruby that to any outsider they must have looked deranged: they smiled too much, they laughed too hard, they would look anywhere except at each other. As soon as Ruby tumbled into her bed, they both stood in the hallway, listening to her gentle snore.

Julian had put his arm around Flora, and although her brain told her to pull back, she found herself melting into him, easy with wine and gratitude because she was under the same roof with Ruby. While she was in New York, she hadn't focused on her loneliness. But here at Stoneham, standing at the landing on the top of the stairs of the Little House, she welcomed the warmth of Julian's body, the voices and laughter coming from up the hill. The string lights were on in the suffering hemlock. Ben had made Ruby flip the switch that night and led everyone in a rousing version of "That's Life." Even though Ruby rolled her eyes when Julian told her Ben was on his way down to re-instate the ceremonial tree lighting, her face flooded with joy when the tree lit up.

"Should we turn the tree lights off?" Flora said, turning to Julian, and he took the moment to kiss her. A long, deep kiss, and she let herself have it. She let herself soften, not only because it felt so good, but because she was testing herself. Could she? Would *this* be the thing that would save them? She pulled away.

"Julian," she said. "I can't."

"Okay," he said, his voice thick. "But, Flora, please don't leave again. Please stay for the show."

The show, the show, the show. It was always about a fucking show.

"I'll see you tomorrow," she said.

In her bedroom, she could hear Julian moving around the kitchen. Unloading the dishwasher. He came upstairs and took what she assumed were sheets and towels from the linen closet. She was so tired. She'd wanted to keep kissing Julian. She'd wanted to undress him and take his hand and lead him onto their bed and let him have his way with her. But not until she understood what she wanted. She crawled into bed and lay still, trying to concentrate on the noises outside, the laughter, the singing in the distance. How different this night would be if she'd never found the ring.

"I would always choose the truth," Maude had said to her, "no matter how painful."

She felt herself drifting off. The screen door slammed. The lights in the hemlock dimmed. When the tree was finally dead and gone, you'd be able to see straight up to Ben's house from the north side of the Little House. The view would feel so bare.

⌒

RUBY CAME DOWN IN THE MORNING wearing gym shorts and a ratty T-shirt after fourteen hours of sleep. Her curls were flattened on one side of her head, and she still had pillow marks on her cheek. The night before, they'd talked about Ivan and his *unjust, unkind* behavior. Finally, Ruby had sighed and put her head on the table and then looked up at her parents and said, "I think he knew I was about to break up with him." She stood and yawned and filled a glass of water. "We were never really connected, you know? Not like this." She clasped her hands together, fingers entwined. "Not like you guys. So maybe it's all for the best."

Ruby downed some coffee, changed into a bathing suit, and went straight to the pond for a swim. When she came back, she wanted Flora to go up to the Farmhouse with her to visit Margot and David. "I'm so happy they're here," Ruby said. "Are you coming?"

"Maybe later," Flora said, keeping her voice even. "I have some chores to do."

"*Chores?* I didn't realize we were on back on the prairie, Ma."

Flora laughed. She'd missed her daughter. "Go ahead without me. I'll catch up with everyone later."

Watching Ruby walk across the lawn and up the hill, Flora could see so clearly the woman she was becoming. She'd acquired a certain grace to her movements. Had it happened in Spain? Probably. She could see a new assurance on Ruby, a kind of swagger that comes from going off on your own. Even though she'd been with Ivan's family, she hadn't been with *her* family. Flora could see her starting to decide what she wanted from the world, from life. She was curious and, Flora was happy to see this in her daughter, too, entitled. Not to things she didn't earn, but to her own desires.

Maybe they had been selling her short. Maybe Maude was right. But Flora couldn't help but think of when Ruby was little and a conversation about—of all things—Babe Ruth had led Ruby to ask what happens after you die. ("You go to the big Bambino baseball field in the sky and try to win a pennant for the Yankees," Julian had joked, trying to change course because when Ruby sunk her teeth into a difficult subject she didn't let go.) No use. Ruby didn't want to hear that "everybody died" or that Flora and Julian would live a long time because they were healthy or that these weren't things for a little girl to worry about. She became so fraught and hysterical, standing in the middle of Washington Square Park, a melting cherry Popsicle dripping down her arm, face smeared with tears and snot, that a desperate Flora had finally knelt in front of her and said, "Okay, okay. I promise you I will not die." As the words were coming out of her mouth, she regretted them, until she saw the look on Ruby's face. Utter relief. "See?" Ruby had snapped at her, still furious. "Was that so hard?"

She and Julian had laughed about it later, but the conversation had haunted Flora. It never stopped being a tiny buzz in the back of her head—she'd promised Ruby she'd *never* die. She thought about it while crossing the street, while sitting on the subway, while driving upstate to Stoneham by herself, while feeling under her arm in the shower and wondering if she felt a lump. There were so many ways to die, to leave Ruby and break her promise. She didn't relax until Ruby was old enough to be reminded of the story and for them to joke about it. Her knee-jerk reaction since finding the ring was to protect Ruby, but why? She wasn't going to tell her the unvarnished truth. Not yet. But she could treat her like the capable human she was becoming.

And Flora couldn't put off talking to Margot any longer. They were going to see each other soon. She texted her: *Want to go for a walk?*

The reply came back immediately: *oh, thank god. yes. yes!*

⌣

"I JUST WANT TO KNOW WHY, what you were thinking," Flora said, after a few minutes of walking in silence down the long, gravel driveway, away from the crowd. They found two weathered Adirondack chairs under a massive maple tree and sat. Margot had one leg crossed on top of the other and was nervously tugging at a shoelace.

"Because I believed Julian when he said it was a terrible mistake. A one-time fuckup."

"A mistake? Did you know it wasn't an isolated incident—Julian and Sydney? It went on for months."

Margot shook her head. "I didn't think it was only once, but I didn't know it was that long. I did think he came to his senses. And, to be honest, I thought you might blame me, too. For telling you. Killing the messenger and all that."

"I still might kill you."

"I know." Margot looked down at her lap. "I didn't know it went on for months. That's awful."

"Everything would have been so much easier if you'd told me then."

"But it wouldn't have," Margot said. Flora looked up at the

sky and shook her head. "Flora, think about it. If I had told you then—"

"What?"

"I think you would have left Julian. I don't think we'd still be friends."

Flora could see the front lawn of the Little House from where they were sitting. A group was rehearsing on the front porch. She couldn't make out what they were saying, but could see Julian pacing as Lopakhin, gesticulating like a good Russian. "But you never gave me the chance," Flora said to Margot. "You didn't give me the opportunity to understand or process or forgive. You decided it all without me, you and Julian."

"I'm sorry. I didn't think of it that way."

"I was blindsided. In the space of a conversation, everything I thought about my life evaporated."

Margot turned to Flora. "I know a little something about that, you know." Margot was chewing on her lip, trying not to cry. "Flora, I couldn't. I *couldn't* tell you. You know why."

"But that's the thing." Flora stood up, her voice louder. "I don't know! I know why you wouldn't *want* to tell me. I don't know why you *couldn't*."

"Because we'd lost so much that year." Margot leaned forward in her chair, looked up at Flora, pleading. "You remember what David was like after rehab, when I was in Seattle; he was like—like a child. I was so scared and miserable. I didn't know what was going to happen. I'd lost too much—" She broke off and wiped the tears from her face with the back of her hand. "I'd lost so much, Flora. I couldn't lose you."

Flora looked at her friend, disbelieving. "But it wasn't about you Margot," Flora said. She walked a few steps away from Margot, who put her head in her hands. "I know," she said. "I'm so abjectly, truly, deeply sorry. I don't know what else I can say. I can only prove to you how sorry I am."

Flora reached in her back pocket and handed Margot a tissue. For a few minutes the only sound was Margot sniffling and blowing her nose and, in the distance, the incongruous staccato bleat of the trombones practicing one of the klezmer tunes.

"Look at those fools down there." Flora gestured at the lawn in front of the Little House where most of the company was rehearsing the hip-hop/Russian Cossack dance. "Maybe two pairs of knees in this entire company can handle that nonsense."

"Was it always this—ambitious?" Margot said.

"I think so," Flora said.

"Can I tell you something?" Margot asked.

"Why start now?"

"Deserved. Deserved." Margot plucked a dandelion from the grass and tucked it behind her ear and did that thing where she twisted her hair in a knot behind her head and it stayed. She closed her eyes and tilted her face to the sun. Her face was blotchy and her eyes swollen from crying. Were those new lines around her mouth or had Flora not noticed them before? "What did you want to say?"

Margot looked at Flora. "I hate it here." Flora laughed. Margot laughed. The Cossacks down the hill laughed and groaned. The screen door of the Little House slammed. Ruby came out on the porch, shielded her eyes from the sun, spotted Margot and Flora, and waved. They waved back. The breeze picked up and the long reeds along the pond swayed in unison, a peaceful dance. A duck flew low over the water, quacking.

"I should go." Flora put a hand out to Margot still sitting in the chair.

"This isn't some kind of Charlie Brown trick?"

"No, but only because I didn't think of it first." Flora took Margot's hand in hers and pulled Margot to her feet, exerting more force than was necessary. It felt good; it felt sad. Margot winced but didn't say anything.

"Will I see you later? Are you staying for the show tomorrow?"

"Yes," Flora said. "But then I'm off. Back to the city for a bit." They started walking back toward the Farmhouse.

"Remember that night at the Chinese restaurant," Margot said, "after *Midsummer*?"

"Of course," Flora said.

"So how does this end?" Margot said, calling back David's question from that long-ago evening, her voice soft and beseeching. "Happy or sad?"

"I don't know," Flora said. "I wish I did."

TWENTY-SIX

T he morning of the performance, Flora woke to the sound of chain saws below her window. Luckily, Ruby hadn't noticed she and Julian were in separate bedrooms. The last two nights Ruby'd surrendered to her jet lag and was in bed before they went to their respective quarters. Julian would rise at dawn, make up the guest bed, and be in the kitchen manning the stove before Ruby was awake. She and Ruby woke to the smell of coffee and bacon. They came downstairs to homemade muffins, pancakes, omelets.

"Bacon," Flora said. "Dirty trick."

"I'm bringing out all the big guns this week," he said, pointing to the huge vase of roses he'd clipped from the bushes along the driveway. She was softening and he could tell and she didn't like it. Or did she? She'd agreed to stay until dinner tonight. *The Cherry Orchard* was a four-act play and at the end of Act Three, there would be a break and the potluck dinner would commence. Act Four would start around twilight. She would slip away while everyone was eating and head back into the city.

She and Julian were telling Ruby a very watered-down version of the truth this morning. She knew she was being a bit of a coward finally telling Ruby her plans on the day of the show— Ruby would be too busy to dig her teeth into the story, poke holes, object, throw a tantrum—but Ruby would be more likely to swallow a thin story on a day where her focus was elsewhere. They could deal with her inevitable interrogation later.

The sound of a chain saw ripped through the cool morning, sending the wild turkeys running across the lawn, hooting and hollering like it was the day before Thanksgiving. Flora got dressed and went downstairs to see what was going on. The little grove of sickly hemlocks at one corner of the house had been decimated in the past few days. A landscaping crew had cut down most of the trees, but not the one right in front, not Ruby's tree. She didn't know how she felt about the complicated remnant of their past still standing there, adrift and alone.

Outside, with her cup of coffee, Flora watched a group of people she recognized from years past, all set designers and prop masters, unroll two enormous tarps on the grass. A young woman wearing loose overalls over a tank top with long dark braids down her back was loosely stitching them together down the middle using an enormous needle and twine. Combined, the cloths had to be twelve feet high, fourteen feet wide. On the tarp, a painted grove of trees—the cherry orchard of the play. Flora walked over for a better look, the mural was truly magnificent. Seurat-like in its execution—all blues and greens and pinks. In this rendering the trees were in full spring bloom, and the depth of the mural was astonishing, the orchard seemed to go on and on.

"Terrific, isn't it?" Charlie said. Good old Charlie, who still came every year and photographed the production. He'd asked

Ruby to work as his assistant today. She was thrilled and Flora was grateful; another valuable distraction.

"It's gorgeous," Flora said. "Helga?"

"Of course." Helga was the gifted, much-awarded set designer and Stoneham regular. Her contributions to the shows were Flora's favorite things. A Helga production was always richer, more creative, and more breathtaking than anyone else's. When Ruby was younger, they would spend hours in the barn watching Helga, who would let Ruby "help" her paint masks, sew puppets, glue feathers to costumes or cardboard wings. One summer they made papier-mâché decapitated heads for *A Man for All Seasons*—a gruesome project that Ruby adored.

Clearly, the mural had been designed with the hemlock in mind, because once they hoisted the tarp in place behind the tree, strung between two metal poles, the painted trees surrounded the real one with perfect symmetry and just like that the bereft hemlock became something else: a part of the doomed cherry orchard. Such a shame, Flora thought, not for the first time, that Helga's creation would be rolled up and stored away and probably never seen again after today. But Flora also thought, not for the first time, how indescribably beautiful that the only people who would have a memory of this orchard were the ones who passed through Stoneham today.

Back in the kitchen, Julian was making blueberry pancakes, Ruby's favorite. He didn't hear Flora come in and she watched him for a moment, ladling perfect circles onto the ancient pancake griddle that had probably belonged to Ben's mother once. He took a handful of blueberries and carefully dropped a few onto each round of batter. Graceful and precise—that was her husband. He turned and saw her and the look on his face— happy, hopeful, wary—tugged. She looked away.

"Hi," he said. He took a step toward her and then stopped. He started to say something, but then—Ruby's feet pounding down the stairs. Ruby in the kitchen, grumbling about how she couldn't find the right lens for today, the super wide-angle, and how was she supposed to take the kind of photos she wanted without that lens? She knew it was here somewhere, she'd had it in Spain unless she'd lost it, accidentally left it in a hotel room or in the rental car, which would mean she'd have to call Ivan or his parents, and forget it! She was definitely *not* calling Ivan.

She turned around, glass of orange juice in hand, and saw her parents, looking at each other and then at her.

"What?"

"Good morning," Flora said.

"Good morning, Mother," Ruby exaggerated, bowing a little, turning toward Julian. "Good morning, Father."

"I'm sure Charlie has whatever kind of lens you don't," Julian said.

"But the point is for me to get the pictures Charlie *isn't* getting."

"So if he's not using the super wide-angle, then you can, right?"

Ruby let out one of her signature sighs, all shoulders and lower jaw. "I guess, Dad." She sat at the table and Julian put a plate of pancakes in front of her. "Hmmmm." She lowered her face to the plate and inhaled, five again. Grabbed the syrup. "Hey, when is our flight home anyway?"

Julian looked at Flora. Flora looked at Julian. This part was hers. "I think you guys leave Monday morning," she said.

"What do you mean? You're coming later?"

"Yes. I'm going back into the city for a little bit to work."

"I don't get it," Ruby said, cutting her pancakes into tiny

pieces the way she always had, brow furrowed. "Why do you have to go to New York for work now? Can't you record at home?"

"I've been thinking of spending a little time in New York," Flora said, impressed by how casual her voice sounded because her heart was galloping like a thoroughbred turning the ninth post. "My friend Michael's apartment is available, and I thought I'd go back and stay a bit and maybe check out some opportunities. Introduce myself to new casting agents, make the rounds."

Ruby kept her head down, methodically eating her pancakes, dipping each forkful into a tiny puddle of syrup at the side of her plate. Julian looked at Flora and shrugged, but Flora knew Ruby was running this information through her brain; she could practically see facts turn into knowledge.

"Are you *moving* to New York City?" Ruby sounded calm, but Flora could see the flash in her eyes as she put her fork down.

"Of course not. I'm considering spending some more time there. I miss our friends." She was proud of herself for the all-encompassing "our," as if this might be Julian's idea, too. "I don't get called for a lot of New York-based work because I live in Los Angeles. I think it might be interesting to explore those opportunities and, you know, be bicoastal." This was the ingenious phrase she'd landed on over the past few days. She and Julian weren't separating; she was becoming *bicoastal*.

Ruby finished her pancakes and a toxic silence started to fill the room. She stood and brought her plate to the sink and put it down too hard. "You guys," she said, turning and crossing her arms, "are *unbelievable*. Do you think I'm an *idiot*?"

"Nobody thinks you're an idiot, Ruby." Julian was stern, but he looked ridiculous dressed in half of his costume—wool pants with hanging suspenders. His hair was slicked back, and he had tiny wire-rimmed glasses on.

"This isn't about Mom wanting more work," Ruby said. "This is about *me*."

Julian and Flora looked at each other, genuinely confused.

"I'm sorry, what?" Flora said.

"You think I don't get what's going on? I go to college *forty minutes* from New York City and all of a sudden you want to be bicoastal? My God, Mom. I haven't even left and you're making plans to be practically in the same town? The same place? You don't even trust me enough to give me a chance? You guys"— now Ruby was on the verge of tears, her chin trembling—"are really not fair."

Flora knew the worst thing she could do at that moment was laugh, but she couldn't help it. It was all so *Ruby*. The one thing she'd worried about in having an only child was Ruby believing the world revolved around her and only her because *it did*. Of course Ruby would see this as about her new life on the East Coast. Flora should have anticipated it, but she hadn't. She started laughing, then Julian. Ruby was incensed. "Oh my God, this isn't funny!"

"Sit down," Julian said. He pulled out a chair for Ruby, then one for Flora. He and Flora were trying to keep a straight face. Ruby was flushed and chewing her lower lip and livid. "Here's the thing," Julian finally said. "Your mom and I are thinking about the next phase of our lives, about the shape of them." Flora watched Julian snap into director mode, easy, believable, drawing out the exact right emotions from their daughter. He was good. "Your mom might want to spend some more time in New York, and *because* you are going away, she can. This is a wonderful thing and would be happening if you were going to college in New York State or in Timbuktu. Our work exists mostly in Los Angeles and New York—we don't have any control over that."

Ruby looked back and forth from one to the other. "But you aren't spending time in New York together?"

"Dad's show starts back up in a few weeks."

"But when Dad doesn't have work?"

"I don't know," Flora said. "This is all an experiment."

"How come you need to experiment?" Ruby said, and now her suspicion had pivoted from anger to fear, eyes filling with tears.

"Because we can," Flora said.

"I don't understand."

"All you need to understand," Julian said, "is how much we love you. We can't wait to bring you to college, to help you settle in."

"And then leave you completely and utterly alone." Flora smiled at her, attempting levity.

"Both of you are bringing me?"

"Both of us," Julian said. "Absolutely both of us. And your mom and I are going to figure out how we want to divvy up the next few years. New York? Los Angeles? We'll figure it out."

"Did something happen?"

Flora took one of Ruby's hands in hers. What to say to her precious girl, now that she'd asked. What to say not to break her heart, to keep her world intact. *I won't ever die.* She looked Ruby straight in the eyes. "Honey, you have to trust us right now. We love you. We're working on things, but the one thing we know for sure is how much we love you."

"Mommy," Ruby said. *Mommy,* the heartbroken one.

Julian took Ruby's other hand, then put his outstretched hand for Flora, and she didn't hesitate. This was for Ruby. "Hey," he said. "It's the three of us, no matter what. *No matter what*. Right?" He squeezed Flora's fingers.

"Right," Flora said, feeling the energy course through the three of them and start to liquefy the tiny hard place inside. She let go of Julian and Ruby and pulled herself inward. Stood and clapped her hands, like a kindergarten teacher. "Let's continue this later. Don't both of you have a show to work on? Come on, this is an important day."

As hackneyed as the expression was, that *the show must go on* was one thing Ruby understood, only child or not.

—

RUBY WALKED UP THE HILL looking for Margot. She was sitting on the porch steps, the same ones from the photo her mother had given her graduation night, back when Ivan was still her boyfriend, back when her parents weren't insane. She remembered then seeing her mother on the sidewalk after graduation looking so angry. She'd been right. Things had been bad for a long time.

Margot saw her and stood up and waved. She bounced down the lawn to meet Ruby; she was wearing a long, flowing sundress with tiny straps. Her hair was pulled back, and her face was unadorned—no makeup, no jewelry. She was so pretty.

"Here she is." Margot gave her a long hug and they started walking toward the meadow, back where the train tracks ran, away from the hordes of people. "How are you today? Ready for the onslaught?"

"Something weird happened this morning," Ruby told Margot. "Mom said she might go back to New York and stay there for a little while."

"She did?" Margot said, not sounding surprised.

"Yeah, she said she's thinking of becoming *bicoastal*."

Margot laughed. "You make it sound like a dirty word."

"I just want to know what's *really* up with them. Something's wrong. It's so obvious, and they won't talk to me about it."

They walked for a few minutes in silence. Margot was looking down at the ground. They heard the *ding, ding, ding* of the crossing gate closing some yards away. They moved farther down the slope of the hill covered with tall grass. They both looked in the direction the train was coming and waited. As it started to rush by, blowing Margot's dress back and her hair around her face, Ruby turned away and covered her ears. She hated how loud it was, how overwhelming. Margot tapped Ruby on the shoulder, and when she turned Margot pantomimed talking, pretended she was telling Ruby something vitally important. She gesticulated widely and grabbed Ruby's arms and shook her a little. Ruby laughed and as soon as the train was fading into the distance and they could hear each other, Margot said, "So *that's* what's going on with everybody."

"Very funny."

They resumed walking. Margot eyed Ruby, so young and indignant. She took her hand and led her to a bench, weathered gray and splintery, that had been built for some Stoneham production years before and still remained. "You know your mom made sacrifices for Julian. I don't think she regretted it. She had you and she always had her work, but she missed a lot. I can see how she feels it's her turn now."

Ruby was fiddling with one of the lenses on her camera. "I

guess. I didn't think about it that way. I still think something fishy is going on."

Margot stood and looked down the empty train tracks. Flora might eventually rat her out to Ruby, but she wasn't going to confess. "Could be," she said. "They've been married a long time. Disagreements happen. It's not the end of the world. David and I disagree all the time, you just don't see it."

"But would *you* live in New York? Away from David?"

She turned and looked down at Ruby, who had her camera to her face and was adjusting the focus. "Don't move," Ruby said, clicking away.

Would Margot go to New York? She always thought she would, but she didn't belong there anymore. She didn't know where she belonged, but she suspected a robe and gavel were involved. (*"Sustained!"*) "No, I wouldn't." Margot made her voice cheerful. "Try not to worry about things that aren't your problem, sweetie."

Back at the Little House, Ruby looked at the pictures of Margot. The sun coming from the side bleached out one side of her face a little, the sky was a punishing blue. She didn't notice when she was taking them how sad Margot's expression was, how wistful she looked.

⌒

FLORA WANDERED THE GROUNDS right before showtime, looking for the little cluster of seats that had been taped off for family members of the cast (some things never changed; even in the alleged utopia that was Stoneham, VIP privileges existed). She knew that no matter what happened with her marriage, she'd

never return to Stoneham, so she tried to take it all in. Coming
back after so many years, she had wondered if she would greet
the effort at Stoneham with disdain or admiration. The answer
was both. The scope of what Ben had put together was undeniably impressive. The dedication he'd inspired by hordes of
friends all coming together to create something so specific and
ephemeral—it was impossible not to be moved by the effort, the
grandeur, the community. But also? It felt a little musty. A little
like something that should have ended some time ago. A thing
they should be reminiscing about rather than re-creating over
and over ad infinitum.

She was in no mood to sit through *The Cherry Orchard*, a
play about a family of Russian aristocrats in denial about how
the world around them was changing and the former serf—
Lopakhin—who would usurp them. She was in no mood to
contemplate the characters clinging to a version of their past,
incapable of moving forward. She sat at the end of a row of
folding chairs. All around them people were settling in. Many
brought blankets to sit on the grass. Flora couldn't imagine
why—this Chekhov spectacular would go on for hours. She
needed a chair. Her seat needed a seat. She felt a hand on her
arm. Margot. David next to her sliding into an empty chair.
"Okay?" Margot said. Flora nodded.

The show started with the cast on the porch of the Little
House, all in vintage underwear, slowly beginning to costume
themselves as the roving Klezmer band played. The opening
was classic Julian and Ben, making theater out of the theater
of it all. Maybe because this year she hadn't been involved in
any of it, hadn't been privy to the hours and hours of rehearsals and discussions over dinner, the dissection of the text, the
yammering over *choices*, watching them block it first this way

then that, she was immediately entranced by the scene. She loved watching the cast (okay, Julian) dress themselves and each other. Helping with long rows of buttons and bootlaces and corsets. It was mesmerizing and focused the audience exactly the way it was intended.

It's not that Flora had forgotten how good Julian was—that would be impossible—but it had been a long time since she'd sat in an audience watching him. She remembered disliking Lopakhin, but Julian was always telling her how funny Chekhov meant the play to be, and Julian's Lopakhin *was* funny, and endearing. Perfectly so, because at the end of Act Three, when Lopakhin enters with the shocking announcement that he's bought the family's cherry orchard at auction, that *he* owns it now and will destroy it and build houses on the land where his father and grandfather were serfs, and become a rich man, Flora could feel the crowd turn against him, feel them absorb the shock, the betrayal. Julian was mesmerizing.

"I bought it!" Julian as Lopakhin gleefully delivered his lines to the devastated Russian landowners. He took a step off the porch. "Mine!" he crowed, walking onto the grass. "Mine!" And then, beckoning the crowd: "Come on, everybody, see how Yermolay Lopakhin will swing an axe in the cherry orchard."

In any other production, the cherry orchard would be off-stage, or maybe represented by an onstage projection. Lopakhin's ceremonial swing of the axe would most likely be a recording. But this was Stoneham, and if Lopakhin promised to swing an axe, an axe would swing. Everyone followed Julian, who was striding over to where the hemlock proudly stood in front of the mural of the cherry orchard. Someone had strung a red ribbon to keep the crowd at a safe distance, because—as

Flora immediately understood—Julian was going to chop the hemlock down.

Back on the porch, Hadley as the aristocrat Ranevskaya was in a state of collapse, sobbing, louder and louder. "She always knew how to milk it," Margot said, "but I can't wait to see her compete with this."

They watched as Julian slowly unbuttoned his wool vest, picked up the axe, and landed the first blow. He gave the handle a strong tug and it released. He reared his arms back and hit the same spot again. A small spattering of wood sprayed on his boots. After a few swings, he was in a rhythm. He stopped and turned to the roving band that had moved along with the audience and delivered his next lines. "What's the matter?" he yelled to the crowd, the universe, Flora. "Music! Play up!"

Two accordions sprang to swinging life, and Flora immediately recognized the opening bars of the melody. Ruby's tree-lighting song. The violins and strings joined in, and the cast and crowd started to sing along as Julian resumed chopping, *"That's life, that's what all the people say, you're riding high in April, shot down in May."* The sound of the axe provided an atonal beat to the lively instruments. Ruby appeared at Flora's side. "I can't believe it," she said, staring in wonder. "He's going to cut down the tree."

"Do you hear?" Flora said, pointing to the musicians.

"Of course," Ruby said, putting her arm around Flora's waist, singing softly along, *"I've been a puppet, a parrot, a poem, a popcorn, a pong and a KINGGGGG."*

Ten minutes passed, maybe fifteen. Julian was starting to slow down, and Flora was starting to worry. He was in good shape, but he was standing directly in the path of the setting sun, the wan hemlock providing little shade. It was hot, and he'd been working hard all week. She knew he hadn't slept well. He unbuttoned his shirt. Removed his glasses. Flora could see he was laboring. "How long does it take to cut down a tree?" she asked David.

"I don't know. It looks like they notched the trunk in the back last night."

Some of the crowd was leaving, heading up the hill toward dinner and the smell of meat barbecuing on the grill. But most people stayed. Julian versus the tree had become the show. He'd removed his shirt now and his suspenders hung from his waist and swayed a little with each landing of the axe. With every whack, Flora could see the reverberation through his shoulders and back. The sweat was running in rivulets down his face and neck. Ruby put her camera down. "Isn't anyone going to help him?"

"Come on, Lopakhin!" somebody in the audience yelled. "Do it for the proletariat!" A scattering of laughter among the largely moneyed crowd. All the actors in the play were gathered now, too, watching. Ben and Charlie walked over to spell Julian.

"Finally," Ruby said.

Julian handed Ben the axe, and took a large, white cloth from his back pocket and wiped down his face and shoulders. He sat for a bit, watching Ben and Charlie take turns wielding the axe. Flora moved to the front of the crowd and Julian looked over and held her gaze. She didn't understand what passed between them, but it wasn't gentle. It was resolute, and she knew then that it wasn't Lopakhin cutting down that tree, it was Julian.

Julian chugged down a bottle of water and walked over to Ben, whose energy was already lagging. "Give it here," he said and turned back to the tree and started swinging the axe with renewed vigor. Instead of going slower, he sped up. The musicians kept pace, the music frenzied now. Everyone who'd stayed to watch was completely transfixed by the sounds, by the strength Julian was seemingly pulling out of nowhere, by how the scene in front of them had stopped being something from *The Cherry Orchard* and had become something they didn't quite understand but couldn't turn away from.

"I don't know who he's picturing on that tree trunk," Flora heard a man behind her say, "but I hope he doesn't see that guy soon."

Flora watched as Julian stepped back and took a long, appraising look at the tree. Ruby's tree. The tree he'd planted so long ago, during what she now knew was a disastrous summer of their lives, the summer of his betrayal. He bent a little at the knees, held the axe low, then reared back and delivered one! two! three! whacks. The tree swayed a little, and the crowd cheered.

"Come on," Flora said, as Julian put two hands on the tree and gave a full-bodied shove. The hemlock fell in one exhilarating arc, hit the fanciful tarp and held for an agonizing second— Flora could see Helga put her hands to her mouth, waiting for the stitches to give way—and tore through the fabric. Slowly at first—they could hear the long rip—then all at once. The tree thundered to the ground, and as it landed, Flora felt a vibration move through her body.

The crowd cheered. Julian dropped the axe and bent over, hands on knees, catching his breath. He straightened and wiped his face with the back of his hand. Turned and looked for Flora. She could see a lightness in his body, elation in his face. Hope.

If forgiveness was an action, maybe atonement was one, too.

"Flora," he said, putting out a hand. It wasn't a question. It wasn't a command. It was a gesture, an invitation. "Flora Mancini."

"I'm here," she said, walking toward him, "I'm here."

TWENTY-SEVEN

The next morning the house was quiet and Ruby was up early, surveying the slaughtered remains of the hemlock. The heat and sun of the day before had vanished with a harsh overnight rain. The morning was cool and wet. The grass of the lawn flattened in spots from the roaming audience, the folding chairs, the blankets. She always loved the property the day after the production. It felt empty but not hollow, the buildings and the trees and the view returned to them. She had her camera and tripod and was trying to decide which angle to photograph the hemlock. It would be interesting in close-up, the grain of the wood, the whorls of the bark, the ferocious split where her father, the executioner, had dealt the final blow.

"Dad, that was *nuts*," Ruby had said to him the previous night. She'd watched his body absorbing blow after blow, his shoulders heaving back as he pulled out the axe. She wasn't sure what she'd witnessed last night, but for the first time since she'd been back from Spain, the tension between her parents didn't feel lethal.

Upstairs, Flora was packing the small bag she'd brought in from the city. Julian was in the shower. They hadn't talked much last night. When dinner and the play was over, she stood back and watched him bask in the adoration of his peers, the amazement from the crowd. Admiration had never been his favorite thing, but she could tell he was pleased. Around the late-night bonfire, he kept finding her, keeping her in his line of sight, and whether she wanted to or not, she felt anchored by his attention.

Was that all she'd needed? Seeing his pain manifest? Maybe. Or maybe she needed to be back at Stoneham with Julian and Ruby. She'd been avoiding a reckoning, but now it seemed like it wasn't going to break her. She'd reached a kind of detente with Margot, and they would try to muddle through. She hadn't said this to Margot, because she didn't want to be cruel, but they would never be the same kind of friends. They might be something, but it would have to be something new and, she was sorry to realize, something different. Like her marriage, she supposed.

A space had opened up in her since the day she found the ring. Something cavernous and scary and black. Watching Julian last night, waking up with him this morning, lying in bed and looking out the window at the clear sky, no hemlock blocking the view, she realized the space was just that: empty. She could fill it as she pleased, with sorrow, forgiveness, bitterness. She always believed, before Julian, that the only person she could trust was herself. It hurt to find out just how true that was, but she could survive it. She had formed herself in the image of her union with Julian. She had given over a piece of her soul (if she couldn't find her way to any stronghold of belief anymore, she did believe in the soul) to Julian's unshakeable love for her, to the story that was Flora and Julian and their unassailable marriage. In its place, she wasn't putting nothing, she was putting broken Flora, Flora with a crack. She didn't know quite what that meant for her, except that she felt tougher and less afraid and the feeling was tolerable. It wasn't as if Julian had chopped down a tree and all was right with the world, but the world had a little more possibility in it—at least this morning, at least in this light.

As she and Julian came downstairs, Ruby was gathering her camera equipment. She had some cockamamie idea to retake the old photo before they all left. Flora had tried to object, but Ruby wouldn't let it go. "Please. I am begging you. Just one picture. It will take a minute. Mom, please. This is important to me." Flora looked at Julian, who shrugged, borrowing the inevitable agreement of David for a minute.

Ruby corralled them all onto the front porch of the big house. A small crowd of actors and crew—those who were awake so early—were cleaning up or packing up or milling around on the porch, congratulating themselves.

"Hey!" Ruby stuck two fingers in her mouth and gave an ear-piercing whistle. "Hey, everybody. If you could clear the stairs for two minutes, I need to get a shot. Won't take long."

Margot and David laughed and Flora looked at them and they all shook their heads in wonder. Where had she learned that? Margot and David sat on the bottom step as they had in the original photo, Flora and Julian above them. "I'm not sure you're going to fit on my lap this time," Margot said to Ruby.

"No. I'm going to sit on the middle step, in between."

Standing behind her tripod, Ruby bent down and looked through the lens. "Everybody squeeze a little closer, please."

Flora let Julian pull her close. She relaxed into his side and he put his arm through hers just like in the first picture. As Ruby looked through the lens, she believed she could see the future as clear as the bright blue Hudson Valley sky; her parents were joined, two parts of a whole. The empty space between Margot and David made her uneasy. David was looking in the wrong direction, away from Margot. Margot was looking at the camera and trying to smile, her hands clasped in her empty lap. Ruby snapped a few quick pictures. She'd never show those shots to Margot or David, but would end up using them in her first student exhibit called *The Space Between*, pictures of couples who, if they weren't estranged, certainly had an air of estrangement to their poses, a vacancy lurking in the middle.

"How long is this going to take?" Julian asked.

"Not long. I'm almost ready."

Margot leaned back and felt herself brush against Flora's knees and sat up quickly. "I'm sorry."

"No," Flora said, "come back." Margot leaned back again, and Flora could feel Margot's shoulders against her legs, feel her body release a long sigh.

"Okay," Ruby said, pressing the timer and running to the porch. She sat on the middle step. Wiggled her fingers behind her. "Where are you, Mommy?" Flora smiled at Julian and took Ruby's outstretched hand. Ruby reached for Margot with her other hand.

Margot to Ruby, Ruby to Flora, just like in the first photo—only different.

"When does this thing go off?" David asked, squirming a little.

"In a sec," Ruby said.

"Are you sure you set it?" Julian asked.

"Be patient, Dad. Wait for it to start flashing faster."

The five of them sat, expectant, silent.

"There it goes!" Ruby could feel everyone around her shift a little and resettle. The tiny little red light on the front of the camera blinked furiously. "Okay, everybody," Ruby said, squeezing her mother's hand, squeezing Margot's, "look up."

And miraculously, everyone did.

ACKNOWLEDGMENTS

I owe the writing of this book to the people who were willing to talk to me about their experiences in theater and television with insight, candor, enthusiasm, and humor. I am indebted to: Mia Barron, Paget Brewster, Jessica Chaffin, Jackson Gay, Jason Butler Harner, Melissa Kievman, Adam O'Byrne, Liza Powel O'Brien (who does double duty as my most trusted early reader), Maria Thayer, and Janie Haddad Tompkins. Rolin Jones has helped me in more ways than he would ever count, but I remember them all, and my gratitude is boundless. I couldn't have finished it without you, Jones.

I was lucky enough to start this book with Megan Lynch and finish it with Helen Atsma, which is more editorial genius than any writer deserves. Thank you, Helen, for stepping in midstream and immediately understanding what I wanted the book to be and shepherding it to the finish; it's been a true joy. I am grateful to all my friends at Ecco/HarperCollins, especially Sonya Cheuse, Daniel Halpern, and Miriam Parker.

Thanks to Henry Dunow for his friendship, humor, and

cool-headed responses to my shitty first drafts, and for knowing that every conversation is better with a Manhattan, straight up. I wouldn't want to do this with anyone else, Henry.

Parts of this novel were written at the utopia that is the Ucross Foundation. I am eternally grateful for the time and space and the friends I found there. Thanks to superstars Rufi Thorpe and Jade Chang for their early and ongoing support of this book and for being brilliant and beautiful humans.

To my husband, Mike, and my sons, Matthew and Luke: you are simply the best and I am the luckiest.